THE EXILED IMMORTALS

BREAKING MORTAL

BY

CAMILIA JOHN

InTown Books

245 North Highland Avenue
Atlanta, Georgia 30307
http://www.intownbooks.net

The Exiled Immortals:
BREAKING MORTAL

ISBN-13: 978-0692525203

ISBN-10: 0692525203

Editor: William Dyson

Cover Art: Michael Dyson
http://www.coroflot.com/guerrilla808

DEDICATION

To my husband Greg, who kept
alive my passion for writing, with
all my love.

ACKNOWLEDGEMENT:

My deepest gratitude to Mr. William Dyson, my friend and my mentor, who always encouraged me and believed in me and my work.

Book 1

The Legend of the Fire Sword

PROLOGUE

Five thousand years ago, to keep the peace and avoid an uprising, our King exiled three Orders of Immortals to the mortal realm: the Warriors, the Defenders, and the Enforcers.

We came from the future and into your past.

Today, we are still here among you.

We are the Warriors.

These are our stories.

1

IT WAS ALWAYS THE SAME dream with the same mysterious man. I didn't know his name but he felt familiar. His scent was strong and tickled my senses with pleasure. His arms were around my chest holding me tight, like he didn't want to lose me. We were both naked on the floor of a dark room, somewhere cold and isolated.

I couldn't move and his body covered mine completely. I was not afraid of him because somehow I knew that he was my lover and I desired him. His body was hot, his flesh was rubbing against mine, and it was pleasurable. When he relaxed his arms, his fingers softly touched my face as he leaned to kiss me.

My whole body convulsed with expectations—I couldn't resist the delirium of a night of passion. But when I opened my eyes to see his face, he disappeared.

Always.

My soul felt emptiness. Every time, dream after dream, I hoped to keep him more, maybe just one more minute in his embrace. For the past century, on some nights, this dream made me wake up confused and upset, and that morning it happened again.

It was still a bit chilly and foggy for the last day in April, quite unusual for the Atlanta area. I decided that I would drive the golf cart and take the dog to the park hoping to clear my mind and spirit. At the age of five, my German shepherd was in his prime, and he loved to run around the park's perimeter. The moment I pulled the cart of the garage, the dog knew what to do and he jumped right into it.

I grabbed my long all-weather coat, filled my pockets with dog treats—and with something I never leave home without: my sword.

From the house across the street, Doctor Samson, my ninety-one year old neighbor, waved to me as he walked slowly with his cane. As he emerged from the shadows of the Bradford pear trees that lined the sidewalk, his small body frame appeared to be that of a young boy.

"Good morning Miss Safira," he saluted me quite jovially.

"Doctor Samson, it's so good to see you. How are you doing?" I asked, so happy to see him.

"Oh, I'm not making any fuss," he answered sincerely, "now that I'm officially an ancient." I smiled. He had no idea about how ancient I was.

I accepted the fact that immortality was an unattainable dream for most mortals except for Amestec. But what would one do to attain it? Hunt and kill all of us? As a

Healer, I had postponed the death of so many people, so many times, but they all died at the end.

As a Warrior, I fought my enemies and I took their lives.

I saw all the ones I once knew or developed an attachment with growing old and dying, leaving me with a scar of pain every time. I saw this world changing and transforming and I wasn't able to keep and save what I once held dear. My spirit was somewhat eased only by moving from one place to another.

"Ruth is ready to cook that chicken casserole you like," Doctor Samson tempted me. "We really want to have you come over for dinner more often."

"I would love that, Doctor Samson."

After a brief pause, he said, "Let me ask you, Miss Safira–shouldn't you be married and have children by now?"

"I am still very young, doctor Samson," I mumbled, surprised by his unexpected question.

"True. But I would surely like to see you situated while I am still around."

"Do you have someone in mind?" I asked him, laughing at the whole idea to having a ninety year old as a matchmaker.

"I sure do," my dear neighbor answered very seriously.

"I promise to come for dinner soon, Doctor Samson." He nodded and slowly turned to walk back to the house.

* * *

Once I reached the park, I parked the cart at the entrance and I took the leash off Lord Arthur. The German shepherd disappeared into the fog. His speed was amazing, but he wouldn't run so far that he couldn't keep an eye on me. I sat on a bench, waiting for him to get his exercise and be ready to return home.

During that time, my mind kept up a steady stream of conversation. The dream was always disturbing to me and I couldn't understand it. I knew what lay ahead in the future and I was ready for it. I was ready for war and but not ready for the unknown master who was supposed to come for me.

Long ago, Andreas, the Immortal man I loved, was forced to choose a different path and his love was lost to me. And for so long I just hardened my heart, guarded my feelings, and waited for my destiny to unfold. But I couldn't stop the hope of ever finding my lover again. The man from my dream was not Andreas, and that saddened me a bit but I wanted him back, even for just a short time.

Suddenly, I stopped my train of thought. Lord Arthur came running back to me quite agitated. I looked around, as far as the fog would allow me, but I could see only vague shapes in the distance. The park appeared to be empty, but I could feel a change in the air. A certain change in the pressure of the wind made me tremble. It had been so long since I felt something like that.

I stood up and faced the lawn and the trees behind our bench. The wind was blowing harder now, from the west. As the tendrils of the mist began to shift and rise, I could see that not far from where we were standing there was something hiding in a tree. I had the feeling that I was being watched from above.

Lord Arthur lay down at my feet and I clipped the leash back on his halter. I unzipped my coat and tied the dog's leash to the bench. I walked slowly along the little alley towards the wooded area and directly to the first tree. I looked up, waiting for a few seconds before I acted on my instincts.

"Come down!" I yelled to the shadow of a man in the tree, "I know you're there."

A tall, slender young man jumped down from the tree and landed in front of me. This young man didn't look like anything I expected. He was blond with ebony eyes, so dark that his irises were indistinguishable from his pupils, with a weary but aristocratic look that made him seem very familiar. Maybe he wasn't what I first thought he was, an Amestec, but how could I explain how he jumped from that tall tree and landed on his feet?

Something wasn't right.

He threw a long, narrow bag on the ground, and after a few seconds of staring at me, he raised his right hand to hit me. As I blocked his swing with my forearm, I knew immediately that he was too strong to be a mortal, but he didn't appear to me as an half- immortal, either. He had knowledge of ancient fighting techniques, but he wasn't faster than me.

At first I only defended myself, avoiding his punches by moving sideways and backwards. After a few seconds of this feinting, I became aggressive and I slammed my arm across his neck. The shock made him bend to the left, but he didn't fall. He attempted to kick me in my stomach a few times, but he was always wide or short of his target. Then I flipped backwards into the air.

My clenched right hand swung around into his face, striking his temple with a crushing blow, but I still couldn't seem to be able to get an advantage over him. It was only when I swung my leg up and I kicked him on his jaw that he fell to the ground. His face became darker and his lips drew themselves into a narrow line as his anger increased. He got to his knees, opened his bag, and pulled out a sword similar with mine.

I knew then that I was fighting for my life. When the swords entered into the mix, this battle would end in either his death or mine.

Behind me, Lord Arthur barked nervously, trying to escape his hold so he could come and protect me, but without looking I yelled for him to sit and be quiet. The man in front of me was not about to be scared by a dog. His eyes, so large and so dark, were staring through me without any expression.

"Who are you?" I asked him as I gathered my hair into a ponytail and pulled out my own sword from my coat.

"You have no idea." he answered as he raised his sword, swinging its arc furiously in my direction.

I was skilled in fighting with every modern weapon, but fighting with a sword has a totally different technique. What you must do is to simply listen to its music. There was a certain sound in the air when it was swung, another when it made contact with the other sword, and yet another when it cut. I knew how to maneuver my sword very well, but so did he.

This meant only one thing—as always, one of us must be terminated.

Lord Arthur wasn't accustomed to being held still while his master was in danger. He barked more intensely, and it was frightening. In the midst of all this, I didn't want to attract anyone else's attention who might be in the park. I had to hurry.

But while I took the time to think about what was happening, I was too slow to block his thrust and his sword cut my left arm, just above the elbow. I looked at my ripped shirt and saw that the cut wasn't very large or deep. I didn't feel any pain and I didn't bleed. I tried to touch the cut with my other hand, but the man wouldn't give me time for that. He swung his sword, aiming for my head.

I ducked down to avoid his blow and then I leaped into the air over him. As my feet passed over his shoulder, I cut off his head. His body fell to the ground and his head rolled a short distance away. I expected blood to be gushing from the arteries in his neck, but as he fell to the ground, there was no blood. I looked over to his head and his eyes were wide open without an expression.

I didn't feel anything like I should have when his soul left his body. His corpse remained warm to the touch.

Lord Arthur was quiet, too. The sudden tranquility was sinister. Only a bird dared to disrupt that moment with its loud and fearless song.

I hid the two swords in the man's bag and I returned to calm the dog. I stroked and patted Lord Arthur, and he settled down and lay on the ground–for him, his master was safe and the danger was gone. I sat on the bench and closed my eyes. I hoped that this wasn't real and when I opened my eyes again, all this would go away. But when my eyes opened in a few moments, the mysterious man was still there near the tree, headless and dead.

I drove the golf cart to where the dead man was lying on the grass. I lifted him up and set him in the back seat, and I balanced his head back on his neck, wrapping my jacket around it to hold it in place. Once the dog jumped in the front seat, we left the park to go home. There was nowhere else I could take him.

I went in the back door of our house and placed the man on the floor of the kitchen. There was nothing for me to do but to wait patiently all day long until Octavian came home. When he walked through the garage door, I took him directly into the kitchen and pointed to the floor.

"Is he dead?" asked my brother, surprised.

"Yes. I cut off his head. He waited for me in the park and he attacked *me* with a sword." The man's head was still wrapped in my jacket and it looked like it was attached to his body.

"And you brought him here, to our home?"

"Look at his eyes!" I took my jacket from around his neck. His head rolled over against the dishwasher, face down. Octavian got down on his knees and turned the face up.

"What is he?"

"I don't know. See, he's not bleeding and he spoke to me with an accent. I hope I'm wrong, but he doesn't seem to be an Amestec, either."

"Don't worry about him right now," said my brother agitated. "We've got work to do. I just located the Fire Sword."

Now was as good a time as any to bring our past to the forefront, to learn to stay focused because our hunters will never stop.

2

IN THE EARLY SPRING OF *1885, Transylvania was an occupied province under the Austro-Hungarian Empire. The Governor of the province was a prince, Lord Milos Martuzon. His seat of government was the Black Eagle Palace, one of the many beautiful castles in the city of Oradea.*

Black Eagle Palace was also my home for the past five years. Other than this plain detail, my presence there was only an obscure story that was whispered among the serving staff, but no one ever told me anything about why I was there. From the outside looking in, it must have appeared to be such a glamorous life, residing in the most important palace in the whole province. As I looked from the inside out, my heart knew nothing but loneliness and unhappiness. I had no other dream than my desire to leave and to be free.

"Lady Safira, come and eat, my dear!"

Nana Saveta interrupted my reverie. She had come into my room with my dinner tray. Like everything else in this castle, it seemed that she was here only to be a nuisance to me.

Nana was probably somewhere around fifty years of age–at least, she seemed that old to me at the time. Her hair had once been the color of the blackest raven, but now it was flecked with random strands of grey. It still flowed softly down to just below her waist, just as it had when I first saw her. Her dark thick brows outlined her eyes that were the color of dark chocolate. Slim in her younger days, it was obvious that she had begun to add weight to her frame as she grew older.

Nana had been my caretaker for the past fifteen years and I still did not trust her. If I had magical powers to make people disappear, Nana would be the first to go. She was the only person I knew who was connected to my past, and even though her caring for me seemed genuine, her loyalty was totally to Lord Martuzon. Her obedience was to the Governor in all things, and I had no freedom of movement beyond the corridors of the castle.

Most of the time we argued over her stubbornness to ignore my questions. I had asked her for years about whom I really was, who my parents were, and why was I here. For years she answered me with only vague replies and veiled hints of my origin.

That evening, though, I had a plan in mind – a plan that took me several days to devise, as I worked out in my mind all the ways that it could fail. So, I quietly ate all of the food she brought me. The more I talked with Nana, the longer she would stay in my room. The less time she spent here with me tonight, the sooner I could put my plan into action.

"Why is it so cold in here?" Nana asked. "Did you open the window?"

I pretended that I didn't hear her question.

"It is still very cold outside, especially at night. Spring is not here yet and winter still holds us in its grip. You should not risk getting sick…"

"From an open window?" It was a beautiful but chilly evening at the end of March. Spring, with its warmth and flowers, comes late in Transylvania.

"Yes, my dear, you are not accustomed to being in the cold air. I know what you are about to say, but until spring has fully arrived; you are not to go outside under any circumstances. After all, I am responsible for your health."

"Then let me go out during the day, at noon, when is a little warmer…"

"No! I won't allow it!"

Nana Saveta showed indignation about my request, but I had begun to make the same request almost every day. A part of me wanted to go outside, but another part of me just wanted to irritate Nana.

Somewhere in the palace, I could hear music, dancing and laughing – the usual sounds that I could hear every Saturday evening. I wanted so much to be a part of it.

"Oh yes, I'm a prisoner here…"

"You are not a prisoner and I will not continue this discussion with you. I know where it's going to lead us…"

"You're right, Nana. Please send Savu to light a fire, if you think it's too cold in the room."

Her victory and my defeat was the end of our short lived spat that evening. Usually I would drag out an argument for almost an hour before I gave in and accepted what was demanded of me. Our arguments always took so much energy out of both of us.

"Spring will never come," I said with a very deep sad voice, trying to soften even more the heart of my 'companion lady'. This was how

Nana referred to herself, but in my opinion, she was employed just to be my shadow.

"It always comes, year after year, you will see. When it's warm enough, I promise you that we will go outside every day."

I didn't doubt her promise. In the past five years I have never taken a walk outside the walls of this palace alone without being in the presence of Nana or some other guardian. I still remember that day so clearly when I lost my independence.

Lord Milos Martuzon, the newly appointed Prince Governor, had entered my private quarters that were in his father's old palace in the city of Cluj. Nana Saveta was teaching me when he ordered us to be taken from there, and we were brought to the city of Oradea. I was given my private apartment in his palace. At the time, I was only fourteen.

There was never an explanation given to me for this radical change in my life, and all of my attempts to learn the truth from Nana Saveta were unsuccessful. The mystery of my circumstances, along with the aching need in my soul to know what had happened to my parents and to know who I am, was the reason behind all I was about to do.

"Cheer up my dear, I have some wonderful news!" exclaimed Nana. "You can't possibly believe who will be the guest of Lord Martuzon, in less than a week."

"No, I can't imagine who it will be. There's no one coming here who can be of any interest to me."

Nana was disappointed in my lack of interest in her announcement, and she pretended to ignore my answer. She continued her conversation exactly where she had left it.

21

"I could not believe it myself, but today Counselor Grunter confirmed it to Savu and Doctor Gales. Lord Martuzon must be so honored to welcome none other than the Prince Regent, Archduke Rudolph himself. Lady Safira! Are you even listening to me?"

The Archduke Rudolph was nothing more to me than another stranger. I had nothing in common with him, and it was useless for me to develop any interest in a royal presence that I may not even get the chance to see, much less to speak with.

"Indeed," I replied, *"this is great news, but it won't affect me in any way. The last time we had a royal visit, when Prince Edward was here, I didn't even set eyes on him during the whole month. Lord Martuzon has not seen me in several months. He hasn't been interested in my person or my wellbeing since he forced me to live here. If he won't pay attention to me, why should I become excited over some visiting royalty? Admit it, my dear Nana – I will have to die here in my living quarters, in this unyielding castle, suffering from loneliness and abandoned by the very people who had sworn to protect me..."*

Nana Saveta stared at me, astonished and wide eyed, frightened of what I was saying to her. Lately, I enjoyed torturing her with my extremely sad predictions of my possible demise. I tried to be as gloomy as a nineteen year old girl could be. But there was nothing else for her to do or to say.

She made sure the water for my tub was hot, collected the dinner dishes, and left for the servant's quarters. Her useful existence was based entirely on how she interacted with me. Whatever she knew about me was buried deep in her mind, and this knowledge was locked solidly in the vault of her memory.

Every night I procrastinated about taking my bath until just before I went to sleep, but that evening my bath was the first thing I rushed to do. I had other plans for later that night. The water was too hot but I removed my clothes and forced myself into it. The heat made my skin turn red immediately, and then I feel good, but sleepy.

I stood up in my little wooden circular tub and splashed the water all over my body. Much of the water wound up on the floor, but I didn't care. I knew that Nana would be aggravated when she saw the mess in the morning, and that pleased me almost as much as my nightly bath.

My game in the tub and my giggling was interrupted by a strange noise. It was the same noise I had heard quite often when I bathed — something like the sound of the wind brushing against a window sash. I had the distinct feeling that someone was watching me, but that notion was impossible. My tub was in a little alcove, a small room with no windows. The only things on the walls were a few intolerable pictures painted with someone's very childish and amateurish art. A curtain separated the bathing alcove from my sleeping area.

That night I could not dismiss the feeling that I was no longer alone. I knew that I had to take the initiative and investigate the sound for myself before I complained to Nana about it.

I got out of the tub, stepped across the alcove, and pulled the curtain — but there was no one behind it. I walked around my sleeping quarters looking for something out of ordinary, but I could not find any evidence of any intrusion. I suddenly realized that I was walking around the room naked and wet.

The floor was spattered with water from my dripping body. Nana wouldn't be happy at all when she saw these puddles in the morning, but I was beyond caring about her feelings. I took my soft towel and dried my body quickly. I dressed warmly so I could continue to follow my plan.

Long ago I had discovered that there was a gap in the established pattern of guarding me. I was totally unsupervised every evening and *night, after Nana left. Perhaps the logic behind this was that the guards were trusted to watch my every movement and to secure the palace each night. I was sure that my thinking was accurate, considering the heavy concentration guards throughout every floor and entrance.*

* * *

About a year ago, I found that I could easily move unseen from my room to an unused side staircase. This spiral staircase took me to a small closet that overlooked the immense apartment occupied by the Governor. From a very small window in the closet I could look into his private parlor where he entertained his closest friends or associates. This is where I spent many of my evenings, spying on Lord Martuzon in the hope that whatever he discussed with his intimates could shed a light on my existence.

That evening I was eager to explore where the staircase would take me beyond the closet, praying that what I so ardently wished for would be true. I left my room quietly and ran as quickly as I could, all the way to the last door in the corridor—the door that was so cleverly hiding the staircase. The two guards were making loud noises on the other side of the corridor adjacent to the main stairs. This told me that they were having their usual dinner and some wine.

As I passed the closet I fought the temptation to enter and spy on the Governor once again, but I continued through the darkness, using my hands to hold on to the old wooden rails. The staircase's spiral made me dizzy for a moment, and I thought about giving up and returning to my quarters. Cold and dark places always unnerved me, but even though my heart was full of fear, I didn't stop.

A few minutes passed as I made my descent, and in my fear and anticipation those minutes seemed much longer than they actually were. I had the feeling that I had been going down for so long that I might be somewhere deep underground, perhaps close to the cellars. It took me a moment to realize that the steps had ended and there were no more hand rails to grasp. That frightened me even more because I had nothing left to guide me. I blindly continued to walk in what I thought was a straight line until my hand touched a wall in front of me.

My heart began to race as it dawned on me that I had found a door. This door was unlocked, and it was real, not figment of my imagination. I was on my path to liberty.

I pulled the handle slowly, fearing that someone would hear me. I was uncertain about what lay ahead—I may have uncovered an old trap.

But when I pulled the door open, there was no trap. The door opened onto a small street that was unknown to me. The street was made of cobblestones, very narrow and dimly lit. I stood there for many minutes, just breathing the fresh air and weeping for joy that I had come this far and that I was safe.

What should I make of my new discovery? I didn't know for now. For me, it was enough that I had found a way to the outside and that I could get there unhindered by anyone else.

To my surprise, returning to my room was not a challenge. I could easily see the stairs and the corridors in that deep darkness. This was so strange – how was this possible? But I didn't stop to think about how or why that happened. I was happy and thankful that my prayers had been heard, and I was grateful to the master architect who built this passage.

So much of my past had been hidden from me, but now, my future lay ahead of me.

I would not despair. Not now, not ever.

3

"GOD'S SPEED, SAFIRA," SAID MY brother, giving me a soft farewell pat on my shoulder. "By the way, would you like for me to bury your dead *friend* or keep him around?"

"Don't touch him until I return–he won't decompose," I answered as I finished packing my gear. "Maybe we're wrong about him. Keep the signal on me at all times."

"I could come with you," suggested my brother putting on a tempting smile.

"No, you are most useful here to monitor the place. This should be easy–I'm not going to fight the man, I am just stealing his sword."

That morning, a search for one of our lost relics had me on a flight to Germany by dawn. I had traveled all over the world looking for the two swords that had been lost in the distant past, the only ones that could destroy my kind forever.

And for the past century my sole mission was to stay alive and retrieve the swords.

Octavian had a clear and solid lead when he located Hans Wagner and the Fire Sword at a farm in a small village in Germany, close to our US military base in Wiesbaden. We offered to buy it but Herr Wagner refused vehemently– perhaps he knew the real secret behind it. We had no other choice but to try to steal it.

My plane was ready and loaded at the Newnan airport. Two hours before landing, the phone rang a few times in the small device in my ear.

"Safira, we have a situation here," said my brother, a bit irritated. "This morning, some crazy idiot took over the Wagner's farm, declaring that it's his territory. He took the whole family as hostage–five of them are small children–and he ambushed some of the Marines passing by the farm who were returning from a recon exercise."

"Are you sure that it is *our* Wagner's farm?" I asked, astonished.

"Yes," continued my brother. "It's all over the news. They don't know who this fool is, but he has a few others with him. The police sent in a German hostage negotiator and he was killed. The police snipers can't get close enough to them and two of their helicopters have been shot down. They've got satellites, motion detectors and monitors surrounding the place. These guys are armed to the teeth. They've got some heavy military style weapons and they're not amateurs–they certainly aren't afraid to use them. Apparently they are planning to send a squad of SEAL's in to ambush them."

"This is insane!" I exclaimed puzzled. I was troubled by this entire situation as well. "Why are these people after the Wagner's property?"

Until that moment I was certain that I could pull off this mission as we had planned all along.

"Perhaps they are just after our military; they are mercenaries. I don't like this at all. Safira, I need you to abort."

"No way! I can handle this," I answered with confidence. "The sword is there. I just have to find a way to the farm."

"The Military base is sending a rescue team," answered my brother and I heard the sound of more computers monitors coming online.

"Aha!" I exclaimed with a bit of excitement in my voice. "The mortal soldiers. I always wanted to try them out. Let's see how good they are."

"You've got your wish—these are the best, the Navy SEALs. And how are you planning to pull that off?"

"Do they have a medic with them?"

My brother finally responded to me while I got permission to land at a private airport close to town.

"This particular team doesn't have one. Here are the coordinates—twenty-six kilometers northwest of the airport—that's where the commando team is right now. The farm is two and a half kilometers off the road, but they can't get any closer. Now, good luck to you, Safira."

* * *

After I landed, I unloaded my car, my favorite dark gray Land Rover from the back of my plane and went through customs pretty fast. Then, exiting the town, I drove on EU 79 for twenty kilometers until I left the highway and I turned right on road 1145.

The German police task force, ambulances, and the Marines waved to show me the shelter they had found, a safe distance from where the mercenaries were holed up. I could hear sporadic gunfire coming from my right side that was more like a warning than hostile action.

I made my way down that narrow dusty country road until I reconnoitered with a truck—a camouflaged troop carrier with two benches on each side of the bed and a canvas canopy overhead. All the men in the truck looked at me with surprised expressions on their faces. I parked my car and waved at them to let me on board. One of the men shook his head, and there was no doubt that he was very much disappointed with my presence.

"I'm a nurse, with the American Red Cross" I said to him, certain that my new cover would keep me safe—at least until I reached the farm. I had volunteered with Red Cross many times in the past and I was sure they had my name on file. I grabbed the medical bag I always keep in my car and jumped into the truck, frustrated that I didn't bring along my own guns and ammunition.

"Report to Commander Grant," the man ordered me without any other comment.

We drove a few more kilometers until we got closer to the farm. Everybody took cover behind a hill that was about twice the height of an average man. It was no more than a grassy knoll, but it could give them some protection and good view.

As soon as I approached the commanding officer to introduce myself, I wished I would have listened to my brother and returned home. My heart started to beat faster at the sight of him. He was tall, with dark hair and blue eyes, like me–like all of us.

At the very moment my eyes froze on him, my spirit was disturbed and shaken. It was eerie how much he resembled Andreas, the Immortal Warrior who I once loved. He stared back at me, but his piercing blue eyes did not allow me to read into his soul.

"Why're you here?" Commander Grant turned and stared at me for a few seconds. I was not wearing a uniform and my dark colored stretch pants and shirt were not quite a fancy fashion statement. The choice of my dark colored clothes was solely to keep me invisible–I came here to steal what was rightfully mine. I had my long brown hair in a ponytail and my makeup was almost nonexistent–not quite the right circumstances if I wanted to impress a young man.

I lowered my head so he could not see the changing intensity of my blue eyes.

"In case you need me, sir, I'm a medic," I answered, trying to calm down the rhythm of my heart and praying that he wouldn't send me back. "There are women and children in the house. The ambulance is further up the road."

Commander Grant turned and looked at me again, even more perplexed. But for just a moment, a current of excitement passed through my body–it was a sentiment of pleasure combined with irritation. I was an old Warrior from a different world encountering a modern soldier, and for reasons I couldn't understand, I felt vulnerable and captivated by his presence.

"Look! I'm not sure about this at all," he said, not entirely convinced but not denying my story either. "This is odd. How long you have been a nurse? What's your name?"

His questions were rather abrupt, but I understood his position. I looked strikingly out of place, and perhaps, I appeared to be too young to be out there.

"Seventy years. Sorry, seven years–I'm very good at my job. My name is Safira Tash." I immediately wished I hadn't given him my real name, but it was too late for that.

"I'm sure you are, Safira Tash, but I'd rather have someone who's also capable of shooting a rifle. This is a dangerous mission we're on," Grant tried to warn me. "You've got to stay behind my men at all times. We'll give you as much protection as we can. Understood?"

"Yes, sir," I answered, amused by his innocent intent to keep me safe.

We crawled to the top of the hill. The snipers took their positions at the highest point of the knoll and made sure their rifles were locked and loaded while they tried to assess the situation. By now the sun had fully set and the night was pitch black–there was no light whatsoever that was visible from the farm. The stars and the moon were covered by heavy clouds.

Commander Grant ordered me to stay several meters behind them, so I could see nothing. Judging by the sounds, though, the gunfire was coming from two directions directly across from us, perhaps from different floors of the building. I tried to do an initial determination of the mercenaries' positions from the sounds I heard, but I needed to *see*.

"Tash, get down!" Grant yelled at me, when I attempted to crawl to the top of the hill.

"Sir, from where we're positioned, it'll be damn hard to hit them", said one of the snipers as he adjusted his night vision goggles. "They know the range of our weapons and they're too far away for a clear shot. It'll be a tough shot from this distance in the dark."

"Lieutenant Pollack," Grant said to the soldier who had the night vision goggles, "the only way out of this situation is to put the snipers on them, but we're still too far away, we need to get closer. They have motion sensors so we have to be fast and accurate."

"Understood."

I could see that once they left our little shelter, they would be going directly in sight of the mercenaries and in their line of fire. There was nothing to offer them protection from our position to the first building of the farm—just an empty field with short, close cropped grass, and the wreckage of the two helicopters. If they tried to crawl and take cover behind the wrecks, it would be physically very difficult. There's no doubt that they would be detected by the mercenaries and shot.

I didn't try to peek over the hill this time, but I distanced myself further down from the top of the hill. I needed to call back Octavian, my brother. There was no chance that I could get closer to the farm unobserved and see with my own eyes what the real situation was. My adrenaline was rising.

"I need you to pin down my location and tell me what's going on around me," I whispered to him in my ear piece phone. "I can't *look* and I'm unarmed. I need you to tell me what you see."

"Sure, I understand," he said defensively. "Here we go; the images are coming in, now. There's a Humvee and a truck in the front of the house. Soldiers are in the truck, but they're trapped. I can't see inside the house. Let me see if I can hack in through their satellite." After a few seconds that felt like minutes for me, he continued.

"OK–it's on. On the first floor there are three guys, moving back and forth from window to window. They're armed with sniper rifles and from the way they're handling themselves they're not afraid of retaliation. There's a fourth guy with them, too, who may be the leader–he's not armed. There're some other people lying on the floor, the Wagner family I assume. On the next floor there are three more guys with machine guns, and grenade and rocket launchers. They're trying to locate you and soon they'll have you totally pinned down."

"Can I reach them from here?" I asked, but I already knew the answer.

"Yes, from the top of the hill. Think fast and *look*. Any weapon will work. I'll keep the signal logged on you."

"What are you mumbling about, Tash?" Grant asked me and from the tone of his voice, I knew he was highly irritated and uncomfortable with my presence. Obviously, at this point I became an unwelcome distraction for him.

"Nothing, sir," I answered as I quickly checked the snipers' rifles.

"Be quiet!"

The mercenaries were shooting toward our position, but they couldn't see us in the dark any more than we could see them. A grenade exploded not too far from our left side. The warning was understood– they wouldn't allow anybody to get any closer than we already were.

I couldn't just lie here on this hill and do nothing– I was a Warrior, after all. I jumped up from my prone position and grabbed one of the sniper's rifles that had a ten round magazine.

By the time the soldier understood my intentions, I was already standing up on the hill.

The bad guys saw my movements on their monitors. At this point, I needed for all of them to come to the windows. Some grenades and bullets were being fired randomly to reach our position, but they did nothing to harm me. The SEALs took cover behind our knoll.

Now I could *look*. I could see. At first my vision was dim and out of focus because I hadn't looked in a few weeks and I was out of practice. But in a moment the road ahead and all the buildings appeared to me as if they were in daylight.

"Yes, come to the windows my friends," I whispered while my finger was ready to pull the trigger. A moment later they were in my sight.

My eyes glowed like two miniature blue headlights in the night. One by one, I shot them all. It only took me ten seconds to finish the job.

Suddenly there was silence all around us. The darkness and the silence were almost majestic.

My eyes had closed to hide their glowing—none of the others could see me, and when I turned around, the glow was gone. I can't remember if Grant yelled at me again, but I'm sure he did.

"They are all down," I said to him. "Go rescue your men, Commander."

I returned the rifle to the sniper who took it back, visibly confused. That type of rifle was not designed to be fired from a standing position. Commander Grant furiously pushed me back down the hill. He looked through his night vision binoculars to confirm that the mercenaries had all been killed, and he gave the order for his men to approach the house with caution.

All the seven men were dead. A couple of them were very young, barely eighteen. I had seen their faces before I shot them, and that saddened me. They were too young to be killed.

I had taken many lives since the day, long ago, when I fought alongside my brothers. But in a war it doesn't matter. Someone's life has must be taken in order for another to survive; I know the meaning of this concept very well.

"Can somebody tell me what just happened?" asked Grant in disbelief. "Medic, what the hell did you do?"

4

FOR THE NEXT TWO NIGHTS *I didn't sleep well as I thought about my discovery and how it might affect my life. I didn't go down to my spying room and watch Lord Milos Martuzon, either. I knew that my discovery of the door to outside the castle had to be kept a total secret, until I was ready to leave for good.*

But where would I go? I didn't know who I was; I had no last name and had even less knowledge of the possible existence of any relatives. That was why I had to wait here in this prison as I painfully searched for more answers. By now I realized that Nana Saveta could not be relied upon for any answers and the one I needed to confront was the Governor himself.

At the beginning, when I was taken to Black Eagle Palace, I believed that my situation at the palace would be temporary. I didn't want to leave my old home, Lord Fers Martuzon's palace in Cluj, the one place where I could remember my mother. I had seen people honoring her when I was a child and I was delighted by the attention she received.

But something happened when I was four years old. That evening, Mother didn't come back to our quarters. I was left by myself for a whole night, until the next day when one of the Governor's aides came and introduced me to Nana Saveta and she became my new family. At that moment I started to pray every day for Mother's return. I could feel in my heart that she wasn't dead, but there was no one who would talk to me about her. Nana Saveta's mouth was sealed. I knew even less about my father who had disappeared before I was born.

I did not know why someone like the Governor, or his son, Lord Milos Martuzon who became Governor, would take an interest in me, to keep me as his own. Since I came here to Black Eagle Castle, my only interaction with him was to observe him through my apartment window, watching his comings and goings. Lately, though, since I discovered the secret closet above his quarters, I had been spying on him in his own sanctuary.

Most people would consider my situation a tremendous asset. I was housed, fed, clothed, and educated in a most grand manner, especially when I thought of myself as being a mere orphan. But for me that was not enough. I had a tremendous inner drive to learn everything I could about my origins and my family.

I wanted to see the Governor, to talk with him, to ask him many questions. But perhaps this was why he was avoiding me, to keep the story of my origins shrouded in mystery. If that was true, what were his motives for doing that? Although he was a total stranger to me, I had no doubt that, Milos Martuzon was more than my rescuer. There had to be a compelling reason that he needed to have me in his palace. I had to find a way to remind him of my presence, to remind him that I needed him to reveal my past and my family's past to me. But how?

*   *   *

Nana Saveta came in early that morning to help me curl my hair. I refused her help because I didn't see any point to it. It always made Nana agitated when I refused to dress and groom myself, and when I started another hunger strike. One day all of my refusals and lack of cooperation would cause her to have a nervous breakdown.

"Why should I dress up, Nana? No one of any importance ever sees me and my only friends in this huge palace are the servants and the guards. They are obligated to try to make me happy, but their opinion of how I look doesn't matter. Even School Master Seles wouldn't notice if my hair was wild and frizzy or if I wasn't properly dressed."

"What is your game today my dear? Are you trying to make me lose my job over your refusal? They will send me away if they think you don't need me..."

I laughed. Nana was trying to use the same kind of schemes on me that I used on her. But this time I was sure that I would succeed and win this argument.

"Nana, no one will ever send you away. I need you and I rely solely on you, but no one else in this world wants me or needs me. My mother almost certainly abandoned me many years ago and left me to grow up as a prisoner. Why, Nana? Why did she abandon me? Was I so hideous to her that she could no longer look at me? I just do not even deserve to be alive!"

"What are you talking about, my child? Your mother didn't abandon you", she said, betraying her oath of silence. But was too late for her to take back what she had said, and this was the perfect opportunity for me to continue with this same train of thought.

"Why I should believe you?" I responded. "You have been avoiding my questions for fourteen years, and anything you say now can't be believed. If my mother died, I was not even given a chance to weep at her tomb. What child deserves this, tell me? Tell me, Nana?"

Nana stood by the window, looking outside with a mindless expression. Many minutes passed before she turned to look at me.

When she turned around, I thought she would lash out at me for having called her a liar. But when I looked at her fully, there were tears streaming down her face. All I saw in her eyes was compassion and love, after all this time. I was astonished!

"Your mother was forced to leave and she didn't have a choice. I speak the truth, now, as earnestly as I can. Your mother is not dead, but this is all I can tell you for now. But I swear on the grave of my own dead child, this is the truth. I don't know what you will choose to do with what I just told you, but if Lord Martuzon learns that I have told you this, I will be executed. I am sorry, my child—I know you have suffered because your lack the knowledge of your past, but in time you will learn everything you have ever hoped to know."

Nana had just revealed one of the most important details to me that I was seeking. That alone was sufficient for me to have some hope.

"Thank you Nana. I will not ask for more information, I promise. I can't possibly dare to think of a better future for me because my life here in this palace is so insecure. The thing I fear the most is that the Governor will decide one day that I no longer deserve to live here and I will have nowhere else to go. I need for him to reassure me that I have a safe haven here and that I am under his protection. Instead, he ignores me completely. I am constantly worried about my fate and I think I might go insane. I am so frightened, Nana, that I will lose his good will. It seems there is nothing anyone can do to give me the hope that he is favorable toward me."

My little speech sounded sincere, and I hoped she wouldn't hear the sarcasm in my tone of voice. I hoped I had convinced Nana about how I felt—that my situation was weak and vulnerable, and my mind was in such turmoil that my sanity was in doubt.

"Don't be worried, Lady Safira. He won't forget that you are in his palace."

"He will!!" I wailed falling backwards on my bed. "He doesn't remember me anymore. And what will happen to me if he decides to get married? His wife would never allow me to continue to live here!"

"You only think negative thoughts."

"I don't know who I am! If Lord Martuzon decides that he doesn't want me here anymore, I won't have any more desire to live!"

"You frighten me now, my child!"

"Nana, I'm so sad, I just want to be alone. Please, go away and don't come back until it's time for dinner! Tell the School Master that I am ill today. Please!"

Nana Saveta left my room believing that I was despondent and broken hearted, but I had other plans. I knew that I must gain access to the Governor, but I had to be either wise or tricky—or both. I had to speak with him in order for him to inadvertently reveal more facts about me and my origins, just as Nana did.

I received the greatest piece of information today since I have known Nana—that my mother still lives, and she didn't abandon me— she was forced to leave. But who was the diabolical person who did this to my family? Someone, somewhere, has the answer to this mystery and I must learn it, and I must find my mother, too.

For now, I had two things to hold close to my heart: the door I had discovered that will lead me to my freedom and a mother who was somewhere, either near or far away.

*   *   *

The Black Eagle Palace was located in the heart of the city. It was shaped like a horseshoe, four stories high, and seventy-six rooms with three entrances into the castle's inner gathering hall. The windows of my quarters were deliberately placed towards the inside court.

The outside view from the castle was a beautiful scene of the Crisu River on the right side and Alexander Street, with its view of many grandiose buildings on the left. From my quarters, though, all I could see were servants going about their daily routines, guards, and many other usual inhabitants of the city who constantly came to the castle for their business.

I spent the entire day sitting at my window and watching the parade of people in the courtyard from my window, and I recognized some of them. Mr. Milea and Mr. Rozan were my favorites. They were both noblemen and both were very much disliked by the Governor. Although they were unwelcome to the palace, and they knew this, they stubbornly continued to come here for an audience almost every day.

Miss Flora Cristea was a regular visitor, also. I would wave at her and she would wave back. She was the only Transylvanian among all the females who visited with and who entertained the young and still single Lord Martuzon. I liked her and I considered her my distant friend.

Miss Anda Kovach was also a visitor on a regular basis—I did not wave at her. She was a very mean-spirited lady, very vocal and very rude. It was not an exaggeration to say that Anda and I disliked each other intensely. She knew I was a ward of the Governor, and my continued presence here resulted in a tremendous amount of rivalry and jealousy.

She came to the palace every day and the rumors were that the Governor was very fond of her. If he were to marry her, the prediction I made to Nana would become a reality. That she hates me is unquestioned. I needed to seek my liberty and get away from this situation soon, but before I did that, I had to discover all that I could about my lost family.

* * *

I went to my secret closet before dinner because Lord Martuzon was in his apartment, preparing for his evening meal. Although the palace has several formal dining rooms, he often likes to dine in his apartment in the company of his close confidants.

As I had watched him for the past year, I came to the conclusion that he was very much a tormented soul, much like me—a loner. His deeper secrets were very well hidden and his fears made everyone around him quite uneasy. Most of the time I didn't understand the deep meaning of his conversations, and all I could learn about him was that he lived his life watching over his shoulder for unseen enemies. There was one thing I was sure of: I felt compassion for him.

That night he was preparing to dine alone—at least, this is what I thought. To my unpleasant surprise, Anda had been invited to keep him company as they enjoyed the repast. I had to be tremendously patient to stay in my closet for those two hours, waiting for that creature to leave. I had no interest in their conversation whatsoever.

They spoke softly, almost in whispers, and all I could hear was her annoying laugh. I could see Milos' face blushing from time to time, a particular sign that he was very uncomfortable with the entire situation.

After exhausting all the subjects of conversation that she knew, Anda left the apartment. Perhaps, too, she was a bit tired of his unwillingness to succumb to her temptations and subtle hints of promises of more physical intimacy. It was in that moment that I began to like him even more.

I was about to leave my hiding place, convinced that there were no other events that evening that would concern me, when Nana entered his parlor accompanied by Mr. Lutz, the Governor's personal aide. I came closer to the window so I could hear them more clearly.

"*Thank you for allowing me to speak to you, my Lord. I am so grateful,*" *said Nana, bowing to him.*

"*What can I do for you, Nana Saveta?*" *asked Lord Martuzon in a very pleasant manner.*

"*My Lord, I have tried not to trouble you in the past for anything. Now I dare to ask you to do me a great favor. The girl you entrusted into my care has had a very difficult time. I have been her only family for so long, my Lord, but now she needs you.*"

Lord Martuzon stood quietly for a moment, trying to understand what it was that Nana was asking of him—or perhaps, just trying to remember me.

"*Nana Saveta, I really don't understand you.*"

"*Lady Safira needs you, my Lord; she needs to see you and she needs to talk with you. She needs to get your assurance that she is safe here...*"

"*Of course she is secure here. I would never abandon her. She belongs to me and everyone here knows it. Did you not tell her this?*"

"*No my Lord; she needs to hear this coming directly from you. She needs to know the truth.*"

"*Absolutely not! I am not ready to talk with this child and I am not ready for any of her questions...*"

"*She is not a child anymore, my Lord, she is almost nineteen. She has no friends—her only acquaintances are the servants and guards—and she feels abandoned by you. There is a terrible spirit of depression and sadness surrounding her that greatly concerns me. Please, my Lord, come and talk with her.*"

"I understand that she is troubled, but I am in no mood for talking to a child who has hundreds of questions to ask me. My time is limited and I have many responsibilities to this country. This is why I do not wish to see her or to talk with her..."

"My Lord! Please, come and just give her a few minutes of your time."

"I will consider talking with her, but it won't be any time soon. Archduke Rudolph is arriving tomorrow, and I do not want his stay here to be troubled or marred by anything."

"How long will it be, my Lord, before you think you can talk with her?"

Lord Martuzon stepped into his bedroom and I could hardly hear him speaking from there.

"Four months, Nana, four months. Can she wait that long?"

* * *

My heart was heavy and sad. I fell asleep late that night and I thought someone was kissing my lips and touching my face. I opened my eyes, frightened. I was alone. Apparently it was only a dream.

5

DO NOT FALL IN LOVE with a mortal.

Some rules are possible to keep; some are not. Mine came down to this one: no mortal can resist us–just a small glimmer in our eyes can sent a powerful signal to their brain and made them act on their instincts. If I had been intentionally grounded for so long, now I was being pulled toward the inevitable–I couldn't restrain myself from being enthralled with him. It could be just the fact that he resembled Andreas or the side effect of my perpetual secret erotic dream.

"Tash, what the hell is wrong with you?" Commander Grant yelled at me again, perhaps just to vent his frustration.

Commander Grant's blue, piercing eyes looked at me in anger and disbelief. As we made our way toward the farm house, he continued to ask.

"You could have been killed. Are you suicidal?"

Lieutenant Pollack, the sniper whose weapon I had commandeered, tried unsuccessfully to interrupt. Whatever he wanted to say, he couldn't find the right moment to get Grant's attention.

"Your AS 50 is a great rifle," I said to Pollack. "Good choice."

"I'll put this in my report," continued Grant following me. "You can be sure of it."

His grumbling didn't disturb me at all. He continued to express his anger by asking me what I considered to be meaningless and irrelevant questions. As one of the soldiers had found the farm's fuse box, we turned the lights on in the house.

I checked the house room by room, pretending to look for the hostages and survivors but hoping to find my precious sword, but the house seemed to been ransacked. First I found the family. There were three males, four females, and their children, tied up in the corner of the living room but none of them were hurt–just frightened. The eight soldiers were all alive, but some were seriously wounded; however, none of their injuries were fatal. One of the soldiers was unconscious, and when I touched his forehead, he awakened.

"You're safe," I assured him. "Are you able to walk?"

He nodded. "I need you to help me with the others."

As the SEALs and the soldier helped with the wounded, they watched me in silence, amazed at how rapidly I prepped the wounds and wrapped the bandages. They realized that without a doubt I knew my craft.

The mortal body was so easy for me to repair.

In a few minutes we had all the wounded in the trucks, ready to return to the aid station. I was certain that they were all out of danger–I made sure of that. Everyone was alive and accounted for.

But Grant would not substitute my work and my silence as an answer to his questions.

"You interfered with an ongoing operation where you had no business," I heard him saying walking behind me. "What was your motive for endangering our mission and our lives? You'd better have a damn good explanation!"

The sniper, Pollack, approached him again and they distanced themselves from me, beside one of the Humvees. I could still hear him as they talked, but his face was unreadable.

"Pollack, what the hell happened? How could you let her get close enough to you to grab your rifle?"

"Commander, she was so fast that she had the rifle before I knew what was happening. But here's the thing. I just looked at all the dead guys and they were shot between their eyes. Those rounds almost took their heads off!"

"What?" exploded Grant. "How can that even be possible?"

"It's not," answered Pollack gazing in my direction. "That was the most fantastic exhibition of marksmanship that I've ever seen, and I've seen a lot. Who the hell is she?"

For a second time I carefully checked every room of the farm house hoping to find what I came here for.

"Octavian, I can't find the sword," I said, knowing that my brother was still listening in. "Where it could be? I've looked everywhere. This place is ransacked."

"It should be on the first floor, in the living room, on the wall hanging over the fireplace. I swear to you– that is where I saw it last, two days ago when the owner put their family's pictures on the social website. It was the Fire Sword, trust me."

"Well, it's not there anymore," I mumbled furiously, "I'm looking at the fireplace, and there's nothing there."

"Check the dead mercenaries," suggested my brother as angry as I was. "Maybe they were looking for the same thing."

I ran up to the second floor to take a better look at the men I just killed. Now, all the rooms were empty. Only the shattered glass from the broken windows remained a solid witness to the horrible event that night.

"Too late," I said to my brother, "I think the SEALs got them. I could find a way to follow them to the base."

A vague suspicion that something wasn't right plagued my mind and I planned to linger behind a little longer. But Grant grabbed me and pushed me into his Humvee. After he made sure that all of his command was safely on the move, we were the last to leave. He was even more hostile with me on the drive back to my vehicle.

"Talk to me, Tash," he said, still angry as his eyes narrowed looking at me. "I need to understand what I just saw. Are you trying to wrangle some kind of medal or are you just plain crazy? Why did you pull such a crazy stunt?

You needlessly risked your life and you didn't even give me or my SEALs a chance to do our job."

"I'm sure your plan would have worked, Commander, but we were running out of time. My 'crazy stunt' as you call it was a better choice."

My answer did nothing to gain his sympathy and I agonized over his indifference to me. I had to firmly resist every temptation of making him interested in me, but it was so hard to control that desire. If I accomplished that, I might have had a moment of delight, unleashing a forbidden passion with him, but where would that have gotten me?

Even so, after over a century of keeping a firm grip on my feelings, I suddenly felt a loss of tranquility in my spirit and I couldn't stop it.

"You're a hell of a shot," he said in an even tone of voice. "Where did you learn to shoot like that? Nobody can see in the dark at that distance, and be so precise and so fast."

His unintended compliment made me smile. Even though he considered me to be lunatic, he couldn't undo my actions.

"Well, I've just spent a lot of time on the firing range," I lied again.

"Do you think I'm a fool? My best sniper couldn't have done what you did. You have an accent—it sounds German. Where are you from?" His sudden interest sounded suspicious to me.

"No, I'm not German, but I was born in Transylvania…"

"Yeah, that's a famous place. Transylvania! Lots of spooky creatures, right?"

I shook my head in denial. I was beginning to get irritated with his questions.

"Safira," I heard my brother's worried voice in my ear device. "You need to turn around—I see some activity back at the farm. There's been movement back and forth from the house to the barn. Did you leave someone behind? I just saw a guy put some detonators in the barn—I have their heat signature on the monitor. And get rid of the SEAL you have with you."

"Commander, stop the car!" I screamed at him. The noise of the squealing tires echoed into the night.

"What's wrong now?" he asked and his voice blasted with irritation.

"I need to turn back to the farm. The barn's got bombs stashed inside—the family will be back in the morning."

"How do you know?"

"Someone back in the States hacked into their monitors."

"I need to report it and wait for my orders."

"Jesus!" I exclaimed frustrated. "There's no time for that. Commander, my brother who is also my source, is never wrong."

Grant hesitated for a moment but made a U turn in the road. I could tell that he didn't like my answer at all. "What a hell," he mumbled.

We drove directly to the massive building on the left side of the house and he killed the engine. I felt my eyes burning, wanting the relief of their being able to open wide and look through the walls. This hidden force inside me acts very much like a self-defense system. In any other circumstances, seeing what was on the inside of the barn would have been so easy.

I suspected by now that Grant didn't fully believe me to be just a medic or a nurse working for the Red Cross, one that has a brother hacking into foreign satellites. But how could I conceal who I really was from him and not get ourselves killed? Moreover, I had to order Commander Grant to stay inside the Humvee where it was safer for him.

There was only one choice: I rapidly twisted in my seat and grabbed his pistol from his holster. I pointed it at him. For the second time that night I was about to serve Grant another helping of craziness.

"Stay in the vehicle, Sir! I mean it. If you get out, I *will* shoot you. Is that understood?"

Grant's face flushed with surprise and anger, but I saw in his eyes that he would listen–for now.

I got out of the Humvee and ran to the building. Once inside, I released the light from my eyes and I *looked*. Now, I could see the location of the bombs, hidden randomly in the haystacks. There were five of them, an act of overkill.

"Safira Tash." I heard his angry voice behind me.

Commander Grant had not followed my order. He came inside the barn, and when I turned toward him, my eyes were still glowing with their soft, mysterious and frightening blue light. The inevitable happened–he was under my spell.

We stood there staring at each other as the glowing from my eyes slowly diminished and disappeared. For me, this was a normal day in my life–in my very long life.

"Commander, you need to go back." I ordered him harshly as I ignored his frozen look.

"OK," he said. "Get back in the Humvee with me. If you're right and there are bombs in here–we've got to call in the bomb disposal unit."

"There's no time for that. You get in the Humvee *now* and back the vehicle up one hundred meters," I shouted at him, still pointing the gun in his direction. My eyes were glowing again and I became impatient.

He ran back and put the Humvee in reverse. I was sure I had humiliated him by giving him an order, but I didn't care. I just wanted him to be safe.

I disabled four of the bombs with all the speed that I was capable of, but I couldn't find the wires or a detonator for the fifth one. As I walked around looking for it, I stepped on something. I looked down and I saw a body of a dead mercenary with a big hole in his forehead and I could see that I was stepping in his brain matter. I looked around and I quickly discovered five more bodies.

"I found the dead people," I said to Octavian in my ear piece. "None of them have my sword in their possession."

"What are they?" asked my brother. "Amestec?"

"I am not sure. Should I bring one home?"

"No, it's too risky."

But there was one mercenary missing.

I saw the timer that would detonate the fifth bomb in one of the dead hands. It was a motion activated timer that started to count down when something moved in its vicinity. Its digital readout showed that I only had three seconds remaining before it would blow. There was no time to run.

As the bomb detonated, the ground shook with the terrible power. For a few moments, debris from the building and the roof rocketed into the air in every direction. The barn and all traces of the mercenaries were wiped out in the explosion and fire.

The blast propelled me high into the air and I sailed over the flames. I landed on my feet through a curtain of ashes and fumes. Grant's Humvee was covered with dirt, stalks of hay, and parts of the barn, but he had already leaped out of the vehicle, screaming my name again.

There was a terrified look on his face as I walked towards to him, like he was seeing a ghost. He started to brush off my clothes and my body. Starting with my face, his hands wiped my neck and shoulders, and then he brushed his palms over my breasts slowing down when he touched my hips.

What he was doing felt almost improper, and at the same time it was extremely delightful. For another long moment he stood there staring at me mesmerized. I didn't have any wound, not even a scratch, but my clothes were badly torn, my skin's complexion was darker and my hair was grey.

There was only one thing that could kill me, and this wasn't it.

"Damn you girl," Grant whispered incapable of hiding anymore his emotions.

He pulled me closer to him, lowered his head to mine, and unexpectedly kissed me fully on my lips. He was daring at first–a little rough–then he relaxed the pressure of his lips and his kiss became softer and more passionate. His lips were hot and tasted like mint as his tongue slid between my teeth.

My blood rushed thru my veins like fire. I didn't try to push him away–my knees suddenly felt as if they were made of rubber–even though I knew that I could kill him with one touch.

But I liked it. I closed my eyes and responded to his kiss, indulging myself in this crazy moment that stirred up every fiber of my body and my soul.

When he realized exactly what he had done, he became flustered, and backed away from me.

"Six of the attackers were inside the barn, one is missing. Somebody made sure that their identity was destroyed," I said, trying to act normally, but in reality I was shaken. Grant pretended not to hear me. He regained his coolness again.

"Jesus Christ," he said clearing the debris form the windshield. "I don't know why you're not dead right now, after what just happened. And give me back my gun."

I passed his pistol to him without looking at him. In fact, we didn't look at each other as we drove back to the main road, where I had parked my vehicle. He had stirred up quite a bit of turbulence in my world, and I'm sure I had produced some disorder in his perfectly well organized and logical life as well.

When we pulled up to my car, he didn't expect any other word from me, not even a goodbye. But before I got out, I said it anyway.

"God's speed, Commander Grant!" I said, trying to sound casual and indifferent.

"My name is Julian. Who are you, Safira Tash?" he asked, and for the first time since we met, he smiled at me. But I turned my back to him and got into my vehicle, leaving without answering.

I was sure that there would be no next time, no more encounters between us. I was returning home, defeated, but my spirit was on fire.

Oh, that's right—we kissed.

6

FOUR MONTHS? *I DIDN'T HAVE that much time to wait for Lord Martuzon to clear an hour or less for me, four months from today. I must confess that his disinterest in me hurt quite a bit, but I couldn't blame him entirely—his duties came first, I knew. I should be touched by my Nana's effort to take a stand for me. For now, it was enough that he was reminded of my existence, but I needed more from him.*

In those interminable hours that I secretly watched him, an unprecedented feeling of attachment for him grew within me. More than that, the desire to be closer to him personally, as his other females friends were, began to stir. In my heart, Milos was both my protector and my jailer—a paradox between friend and enemy—and I could make no sense of it.

How could I be noticed by him when I was not allowed to have any company, when I was not invited to any of his dinners or balls? I had to consider exactly what Lord Martuzon feared about me. Unpleasant questions came to my mind regarding my presence in the castle. Nana was my one tormented witness to it. I needed to change some things, and I must take a different approach.

By now it was clear to me that I was surrounded by a terrible secret, and I would never unravel it if my manners were repulsive to him. I certainly considered myself innocent of any manner of wrong doing in my relationship with Lord Martuzon, but at this point, that didn't matter. Now I must change all that.

* * *

Nana found me in good spirits that morning and that made her happy, too. However, this was a ruse that I had to maintain in order to keep my own secrets well hidden. I couldn't express any gratitude for her intervention, or she would know that I had spied on her visit with Lord Martuzon.

But now, for the first time since we had been together, I opened my heart to her, allowing myself to have some love and compassion toward her. I had stubbornly repressed these feelings for so long, pouring out all of my bitterness for my unjust life onto her. But as I began to mature into my late teens I needed to be loved, to be cared for, and to love in return. I would never cease to look for my missing parents, but I could not search alone, with no assistance.

"Oh, Nana come and see! There are so many servants who are gathered in the courtyard!" I said as I gazed out of my window.

"The prince must have arrived," she answered without bothering to rise from her chair. "It is best to remain where we are for now, and to not be in the way..."

"In the way?"

Nana's words involuntarily instigated an idea that I couldn't contain or have time to think about.

"Nana Saveta, please, grant me permission to go and see the prince! Please—I will come back right away! No one will notice me, everyone is so busy. Please!"

Nana stared at me, astonished by my request. I could see her fighting within herself over such daring, yet simple, request. But since I was on such good behavior for the first time ever, she couldn't refuse my fervent desire. She was so flustered that she didn't even accompany me.

I ran outside my room and through the long corridor to the main stairway. The guard saw me as I passed him, but he didn't question my unaccompanied movement in the light of day. This was the very first time I had wandered alone on this side of the palace. I only had an intuition of the direction in which I was supposed to go, from what I had observed from my window, but all the action in the courtyard created a loud noise. I followed the sounds and other people who were headed in the same direction.

It was a bit chilly outside, a rainy day in early April, and I soon regretted leaving my room so suddenly without my shawl. I tried to keep my promise to Nana and stay far away from the prince's arrival, but my curiosity got the better of me and I pushed closer. All I wanted at this moment was to see the royal guest; otherwise, a chance like this would never come my way again.

His Highness' carriage stopped in the courtyard and a multitude of servants were dispatched to help with his numerous trunks of luggage. He did not come alone, but he was accompanied by his own loyal servants. As he made his way to the entrance of the palace, the palace servants assisted with his personal belongings.

As people moved forward, I was caught up in the crowd. I didn't mind this because I was trying to get a glimpse of the prince myself. Suddenly I found myself face to face with Prince Rudolph, and he assumed I was a servant, so he handed me his hat. I took it with a mechanical movement without thinking, but I was frightened by this close encounter with him. At that moment, Dina, who recognized me, came to my rescue.

"My Lady," she said, bowing to me, "let me help with your burden!"

I stood there, motionless, trying to understand what had just happened, but the servant's behavior toward me did not escape Archduke Rudolph. He was an impressive young man of twenty six, tall, with dark penetrating eyes, and hair colored a mixture of copper and blonde. He wore an imposing moustache that he displayed vainly. I bowed to him, embarrassed and fearful over my stupid and thoughtless action, but he bowed to me, too.

"What is your name, my Lady?" he asked me German, which I spoke fluently.

"Safira, your Highness!" I answered as calmly as I could, but underneath my dress my legs were trembling.

"It is my pleasure to meet you, Lady Safira!"

This time I didn't answer him, but I bowed, hoping that our conversation would end here and I could run back to my room before others in the palace were aware that I was here. He moved on into the palace, indeed, but not before turning back to look at me once more.

I did not run back to Nana—I could barely walk; my legs were shaking and my heart was beating so fast. I couldn't make it slow down, and I had to gain some composure before I could face Nana.

When I finally returned to my room, Nana was still there, waiting for me.

"Did you see him?" she calmly asked, smiling and delighted that I had returned safely.

"Yes, Nana, I did! Thank you for having faith in me, but I know I must have terribly disappointed you. Will you please forgive me?"

As I begged for forgiveness, I told her immediately what had happened. Before today I firmly believed that Nana was against me and that I must keep everything from her, but now I realized that it was better for me to be completely honest with her if I wanted to gain her trust.

"What will happen now, Nana?"

"Well, the prince will be received with honor in the ballroom by all the noblemen in the province, and of course by the Prince Governor, Lord Martuzon. Then they will all continue to socialize while the prince has a short rest. After that, he and Lord Martuzon will..."

"No, Nana, I am speaking about me! What will happen if Lord Martuzon finds out about my escapade? I am not afraid for me, but I do not want him to punish you, my Nana..."

Nana Saveta appeared sincerely moved by my sudden affection for her and she came over to console me. Her right hand softly touched my shoulder.

"I will take all that upon me my dear. Do not be afraid."

*   *   *

After my evening meal I went to my secret closet early. This was the only place where I had any patience without it being a request. I should be safe, though. I hoped that Dina would not tell the prince anything about me other than my name, and I was sure that the prince had already forgotten he had met me.

Seconds after I had reached my secret closet, Lord Martuzon came into his apartment, accompanied by the Archduke, Prince Rudolph.

Mr. Lutz served both of them coffee and wine. Seeing the two men together, I could only confirm that my attraction to Milos was real, despite the strong impression that the prince had made on me earlier in the day. Lord Martuzon was still so young in appearance, with dark hair and green eyes. He barely looked twenty when he was probably closer to thirty.

"It is an honor for me that you have accepted my invitation, my Lord!" I heard the Governor saying to his guest.

"For goodness sake Milos, what are you doing in Oradea?" asked the prince, quite intrigued. "You should be in Clausenburg at least, or even in Budapest. Why are you still here?"

"The City of Cluj proved to be fatal to my father and I did not want it to be fatal to me, also. Here, I am on more neutral ground...I love this palace. The Black Eagle palace suits me quite well."

"Certainly Oradea, is a great and majestic city, but I am not sure of how being here will advance your career. However, I trust your judgment upon this matter."

"I assure you that you will like it here in Oradea," insisted Lord Martuzon. "The people are friendly. Even though most Transylvanian nobles tend to be judgmental, the people here trust me and love me. But I will not bore you with such things. We could speak on this subject for hours. How is His Majesty, the king? I trust all is well with him. And may I also inquire about the Archduchess...?"

The Archduke did not answer him immediately, but he settled himself in his chair to drink some more wine.

"I will have this conversation with you when you're married, my friend," he said sipping the wine. "Until then, you will not understand my answer. Your marriage will be soon, won't it? Is there a good surprise in store for me?"

I held my breath waiting for his answer, hoping it wasn't a positive response.

"I am not in any hurry, your Highness!"

"All right. I still have some hard feeling against you for refusing Lady Edith. She is from a very distinguished family, exactly what you need if you want to have a strong hold on this country. You need to marry into royalty. I will renew my offer my help again, if you wish it."

"Thank you my Lord, I will ask you for it, if I need it…"

"Perhaps you don't need me to help you select a bride," concluded the Prince. "I am sure you are surrounded by many beautiful women here. Upon my arrival this morning I encountered a very lovely young lady, with long brown hair and amazing blue eyes. I am sincere when I tell you that she took my breath away…"

Lord Martuzon was perplexed by this description. Even after a few long minutes he couldn't associate any of his female acquaintances with it.

"I apologize," the governor mumbled, "I do not believe I know a lady of that description."

"Oh, I can help with that! I learned that her name is Lady Safira."

In the secrecy of my closet I closed my eyes so I couldn't see Lord Martuzon's reaction or his face when the prince revealed my name. It was over. There was no question that I would be punished. It would only take a second for my unwise decision to observe the prince's arrival to ruin all the chances I had in the future of finding a way to the heart of the Governor. After a few minutes I heard his answer.

"Oh, her! Lady Safira is my goddaughter. She is a very troubled child, at the very least. I took her under my care at my father's last wish…"

"Wonderful," smiled the Prince, satisfied with the answer. "I suppose you dine with all of your relatives. Am I correct?"

"My Lord, I can assure you that Lady Safira is quite a bit shy. I am afraid she will not make a pleasant dining companion for you."

I could swear that at that moment a great amount of nervousness echoed in Lord Martuzon's answer.

"Shy? Perhaps. But I truly believe that today this beautiful creature deliberately ventured out into the cold weather with one sole purpose – to meet me. I want to delight in her company, Milos. Are you going to deny me my wish?"

7

I LOVE COFFEE. YOU COULD say that I've been addicted to it since 1909, the year we came to America. We were on board *The Carpathia* when we met a very nice American couple from Boston. She was a painter and he was a music teacher, and they befriended us immediately. Miss Geraldine loved to paint Octavian's portrait—as a matter fact, she painted him twenty-seven times over the course of the years. I think we may still have some of those portraits.

Mr. John Glassworthy was a piano and violin teacher. He and Miss Geraldine were childless, and they took us in as their children. He was a very intense person who lived and ate like there was no tomorrow, but he never seemed to gain weight. He remained tall and slender the entire time I knew him. Coffee was his weakness—his cure for every illness—and I could never say "no" to him when he invited me to join him for a cup or more.

We lived in their house for seventeen years before my brother and I inherited his estate after he and Miss Geraldine died. While we lived with them, I truly believe that I drank several hundred gallons of that black miracle.

Our lives were very simple. We lived alone when we could afford it, moving from state to state, but most of the time we roomed and boarded with good hearted people who took us in.

We stayed long enough in a place until the people around us began to raise some questions about our unchanged appearance, but our real motive for moving was to cover the trail of chopped-off bodies we left behind–my hunters.

By mere chance, over twenty years ago, our luck changed dramatically when we were adopted by an older gentleman who was very nice and very rich, but quite eccentric.

That day, we boarded a bus from Arizona to Texas, our new destination. It was shortly after midnight, as we were crossing the New Mexico border into Texas, when our bus collided with something. The bus rolled over twice and its fuel tank exploded. The bus driver had dozed off and didn't see that the eighteen-wheeler in front of him had stopped in the middle of the road. Of the forty people in the bus, no one survived except us, and we merely sustained some minor burns and bruises.

Our story of survival, of how the impact had thrown us out of the bus through a window before the explosion, was in all the newspapers and on the nightly news in Dallas. Because of our very young appearance, it was assumed that our parents had died in the accident, burned beyond recognition. We didn't confirm or deny it.

A few months later we became a part of the household of Mr. Roger Tash, the billionaire oil magnate. His grown son, who was married but childless, was appalled by his father's daring and reckless decision to adopt two teenagers. However, Mr. Roger Tash boldly defended his unusual decision of charity.

Octavian and I loved Mr. Tash. We enjoyed his comforting attitude and we called him our grandfather. Mr. Tash died two years later, after a valiant struggle with brain cancer. The pain of our loss was terrible, but our trust fund was enormous: fifty million dollars each for both Octavian and me.

Seven years later we moved to Georgia. Our home in Peachtree City, a quiet suburb on the south side of Atlanta–overlooking the vast Peachtree Lake–became our fortress. Octavian invested in any security system, weapons, and gadget that money could buy. But in all circumstances, we were ready for a different kind of war.

* * *

I needed more than two cups of coffee before I went down to the basement where we had stored the man I killed in the park.

The dead man's body lay on the cold cement floor in our basement, but he was still warm to the touch. Curiosity is embedded in human nature, and all my senses are human. I wasn't so curious about his lifeless body, but I had to know where his spirit was lurking. Still, as I observed his head, his face had a familiarity that was carved into my memory. His eyes were still open. Perhaps he could still see and hear me– or perhaps not.

I closed his eyes. They had a strange glow in them, a combination of light that was hollow and dark, like pools of water in a cave.

It had been three days since I returned from Germany and I had become a bit restless. Only time will dissipate the memories I came home with and eventually I will lose the awakening that Julian Grant stirred in my heart. It was like a burning coal in my soul, one I can't remove, and one that doesn't heal by itself, as my own flesh does.

At the same time, my attempt to recover one of my precious relics, at that farm in Germany, was a complete failure. Someone got there ahead of me.

"I still don't understand what happened in Germany," I said to my brother, who laid the man on a flat table. "How in the world did the mercenaries get into the barn and how was it possible for that sword to disappear? Do you think that the Amestec is after it and knows its secret?"

"I think that someone, Amestec or not, somehow got away from your shooting and has the sword. That's a powerful weapon if they intend to catch you alive."

My brother moved nervously around the man, pointing his finger to the man's forehead.

"Octavian, what's going on?"

"Beside the fact that this dead man is an experiment, there is something bizarre going on. In the past week, four young girls, aged from eighteen to twenty-five, were kidnapped and then released after a few hours. There was no demand for ransom—they were just snatched, photographed, and then released."

What my brother told me was definitely out of the ordinary. Were we looking at a genetically transformed human fighter? No mortal can do that. And the fact that someone was deliberately abducting these girls just for a photograph raised doubts in my mind that this was being done by someone as a prank.

"Well, what do you think is going on?" I asked, a bit distracted.

"The girls are being selected only because of the color of their hair and eyes. So far, every girl who was taken had blue eyes and dark hair–like you. Although all Immortal Warriors, male and female have dark hair and blue eyes, some mortals resemble us too, like Nelda, my girlfriend, for example."

Octavian turned to me waiting for my reaction. My answer was slow after more than a minute of mental debate.

"I see what you mean. They're looking for me. But the Amestec always find me by my scent. Why the kidnappings?"

I felt a little chill traveling down my spine at the thought that the kidnapped girls fit my description. That could be recipe for disaster. I had a dead man in the basement, a reminder of all the things to come.

"I need you to speak with the girls who have been kidnapped, and the witnesses, and get more details about the abductors."

"I did," he said, with no significant change in his tone of voice. "The girls are just frightened and confused. But I saved their cell numbers."

Octavian is very handsome and he knows it. Actually, the word 'handsome' is not nearly strong enough to describe him. Most girls think he's gorgeous–perhaps a bit too tall, but he's very fit.

His sparkling blue eyes, his long wavy dark hair that he sometimes wears in a ponytail, his contagious smile, and his charming European accent, combined with a good sense of fashion and money, had always been an ongoing challenge with the young ladies.

Many times in the past, the girls thought that his attention to them meant more than he really felt, as my brother was just seeking pleasure and giving pleasure in return.

However, decade after decade, the girls chased him, powerless to resist his spell. I realized that I had to tone down his love life. As of a year ago I reminded him that we were running out of time, and after a century we had yet to accomplish our mission. Reluctantly he agreed with me and concentrated only in locating the swords. He's kept the same mortal girlfriend since then.

"He's a lot older than he looks," concluded Octavian, brushing his fingers over the corpse. "I can feel a few scars on his body. He's been wounded several times, but he was healed by someone else. Look at this deep scar on his neck. The letter A's engraved–it was done deliberately. There's something very wrong here–he really shouldn't exist. He's definitely a hybrid."

"A hybrid? Do you mean an Amestec? The letter 'A' could signify that he is Amestec," I corrected my brother.

His words disturbed my spirit. The Amestec, also known as the half-immortals, were constantly hunting me and my kind. And because they barely live over one hundred years old, some became quite desperate to find me.

My gift of healing could give them immortality since they were the only ones of the mortal kind who possessed half of our DNA already.

However, they would rather kill me to steal my spirit and obtain my healing power, the power that could grant all of them life everlasting.

Twelve men from Vienna, seven from Hungry and fourteen from Frankfurt followed me to Paris and London. Octavian and I killed them all. One hundred traveled with us on the *Carpathia*. Several were females, and I lost them when we arrived in New York. Many more came after that and we defeated all of them. Most Amestec doubted their ability to capture me alive singularly, so they joined forces.

"No, he's not an Amestec—he's an experiment," he started to explain. "He wasn't born that way. Amestec are those who were born from one of our kind and a mortal. Hybrids are humans who have been killed and then revived by a wicked power. Amestec and hybrids physically resemble each other—tall, a light complexion, and like us, they cannot keep short hair. But there's one major difference—the hybrid is no longer alive and he cannot be made immortal. Hybrids are without a conscience—they just follow their master's orders. By the way, hybrids can easily be killed. You could have just shot him."

"Well, I didn't have that choice, did I?" This new creature intrigued me, but for the wrong reasons.

"Octavian, if *this* Hybrid is just a manmade soldier, who is his creator?"

Now, a whole new and an enhanced generation was on my trail. The man lying on my basement floor was the proof of that.

"What are you doing?" I asked my brother, who had stopped his examination and begun to attach the head to the body. He touched the skin around the man's neck with his finger and it healed in a perfect connection.

"Let's ask him who his master is," Octavian suggested, while he dragged an old sofa into the basement from the storage closet and sat the man on it.

"You can't be serious," I said, as I lifted my hand in an attempt to stop him. "You shouldn't revive a hybrid. It's forbidden!" My concern was not just for breaking our rules but the possibility that we might unleash unknown powers buried deep within this new creature.

"He's only a hybrid, Safira. Reviving him won't turn him into an Immortal. Even if you can awaken his dead spirit it just won't stay revived for too long. Once we get all the information from him that we can, we can kill him again and let him dry into dust. We need to know why these hybrids exist and who sent them. According to my calculations, there are over two hundred living Amestec out there looking for you right now. Somehow, one of them has this little unconventional army at his disposal. This is means we're at war and this is just the beginning."

8

LORD MARTUZON'S GODDAUGHTER? WHAT DID that mean?

I doubted that we shared any sort of blood relation, but in my case, his act as a benefactor toward me would have some meaning beyond my understanding. So, where was this new discovery taking me? I knew for a fact that I was not a servant, nor had I ever been under the impression that I belonged in that class. That I was called "Lady" by the servants meant that I had a kind of class or rank. But what was it? What was my last name? Who was my father? Why did Lord Martuzon keep me hostage here if I was, as he declared, only his goddaughter?

Archduke Rudolph's arrival proved to be beneficial to me. Our unexpected encounter brought to my landlord another reminder that the time had come for him to acknowledge my existence. It seemed to be shocking to him that he could not recognize his own kin in the embarrassing moment when my description was given to him by the Archduke.

But all my excitement was put to the test again in the next few days. I could only see him arriving into his quarters at a very late *hour, and then he went directly into his bedroom. I could only assume that he spent his evenings somewhere in the palace in the company of the Prince, dining and conducting business with him and with others.*

It was necessary for me to admit how disappointed I was to be forgotten already. I needed his attention; even if it came in the form of a rebuke. My behavior must not have been so out of the ordinary, though, because I didn't capture the Governor's attention just by meeting the Archduke. What more could I do to provoke a glimmer of interest from him?

* * *

One night I went down to my secret door, thinking that I might go outside for a short while where I could breathe freely and roam a short distance through the city. Once I had stepped onto the narrow cobblestone street, however, I became undecided. What would happen if I should get lost? What would happen if I couldn't find my way back to the stairway and be trapped on the outside? Would Lord Martuzon look for me? Would he even care?

I stepped back inside, frightened by the idea that he would not even come looking for me. He was very indifferent towards me and I had nowhere else to go.

It took all of my fortitude to gather my courage and leave, and if I didn't find my way back, so be it. Sooner or later Nana Saveta would tell him that I was missing and this would make him come looking for me. Yes, this was my plan for tonight, and I had nothing to lose by trying.

This time I made sure that I was amply supplied. I had saved some bread from my meals for nourishment, just in case my prediction came true, and I dressed warmly in case I had to spend some time outside. Then, I left.

It was still puzzling for me how easily I could move in the dark and how clearly I could see in the dark—it was as if I could see as well as on an ordinary cloudy day. Out in the street, I looked both ways, up and down, to decide which way I should start my adventure. Neither way was too appealing to me, so I just turned to my left and began to walk into the city. The buildings I passed were old and rough, and they looked like they were abandoned.

I was frightened, my pulse was pounding in my ears, but I thought that at the end of this street there must be something else, something better.

After a seemingly interminable walk, there was still nothing on my path except some cats that watched me curiously, and I could hear some dogs barking nervously in the distance. By now it was late at night, and from somewhere I heard a church bell chime eleven o'clock. I realized now how imprudent my action was and I regretted very much that I didn't do this exploration during the day.

I knew that I should return to the palace and try this again, taking my chances of being discovered outside in the daylight. I would surely get in trouble, but I would be able to see some of the city without being so frightened.

Suddenly the noise of steps made me realize that I was being followed by some dark shadows, and when I turned to see them, three men stood behind me ready to accost me. They were dressed like gypsies, with scarves wrapping their heads and gold rings in their ears, and they were carrying knives.

I started to run, but the toe of my foot caught a rough spot and I fell down on the cobblestones. I curled my body as tightly as I could into a ball in an attempt to protect myself.

"Oh, look!" said one of them, the tall one and quite young by the sound of his voice, "it's a woman! We're lucky tonight. It'll be easy enough for all of us to take her."

"I bet she's rich too," said another one, older and heavier, coming closer to me. I smelled his bad breath from distance. "She looks like she's got plenty of money, or at least, some jewels."

"Please, don't hurt me," I tried to reason with them, "I don't have any money, I swear. I am very poor."

"Poor?" snapped the third one, who had missing the right arm. "I don't believe you, stupid—don't think we're fools! Come on; give us your jewels and your clothes!"

"Please, I don't have any jewels…" I answered them back in Romanian.

For a moment I thought of how foolish I was to leave my sanctuary and to place myself in this kind of trouble. I knew that I was as good as dead, here in the street at the hands of these awful people. I had no doubt that this would be my last night among the living. All this time I dared not look up at them, hoping they would just leave me alone.

"Get those clothes off!" another one of them yelled. He kicked me in the ribs with a steel toe boot and reached down to rip my dress away from my breasts. I didn't cry out or say anything. Suddenly I felt a strange burning in my whole body, something that I had never felt before.

My first impulse was to stand up and defiantly look at my assailants. I felt another sensation for the first time—my eyes began to flash with lightning. Surprised at my daring move, they jumped back and looked at me in astonishment, along with a little fear.

"What the hell are you, a witch?" one of them asked, waving his knife in my face.

But I didn't have time to respond—not that his question could possibly produce an answer from me. At that moment, another shadow of a man jumped from the building behind us and landed on his feet between me and the men. A moment later, the gypsy with the knife was on the ground with his throat slashed, and a second man was stabbed with a sword.

Then the shadow's feet left the ground. He took several running steps up the wall of the building, did a cartwheel in the air, and stabbed the third man, who, by this time, had pulled out his pistol and had tried to shoot the shadow.

Everything happened so fast, I was hardly able to even take a breath between the deaths of the gypsies. How could someone be so fast and kill those men all alone? It was like he had the power of a small army.

I was still in shock. All I could think of was that someone had just saved my life and I wasn't even capable of believing that it had happened. My hero's back was still turned toward me as he wiped blood from his knife and sword.

"This is not a place for a young lady to wander at night," he said to me in the Romanian language as he turned to face me. "You must be very careful. You're lucky I was around! Those men were the worst kind, very dangerous. Are you all right?"

"Yes! Yes! Thank you so much," I rambled on as I fell to the street again.

I had never seen dead people before that night. The bloody sight of these attackers was gruesome, and I had no stomach for it. I threw up. I made an attempt to get up but I fell back, lightheaded.

Before I lost consciousness, I saw for a brief moment the face of my savior standing over me. His hair was dark and long, but his eyes were like bright stars in the sky, illuminating the darkness with a blue light.

"Who are you?" I asked, and for the second time that night, I was given no answer to the same question I had asked.

*   *   *

When I awoke, I was in my room in the palace, lying on my bed, wearing the clothes in which I had ventured out from the palace. I had wanted so badly to get Lord Martuzon's attention, and at first I decided that I must have dreamed everything. But it was obvious, from my dirty hands and my torn clothing, that I had been outside and that everything had certainly happened the way I remembered it. Everything was still fresh in my memory, and the last image that I remembered seeing was the face and the eyes of the mysterious young man who saved me.

An hour later, however, I began to think differently. Yes, I had to admit that I did wake up dressed for town, and perhaps I did have the intention of leaving the palace, but again, I didn't follow through on my plan. My hands were dirty and my clothes were torn, but that could have been the result of a sleepwalking dream.

If I had been outside, how could I explain the fact that my windows were closed and secured, and that no one in the world could have possibly passed by the vigilance of the guards? So, I had to accept that it was all just a dream. I had never left the palace and no one had saved me by killing three people in a matter of seconds.

What a disturbing notion.

Nana came in that morning, jovial and talkative. She walked around the room singing and smiling, trying to stir up my interest so I would question her. I didn't comply, because I was still disappointed *by my nonexistent nocturnal adventure. As usual, she couldn't wait to burst out in excitement.*

"Oh, Lady Safira, I have great news for you—great news, my dear. You have been so impatient to have an encounter with Lord Martuzon, and now it is going to happen…"

"What are you saying, Nana?" I jumped off my bed and grabbed her arm.

"You are going to dine with Lord Martuzon and the Archduke tonight…"

9

THERE IS NO PROPER PLACE to hide a gun when you wear an evening dress. Since I couldn't take my sword, I decided to simply store my gun in my purse.

That evening I was on my way to the Hilton Hotel in Atlanta, on another wild chase to find our magic swords. This time, Octavian had several reasons to believe that Mr. Nagoshi, a Japanese business man, known for his unconventional acquisitions and who was a guest there, was in the possession of the Silver Sword. That was because he posted a picture of himself holding the sword. And from the look of it– we had no doubts.

So, here I was, again, following another lead as I had done a hundred times before. My plan was to strategically wander around the hotel lobby, find this person, and take a closer look at his belongings.

A corporate party was being held in the most glamorous space, the largest ballroom of the Hotel, and the person I was looking for was among the attendees.

Pretending to be one of the participants, I grabbed a glass of champagne and I made my way through the multitude of people, all of whom were so finely and elegantly dressed–especially the women. Their beautiful long dresses displayed a bit of cleavage as well as obviously very expensive jewels. Some of them waved at me when they thought they recognized me.

When I came to a stop, I stumbled and fell into the arms of a young man who was dressed in a perfectly tailored tuxedo. His long shoulder length hair was a mixture of brown and blonde gathered quite nicely into a ponytail. His face was a bit pale and his skin seemed translucent. He didn't have any facial hair and he had a strange, recently healed large scar along his forehead, making him look bitter and unfriendly.

The stranger gazed at me with a pair of dark eyes that made my smile morph into a somber and sober look. At first he appeared to be quite disturbed by my intrusion into his circle.

"I apologize for being so clumsy," I said, embarrassed and refusing to look into his eyes.

"Absolutely," he said, trying to sound enthusiastic. "It's certainly my fault–I always seem to be in the way. May I introduce myself? My name is Albert Solberg, I am from Liechtenstein."

The mention of this particular country had a significant importance to me. It was the location of the Secret Mountain, a shelter for many centuries for the old order of Immortals. But the man I was looking at had no scent, either as an Immortal or Amestec.

"Nice to meet you Albert. My name is…Megan," I said catching the name tag of one of the lady who passed by me.

The young man bowed to me, but he didn't reach out to take my hand that I offered to him. Then, almost immediately, he regained his suave demeanor and expressed his delight to meet me. His dark eyes seemed to be pools of tar as he took my measure. He finally focused on my red dress, and a moment later he took my hand and kissed it. His lips were cold and wet, and I felt his tongue slithering down my skin. I stepped back, trying not to show my intense displeasure.

"Are you enjoying your time Atlanta?" I asked him, after a moment of awkward silence. My mind struggled to make sense of the sudden feeling that I had seen him somewhere before, and not very long ago…

"Yes, I am, very much. Unfortunately, I am returning to Europe tomorrow. Megan, you are the most beautiful young lady I have ever seen. Your blue eyes and dark hair are an amazing and mesmerizing combination."

"Thank you," I murmured, knowing that he wasn't being truthful, feeling a bit edgy and troubled by the whole encounter with this bizarre stranger.

At that moment we were so close to each other that there wasn't sufficient space for us to maintain a reasonable and respectable distance. I could feel him breathing deeply over my forehead and I lowered my head so his breath struck my hair. The few people who attempted to interject themselves into our circle of two were stopped by the young man's companions.

To my total surprise, then, he did something that was completely unexpected—he removed his cell phone from his jacket pocket and took a picture of me with its camera.

"With your permission, I would love to take the memory of you on this night back with me." he said, as he saw the indignation on my face.

"I really don't want you to..." I began to reply, unsettled by his strange actions.

"May I dare to hope that you will join me for dinner?" he interrupted me, and for the first time that evening he smiled. When he bared his teeth, his smile appeared to me to be a ferocious snarl, one that you would see on a wild and feral dog.

"Certainly," I agreed, quite happy to move around again and away from his closeness, to be free to pursue the Japanese gentleman in whom I had a specific interest to make his acquaintance. Albert left me there, but not before he took my hand and kissed it once again. That kiss felt as repulsive as before.

The fact that he photographed me made me very suspicious. I turned to walk away from him, but then I turned back and followed him from a safe distance. He met with many other women but he didn't take their photographs. He completely ignored some pretty blonde women who surrounded him at all times.

After a few minutes I stopped watching him and I walked around the room to continue my search for mysterious Mr. Nagoshi. But so far, I could not locate him anywhere—as a matter of fact, none of the guests matched his description.

It was not long before I realized that I was the one who was being followed, not only by Albert but by his personal guards, two young men who strongly resembled him. At first I was annoyed, but I didn't let myself worry—it was all a game for me. But when I left the ballroom to go and powder my face, they followed me down the long corridor until I reached the powder room door. I sensed that something more sinister was being prepared for me besides a dinner invitation.

It was time for me to leave before someone got badly hurt—and it wouldn't be me.

I was about to step out into the hallway when I spotted the two young men standing a few feet away with their backs turned to the door. I continued to spend time staring at myself in the mirror.

I am taller than the average girl and I have a fit body. My muscle tone is evident, but at the same time I have curves. I looked very young and sometimes, if the circumstances require it, I could pass as a teenager.

I waited for one of the ladies to return to the ballroom after she had adjusted her dress and touched up her makeup. When she turned the corner, the hallway was empty.

As I pulled the door toward me I realized that the bodyguards were in the hallway once again. I quietly stepped out from the powder room and pulled out my revolver from my purse.

In rapid succession I hit both of the bodyguards hard at the base of their skulls with the butt of my pistol. The men collapsed to the floor, unconscious. I turned to my left and ran to the rear exit of the hotel. Before the valet could bring my car around I saw Albert Solberg watching me through the glass door from inside the lobby.

I was pretty close to home when I realized that I was followed by a black Expedition with dark tinted windows. I stopped at a gas station and waited for them to pass me. They stopped and parked a short distance behind me. I got out of my truck and I slowly approached the Expedition's window on the driver's side, hoping he wouldn't immediately drive away. I bent my head so the driver could see me and I rapped on the glass with my knuckle.

No response. I put my face close to the window again so the driver could see me.

The driver's side window came down.

The man stared at me in astonishment for a second; then he turned on his ignition, revved up his motor, and sped off. I let him go.

The man in the car looked exactly like the corpse in my basement.

My soul shivered—he also resembled Albert and his strange body guards.

10

THAT DAY WENT BY SO *slowly, like a nightmare that never ends. But when Mr. Lutz came to escort me to Lord Martuzon' apartment, I knew that was about to end. At first I doubted Nana, then I anticipated all the reasons for which he would withdraw his invitation, and then I imagined that he would invite a hundred other people to the meal, just so he wouldn't have to talk with me face to face. But my doubts and my fanciful imaginings didn't materialize.*

I dressed nicely, as a result of Nana's insistence that I wear something European. She selected a blue dress for me, with very low-cut shoulders designed to show some cleavage. I knew that a young lady should always be aware of her appearance, and I also knew that the man who was keeping me in his care must find me acceptable and pleasant, but it was beyond my understanding why a dress should be the means to capture his attention.

I had imagined this moment so differently before that night. Each time I would dare to wish or imagine how our meeting would be, I became quite restless and ravished by conflicting emotions. That night, as I was following Mr. Lutz, I could feel nothing! Why was I so devoid of any fervor?

It was the Archduke who first arose from his chair and came to welcome me. Lord Martuzon did not show any indication that he was happy to see me and his manner was cold and austere. For a moment it seemed that all he wanted was to remove me from his presence. But, he too stood and bowed to me.

It only took a few moments for my instincts to be totally in agreement with his reaction. For the first time in five years he and I were facing each other. To me, it seemed so easy because I had been watching him in secret for so long. I knew, from his frosty attitude that I must prove I was equally as qualified to stand in his presence as Miss Anda. I bowed to them both and expressed my gratitude for the invitation.

"Lady Safira, what a pleasure it is to have this opportunity to dine with you," said Prince Rudolph, as he held my chair for me to sit. With a subtle motion, he moved my chair so I could sit closer to him. "Milos is a very stubborn man when it comes to your protection."

"What am I protected from, Lord Martuzon?" I asked him, but I did not look him in his eyes. I regretted the question immediately because I had broken my own code of principles, including not asking him any question directly related to me.

"It's obvious that he is protecting you from me, because he has kept you hidden from my sight!" was the Prince's answer. "It is well known that I am a total menace when comes to beautiful things or beautiful women. You must agree with me, Milos! You know me very well by now. You see, my dear, Milos and I grew up together, and he has learned from past experience to keep beautiful young ladies away from me. I am so impressed that he has remembered this rule about me."

This was the very first time that I ever heard a male announce so all could hear that I was beautiful. At this point in my life, I was innocent about my appearance. Perhaps this was because of Nana's attempt to keep me humble—my room contained no mirrors. I had only seen my reflection in the water of my bath. I was a little at a loss for words by such an enthusiastic and unexpected proclamation.

"Thank you, your Highness!" I answered softly, "Coming from you, this is an enormous honor."

"My Lord," intervened the governor, "please allow my goddaughter to eat! She will have enough time later to be fully convinced that you are a brilliant charmer. She is not accustomed to hearing such flattery, especially from one such as you. Bon appétit, Lady Safira!"

"Merci, Monsieur Martuzon (Thank you, Lord Martuzon)*," I answered, astonished by his sudden change of attitude towards me. Perhaps he was just motivated by a desire to rush through this dinner so I would be dismissed as quickly as possible. He carefully avoided looking at me directly or addressing me during the meal, leaving it open for the Archduke to prey upon my unguarded mind.*

"I see you have mastered the French language, my lady. This is wonderful! I believe you would make an excellent companion for my wife."

"Vous etes tres gentil, Monsieur! (You are very kind, My Lord) *That is a most appealing thought, Your Highness!" I added, very excited.*

All of these compliments and the interest that was coming from the Prince were raising unprecedented hopes for me that I might break free, not only from this palace, but from the Governor. I hadn't mastered the French language at all, but if that's was what it would take for the next ruler of the Empire to transport me from this prison, I would apply myself and I would learn it better than my first language. .

"I will write to my wife tomorrow and present this proposal to her. I am sure she will be delighted. She enjoys having special kinds of

females in her surroundings. You will be quite welcome: you speak German, French and Romanian. Extraordinary! May I hope for a positive answer?"

I could not answer; even I wished to do so. The entire time Prince Rudolph was gazing at me and carrying on this fancy conversation designed to praise me and to capture my interest, Lord Martuzon's face was displaying changes that ranged from indifference to anger.

"Before committing to a letter of acceptance from the Princess, I must warn you, my Lord that my goddaughter and I must firmly establish the guidelines necessary for her to become what is expected of her..."

"Which is what, my dear friend? It is obvious to me that she is already an accomplished Lady. You must allow her to follow her heart's desire and give her some freedom. She needs to be at the royal court. That is where she belongs! My friend, you act more like her father than her godfather!"

"Let me be the judge of that! Your Highness should not judge my actions too rashly."

"Are you insinuating that my opinions are superficial and have no merit?"

The prince's voice had radically changed. What was the true reason for this little adversity between them? It couldn't possibly be only me. Something else was underlying their spat.

"Gentlemen!"

They both turned their attention to me. Their sudden inability to carry on a civil conversation in my presence truly startled me.

"May I be granted permission to retire? I am feeling a bit weary..."

"So soon? Please stay longer! You have not even finished your soup, and the main course is yet to arrive," cried the Prince.

"Please, your Highness!" My words could not express my sadness and disappointment that the dinner had ended so abruptly.

"You are right! Please forgive me and Milos for behaving badly. But perhaps a walk through the city tomorrow is within the acceptable limits of your guardian's...guidelines..."

I turned towards Lord Martuzon. His eyes were looking at me, but his mind was elsewhere and he was not thinking about me.

"That will be acceptable", he murmured. *"Good night!"*

"Au revoir! A demain! (Goodbye. I will see you tomorrow*)",* *I addressed them both in the hope that the planned outing would happen.*

* * *

I didn't want Mr. Lutz to accompany me back to my quarters—I had other plans. But I couldn't override Lord Martuzon's orders, so I rushed to my room and Mr. Lutz returned to his master. Several minutes passed before I could safely slip down to my secret closet. I was certain that this evening would trigger more interesting conversation between the two friends in my absence, and I didn't wish to miss this opportunity to hear for myself what kind of impression I had made on my landlord.

Apparently their appetite did not increase after my departure—they were drinking wine in the parlor, and the main course was still untouched.

"What is the meaning of this madness, Milos? You have acted so strangely the whole evening. I am absolutely positive that your

90

goddaughter did not enjoy her time in our company. I did my best, at least, to entertain her, but your behavior was quite unseemly…"

"Please forgive me, my Lord, but I am quite disturbed," admitted Lord Martuzon.

"All right! Perhaps you could share your disturbances with an old friend."

"I believe they are back, Rudolph! They have returned, and I know what they want."

"Who are talking about? Who has returned?" The Prince had no idea where this topic of conversation would carry them.

"The people who killed my father! They are here, in this city. They have been seen by my spies, and last night one of my guards was found unconscious. They are infiltrating here in my own palace, and I feel powerless."

"Milos, this is absolutely unacceptable! You are a powerful man now, a leader of a country, no longer a young boy. It should not even be humanly possible for someone to enter in this place without being intercepted. You talk about these people like they are some sort of greater beings."

"They are! And they have returned!" Lord Martuzon became angry again. "I will not endure the fate of my father and I will not allow them to take her away from me. I love her, Rudolph, I love her very much."

"Who? Milos, who do you love?"

11

"WHAT'S GOING ON?" ASKED OCTAVIAN. His eyes grew wide with surprise when I told him about the driver of the SUV, Albert Solberg and his body guards. "Are these guys coming off an assembly line? Damn Nagoshi too. He was supposed to be there."

At that moment Octavian's cell phone rang–the one we keep for others to reach us.

"It's Nelda," said Octavian, alarmed. "She is at the Dance Academy and her car has four flat tires."

"The stupid hybrids may be after her too. Tell her to lock herself in the car." As I waited for her answer I became concerned. I didn't want an innocent, young girl to be mistaken for me and be abducted.

"She thinks she's safe, though," said Octavian and his voice trembled. "A squad car is still there in the parking lot."

"We need to hurry. Tell her not to talk to the police."

This time we took the Land Rover. My love for big cars has always annoyed my brother, who always drives fancy sports cars, and my metallic gray special edition oversized Rover was my favorite car.

My brother's hands squeezed the grip and barrel of the Glock 19 that he held tensely in his lap. I suspected he was blaming himself because Nelda was hunted by the hybrids, and that she was his responsibility.

"You love Nelda, don't you?" I asked him without warning. Octavian looked at me, nervous and somewhat unsure.

"Is this a trick question?" he asked me cautiously. "What's on your mind?"

"Remember the SEAL officer who I encountered in Germany at the Wagner's farm?" I started confessing to him unexpectedly. "I didn't think it was possible that I would feel like this again, but I can't stop thinking at him. His name is Commander Julian Grant."

My brother couldn't hide his smile. He knew that I was trying everything to take his mind off what was worrying him about Nelda. Anything could happen to her by the time we arrived to her rescue.

"I know what you may think," I continued my confession, "that he had to be some sort of warrior to attract me. I wanted to impress him, but he caught the glowing from my eyes–it was unintentional. Since I've gotten back home, I've found it very hard to get him out of my mind, and my emotions have been on edge since then."

"Did you fall in love with a mortal man," asked my brother, surprised. "What would you do about Andreas?"

"Julian is the forbidden fruit," I said, trying to keep my voice steady. "I acted crazy. It doesn't matter anyway. There's no way we'll ever meet again. And for me, Andreas is just a shadow. I am still in love with a memory, a century old memory. Julian was real, for that moment in time."

* * *

The Dance Academy was only four miles away from our house, tucked away at the corner of a U shape shopping center, adjacent to St. Paul High School's athletic field. The field had an eight-foot high chain link fence surrounding it, with a gate near the Academy.

I parked the Land Rover at the corner of the next street and walked to the chain link fence that surrounded the St. Paul athletic field. It was no feat for us to vault over the fence. We crossed over the athletic field to the chain link fence that bordered the property where the Dance Academy was located, and we vaulted over that fence as well. We began to scan the parking lot for any danger.

The parking lot was almost empty, but the police car was still there.

Good. I saw that Nelda's car was still parked in the same spot it had been in earlier. I motioned for my brother to go around to the front of her car while I came up from the back.

In the half dark of twilight I spotted people in the police car. There was a figure in the front seat and a shadow that might have been someone in the back.

"Octavian, don't let him leave," I whispered in my brother's ear set.

At that moment, one of the parking lot security lights came on and its strong light illuminated my brother's position. The police car's motor suddenly came alive and the vehicle began to roll slowly towards the exit to the street. Octavian ran straight toward the car's hood while I held my breath. At the last moment he stepped aside to allow the car to pass, but as the driver's side passed him, he grabbed the door handle and snatched it open.

The car veered to the right, hit the curb, and stopped. Octavian had maintained a grip on the door handle as he trotted alongside the barely moving car. When the car came to a stop at the curb, Octavian grabbed the driver's coat collar with his other hand and pulled the driver from behind the wheel. The driver went sprawling on the pavement.

It wasn't a patrolman–it was the man I had encountered earlier in the afternoon–hybrid number two.

"Where's the girl?" Octavian demanded, pressing the driver's head to the asphalt with his foot.

While Octavian made sure that the hybrid couldn't escape, I opened the rear door of the car. Nelda was lying on the seat, unconscious, and the police officer was sitting beside her with blood slowly oozing from his abdomen. I checked his pulse, and it was weak–he was barely breathing.

I moved his body so I could get a better look, and I saw that his wound was deep. The bullet had gone into his abdomen and out his back. The patrolman's spine had just been missed, but he had lost a lot of blood. It looked like he'd been shot not long ago with his own gun.

My mind raced as I thought about how to spin this event and make it logical for everyone else. I had a wounded police officer, a young girl who was unconscious, and a stranger who was identical to the dead one in my basement on my hands. I touched the patrolman and my touch caused the blood around his wound to clot. He wouldn't lose any more blood, but he needed to get to a hospital soon. I moved over to Octavian and I pointed my pistol at the stranger.

"So, you do exist," he responded with a slight foreign accent.

"Get up!" I ordered him. My gun touched his face but there was no reaction from him. "Who are you? Answer or I'll kill you."

"My name is Marin. I'm unarmed, but it'll take more than your weapon to kill me."

"You're wrong," I snapped at him. "You're not the real deal. Somebody lied to you. Who're you working for?" I asked him, irritated.

"You have no idea."

That was the same answer I had received earlier from his twin, but I did have an idea. I looked at his neck and his hair was gathered in a ponytail. Underneath it I saw the same large shaved area and the letter A in it–exactly like the hybrid in my basement.

I lowered my gun. Threatening Marin with it wasn't getting me anywhere. He wasn't giving me any information about his master and I couldn't penetrate his cold spirit: these were the ones who didn't fear death.

"Kill him, Octavian, we can't use guns here. And do it fast."

The young man smiled ironically when Octavian stood up to challenge him. It took him by surprise when Octavian's hand flashed across his throat—he knew had met his match. My brother was strong and fighting the Amestec in the past always gave him the chance to sharpen his skills.

In the meantime, Nelda had regained consciousness and started to scream at the sight of the bloody policeman. She raised her head and saw Octavian fighting the stranger, and she froze with fear.

"Nelda!" I said, getting in the car to check on her. "I need you to call 911 and tell them that someone tried to kidnap you and shot the police officer. Can you do that for me?"

The girl nodded. She had a few scratches on her face, a large bruise above her elbow and she was shaking, but she called. After she made the report to the 911 operator, I helped her out of the car. She looked at me in fright and pointed with her finger to the man Octavian was fighting.

"He was the one who did it," she screamed, "he killed the officer."

"It's OK. You see? Octavian can handle him."

My brother was strong and his blows pounded the other man with great power. His closed fists hit his opponent in a hammering motion to his thorax. Marin backed off. Then he raised his knee and rotated his body trying to extend his leg to kick Octavian with the outside edge of his foot. My brother bent into a crouch and grabbed him by his foot. He slammed the hybrid to the pavement.

This is how we fight–there is nothing our body or our weapons cannot do if our mind commands it.

Octavian allowed the man to get up. They squared off again. Octavian's final blow came when both of his legs flew forward, with his feet landing squarely on the hybrid's larynx. The hybrid fell with a broken neck. But as he did, he gazed at me with his ebony eyes livid and swarthy.

Octavian came slowly toward us. In the next moment, Nelda was in his arms with her hands around his neck, holding him tight. My brother began to stroke her hair and try to sooth her, but he was tenser than when he fought.

"Are you all right?" she asked him, kissing his lips.

Police sirens were sounding in the distance, coming towards us in a hurry. We would see them in the parking lot soon, along with other emergency vehicles.

While Nelda's face was pressed into Octavian's embrace, I lifted Marin's body and heaved him over the fence onto the athletic field.

"My sweet baby," murmured Octavian, holding tight his girlfriend. "Unfortunately, the guy ran away. I thought I could hold him down until the police got here."

"Oh, he ran away," she exclaimed. "But it looked like you'd killed him."

I wasn't worried–she would remember exactly what Octavian would tell her had happened, and not the reality of the events.

"Nelda," I said to her, "Octavian will stay here with you and help you with the police report, and then he'll take you home."

The girl smiled at me appreciatively, but my brother's response to me was a flash of blue lightning in his eyes. Facing Nelda's parents was what he had avoided for the longest time.

I vaulted over the fence, found the corpse, and threw it over my shoulder. I crossed the field in the dark until I reached the fence on the other side. I threw the corpse over the fence and vaulted over it once again. I dragged him over to the Rover and loaded him onto the back seat. Like his twin, he was still warm to the touch.

One more body for my basement. How many more would find their way onto that cold concrete floor before this was all over?

12

To the left of Black Eagle Castle was a very imposing cathedral called "The Church with the Moon". The church's name was derived from a sphere in the tower that simulated the moon's colors and rotation, and the sphere's motions were very accurate. To the right of the church was the bridge that crossed over the Crisu River, leading toward the theater and commercial districts. That was where Archduke Rudolph and Lord Martuzon were taking me that day.

My heart sang with pleasure and enjoyment. These streets were familiar to me because Nana Saveta had brought me here many times, but she would walk me rapidly past every shop and store window, almost running. It was good exercise for my body, but my heart was left heavy by the experience.

But not that day.

That day I walked slowly in the company of these great men and I wanted the whole city to see and recognize me, especially Miss Anda. To my surprise, she was not as frequently invited to participate in their activities as I would have thought. But I couldn't waste my energy thinking of others, especially her. If there was a force in nature that *created a balance, I believe that this little moment forcefully propelled me above other females' accomplishments.*

Lord Martuzon had never taken a walk in the city accompanied by a young lady—but he did it for me, didn't he?

I must say that I was very disappointed in the fact that I wasn't the subject of their conversation last night, but reflecting upon it, I was led to believe that Milos's life was very complicated. The mention of his father's killers and his love for a mysterious woman, affected him profoundly. As I enjoyed my little victorious freedom, it was clearly in the wake of the return of his enemies, and I was no match for this new rising terror within him. Who could be so fierce as to terrify the governor? There was an army of guards protecting the palace and his person, so why was he not taking comfort in this fact? And who was the one he feared to lose? It wasn't Anda, I was quite sure of that, and that simple notion cheered me considerably.

"Lady Safira, what is your heart's desire?" Prince Rudolph asked me. "What do you want to see?"

"Un magasin de vetements," I answered in French to please the Archduke, "et un magasin de chaussures." (A clothes shop and a shoe shop.)

Both men turned to look at me.

"Lord Martuzon, vous permettez?" (Do I have your permission?)

It had been so long since my curiosity of stepping inside of one of these wondrous stores had been satisfied under Nana's strong influence. So far, all of my clothes had been brought to me without my having the opportunity to choose something of my liking, and not much thought was given to their cost. But the offer had been made to me and if I had to choose between acting as a mature young lady or like a child, I would not fail myself. Self-denial was not among my multitude of faults, and Nana Saveta was not here to supervise my ladylike demeanor.

It was obvious that this ordeal appeared to be boring for my benefactor. He was quiet and reserved the whole time, to the point that I forgot he was there. The only person who deserved my attention was the Archduke. I was thankful to him, not only for his undeniable kindness and interest in me, but as the source that ignited all these changes in my life. If he was sincere in helping me leave Transylvania, I must do my part to express my gratitude. But how could I ever repay him for such great favor?

For now, my focus was on acquiring some beautiful garments. My desire to be beautiful and pleasant in Prince Rudolph's eyes made me change my whole attitude about my wardrobe.

"Of course you have his permission," the Prince answered instead. "Milos, allow this lovely lady to indulge a bit today. She needs a new garment for this Saturday's ball. My lady, go in and choose all that you like. I am paying for everything. Please, it will be my pleasure."

I left them out in the street, perhaps arguing over the Prince's involvement in making such a decision on my behalf. I went into the shop, and within a few minutes a large pile of dresses were selected to be delivered to the palace and taken to my quarters. The Prince, indeed, paid for everything.

Milos seemed to be very unhappy that his control seemed to have been diminished, and he insisted that he should be the one to pay.

* * *

They decided to return to the palace and I was walking slowly behind them, still enjoying my outing and unwilling to make the palace my destination. At this moment I was the queen of the city. The fact that there would be a ball on Saturday and that I would very likely receive an invitation made me giggle. Lord Martuzon couldn't control Prince Rudolph's desire to make me his constant companion at events like these.

What a wonderful life was ahead of me from now on! I must maintain the prince's good will at all costs. But that would be difficult, because I had no understanding of what there was about me that kept him attracted to me. But now, my mind was not making the attempt to understand this complex labyrinth called human attraction. I was too new to this life, as if I had just been reborn.

I had seen my reflection in a mirror for the first time while I was in the dress shop. I had to move my hands and my head to confirm that was me I was seeing. So this was me! This was how I looked to the world. I didn't look anything like I imagined—nothing like the blonde Anda or the pale, red-haired Flora.

I stared at my reflection for a long while, not knowing what to think. Was I attractive to others, especially to men? But at that moment saw Prince Rudolph looking at me so intensely. He seemed to be fascinated, and my heart was at peace.

We were just about to cross back over the bridge when I felt something pulling my dress from behind. I thought that in my clumsiness I had caught the cloth on some part of the bridge. I jerked the dress and I tried to move forward, but I couldn't. I turned to see what was holding my dress and I saw that a hand was grasping its hem very tightly.

"Please, my lady, have mercy on a poor soul." I heard the voice of a man coming from what appeared to be a pile of rough clothes lying on the bridge. I screamed for help, but before Prince Rudolph and Lord Martuzon could turn around, a man turned his head to me before he was forced to leave by my silly reaction.

I froze.

It was the same face, with long dark hair and piercing blue eyes that I had encountered the night I left the palace on my own. By the time Lord Martuzon and the Prince came back for me, he had vanished, but the Governor had caught a glimpse of him.

"What happened, my dear? You look so frightened," asked the Prince taking this opportunity to hold me close to his chest.

"Someone attacked her," responded Lord Martuzon angrily. "Your Highness, we must return to the palace immediately. I will send solders to hunt him down…"

"It was only a Gypsy begging for money, my Lord. Please forgive my hysterics—it will not happen again," I implored, fearful for the man's life.

Milos appeared to be completely in a rage over this incident and my response did nothing to calm him. We both knew that I hadn't encountered what I had said.

"Beggars!" exclaimed the Prince, unwilling to release me from his embrace. "This city is the home for many of them. But why they would attack a young girl?"

"I had no money to give him, but he didn't know that," I answered, and at that moment Prince Rudolph pressed a handful of coins into my hand. I didn't have any knowledge of money, then, but I was sure the coins were worth a lot. That only increased the irascibility of the Governor, who ordered everyone to stay inside the palace for the remainder of the day.

* * *

Nana Saveta had waited for me in my room, mending a curtain that had torn. She was a bit sad that she had not been allowed to accompany us, but I was too preoccupied to be sympathetic to her. I briefly described the events of my outing to her, and I carefully avoided mentioning the man who had caused disruption for the whole palace. I stubbornly ignored this strange incident, and I chattered on about the wonderful experience I had. Then I mentioned to her about the Saturday's ball and that I expected an invitation. Nana was not surprised.

"It is all because of Prince Rudolph's kindness to me," I added, "Lord Martuzon is still reluctant to show me any consideration. Why, Nana? Am I such a disgusting person? I thought you raised me to be a lady…"

"Oh, my child, do not judge him by his actions…" started Nana Saveta.

"I try not to, Nana, I do. But he is not making any effort to reconcile. Why is the Prince so nice to me, but the Governor isn't?"

Nana shook her head, but she continued to mend the torn curtain.

"When did that curtain tear?" I asked, quite distressed.

"The other night."

I lay on my bed, tired of my own insecurities. I had experienced little victories, but they were all wrong or they were going in the wrong direction. I sensed uneasiness in Nana's voice when I mentioned the Prince.

"I suppose Lord Martuzon will never like me. Isn't that true, Nana?"

"Oh no, my dear! Listen to me carefully." Nana dropped the curtain on the floor and came to sit by me. "I educated you the best I could and I am proud of you. But there is a lesson you must learn for yourself: it is the heart of a man. I cannot teach this to you, nor can I protect you from it.

"*There is a change coming for you. You are not a little girl anymore—you are beautiful and smart. From now on you must find one man who will keep you and protect you. I was told that from tomorrow on, you will no longer be in my care...*"

"*But why?*" I asked, sincerely astonished.

"*I suppose this is gaining a part of your freedom. But is it only right. Many girls of your age are already married...*"

"*Nana, I don't understand...I have no one who cares for me and who would want me for a wife. Why shouldn't you be allowed to take care of me anymore?*"

"*Because, silly girl, you must get married. Have you not heard a word that I just said?*"

There was nothing reassuring to me in this conversation that did not produce panic about my future.

The thought of not having Nana around any longer gave me chills. What would I do? I had no one other than her and I felt like an orphan again. And what was that stupid thing she had said, that I must get married? Would I be forced into it by the Governor?

And who had been chosen to be my husband?

13

MY CONVERSATION WITH DETECTIVES JOHN Morris and Robert Gibb was shorter than I expected. In reality, they didn't talk much. They asked a few questions about our security system and then they praised my brother for his heroism in stopping another abduction. They were disappointed that the criminal ran away, but they weren't at all anxious to leave–they enjoyed lingering in the house.

They took a quick tour of the first floor, but soon discovered their favorite spot.

Our living room was a perfect picture of domestic comfort. The ninety-two-inch LED television screen that Octavian had left on a sports channel, and the candy bowl full of peanut M&Ms, was the prime attraction for these policemen. After fifteen minutes, however, they realized that this was all the pleasure they could allow themselves to have in one day.

After they left, there seemed to be little for me to do and I felt restless. But what could keep my mind occupied more than an unknown threat? My basement held two of them already, and I was well aware that whoever those guys in my basement were, my enemies were getting closer to me. The first one that I had killed had tracked me to only half a mile away from the house, and the second one had stalked girls who looked like me.

When Octavian came home late that Friday night, his face was harsh and his otherwise soft and gentle features were extremely serious.

"I assume Nelda is home and safe," I said, not knowing how to interpret his unusual expression. I continued to knit a blanket, a craft that I had learned from Mrs. Mary Goldenberg over seventy years ago.

"Yes, and you are looking at a hero—at least, one who can't explain a dismantled police car door. They asked about it, but I had to play stupid."

"All right—I get that. What else is bothering you? I can read minds, you know."

Actually I couldn't, but I could always tell when someone was lying or telling the truth. I moved to the couch and sat beside him when he got up from the floor. Lord Arthur joined us immediately.

"Mortal girls are so passionate," he said, and his eyes shone a bit too wildly. "Nelda is a beautiful eighteen years old, full of life, and I'm her worst enemy. All I'm looking for are moments of sublime wild passions, not a relationship."

He put his hands behind his neck, laid his head back against the couch, and gazed into space. "Safira, you know how hard is for me to stay attached to a girl. Even if I would truly love Nelda, what can I tell her about our future? Before long she'll want to know where she stands with me, and our relationship can't go anywhere."

I nodded. My mental argument about her was that Nelda was young enough for them to enjoy some life together. He was right, though. I must admit–it hadn't worked for any other Immortal before us.

"Anyway," continued Octavian and his facial expression became worried, "Nelda's parents invited me to come to their house and have dinner with them tomorrow, as payback for helping their daughter. Will you come with me?"

"No, I won't. You'll do just fine. Your manners are excellent and they'll be very impressed."

"That really isn't what I'm concerned about."

* * *

We both went to bed that night submerged in worries. Octavian was worried about being in love with a mortal while I was worried about never finding love again. I grew tired of being awakened by a dream that would never become reality.

Nevertheless, there was that shimmering feeling in the air that I couldn't understand, but it gave me chills. Perhaps everything was coming to an end–or to a new beginning.

* * *

I was restless in my bed and I couldn't fall asleep. After an hour of tossing and turning I got up and went outside. I stood on the patio and watched the lake water reflect the light from the stars and the world from the other side, the one place where all Immortals came from. Invisible to mortal's eyes, the world is real and I could see it.

It would soon be summer again, I though. I love the warm weather. Something inside me opens for a renewal of my spirit; otherwise, I can't really live–I just exist.

As I was deep in thought, someone touched my shoulder. I spun around in a defensive posture, but it was only Octavian.

"Come inside with me. There's something you need to see."

I followed my brother to the basement and into the security room. He pointed to one of the screens that showed the front of our house. There was a car parked outside, in plain sight. It was very unlikely that Doctor Samson and Ms. Ruth, our across the street neighbors, would have a visitor at this time of the night.

"That car's been there since I came home," said Octavian, zooming on the monitor's image.

"And now it's after midnight," I commented, on edge by this new uninvited visitor.

"Do you think it's an undercover police car?" Octavian asked intrigued.

"The detectives who were here this afternoon would have told me if they were planning to keep an eye on us. This may be another one like Marin."

"Negative. There is a guy inside that car who crosses the street and comes to the gate every thirty minutes or so.

He stops at the gate but he doesn't ring the bell. He's more than likely a coward, but he's not a hybrid."

"Well, then, let's go make his acquaintance." I said, grabbing a Desert Eagle Magnum from the closet.

"What are you going to do?"

"Go outside and shoot him," I plainly answered.

"Is that your best plan?"

"I don't need a plan. You said he is not a hybrid. You stay here and watch," I advised my brother.

On the way out I stumbled over Marin's dead body. I bent to lift him up and move him out of my way. When I bent down, I took a quick look at him–tears were rolling down his cheeks. I backed up, startled.

"Don't touch him," said Octavian, dragging him out of the hallway by his legs. "His neck is broken, but he can easily come back to life."

"Can he move?" I was sure I left him in the closet on the sofa and now he was out in the hall. "I thought he was dead."

"That kind of injury isn't fatal to them. His injuries and other wounds are healing because of the energy from our presence. This gives him some limited mobility, but he's not dangerous. We may need him later, but for now it's safer to leave him in this state. We'll revive him when he becomes useful to us."

"OK. Silence the alarm, please."

I exited through the back patio door and walked around to the front yard. I jumped over the fence and went over to the rear of the car. It only took me a few seconds to reach the car, break the front window of the passenger side with my fist, and put my gun to the man's temple.

"Put your hands in the air and don't move!" I yelled at him. The man cautiously put his hands above his head. "Now, slowly turn toward me."

When he turned and our eyes met, a flush came over my face. It was Julian Grant.

"Commander Grant, what are you doing here? Do you have a death wish or something?" The surprise of seeing him made me stutter.

Grant exited the car brushing broken glass from his clothes.

"Good God, woman. What's wrong with you? Just stop threatening me with that gun," he said holding his hands high.

All at once I was surprised, happy, and frustrated, but I put away my gun.

"You've been sitting out here for the past four hours. Couldn't you just ring the bell? How did you find me?"

"I didn't know for sure," he answered hurriedly. "I thought I had the wrong address. I was wondering whether or not Safira Tash lives here in this big house."

"This is my house, Commander. What are you doing in Atlanta and why are you looking for me?"

"May I take you to dinner tomorrow?" he asked me with an expressionless face.

"What?" For the first time ever I didn't trust my hearing.

"I would like for you to have dinner with me tomorrow," he repeated, this time a bit intimidated. "And if it's possible, without any firepower."

Everything about me was trembling, not only my legs, but my voice, as well and I hated it.

"Yes, sure," I said in a hoarse whisper, "I didn't expect to see you anymore, Commander Grant! This is quite a surprise!

I'm sorry about your car. You can borrow my truck; my brother will take yours in to be repaired tomorrow."

"Thanks for the offer, but..."

"I insist," I interrupted him. "It's my fault–I overreacted."

I reached out for the touch pad that would open the gate, and my hand was still shaking so much I could hardly enter the code. Finally the gate swung open and he followed me up the driveway, into the garage.

With an almost timid voice he asked, "Is six o'clock alright with you?"

"Six is fine," I agreed rapidly, trying to regain my coolness. "Here are the keys for the truck. Good night, Commander."

He started the truck and backed slowly out of the garage, perhaps unsure of himself. I waited until he was out on the street and I closed the gate. My brother was waiting for me in the doorway. His smile was larger than usual.

"Wow! Commander Julian Grant himself. The guy came to look for you. Do I smell love in the air?"

14

SATURDAY FINALLY CAME. THE PAST three days had been like a prolonged nightmare. I had struggled to fall asleep every night, and then I fought the loneliness during the day. Nana Saveta was no longer to be my companion, and I felt lost and abandoned without her. Indeed, all this was happening the wrong way.

So many times I had dreamed of my freedom, and that included my desire to end Nana's supervision of me. Now, I was a victim of my own wishes as they were so terribly coming to life. I could choose to allow these new circumstances to consume me until my life dwindled away, or I could choose to take care of myself as I promised Nana.

A guard was posted at my door, and that upset me even more than my isolation. I hadn't had any contact with Lord Martuzon since that day we went for a walk in the city, and with the guard assigned to my door, I couldn't go out to my spying room. I was treated like a prisoner in solitary confinement, unaware of what was happening outside my room.

Had that man from the bridge been hunted or caught? My little adventure outside of the palace that late at night forced me to admit that *his capture might have happened. My solitude was now causing me to imagine the most bizarre things. That man had saved my life but I may have put his life in danger.*

I became obsessed by the thought of him. I wished so much to know more about him, to meet him again.

Dina came every day to bring me food but she was not like Nana. She didn't talk to me very much and she was too slow to observe what happened around the palace. She spent so much time in the company of the other servants that she was uninterested in the details of everyday life in the palace, and to try to engage her in a conversation about those things was useless. I tried to listen through the wall on my right where Chancellor Gunter's family lived, but the words I heard were indistinct and meaningless.

Nana had not taught me the art of dressing formally or creating hair styles, so I knew these tasks would present me with a formidable challenge. The dresses I had selected in the shop were beautiful indeed, but I had no sense of fashion. I chose my favorite to wear to the ball, but I had no knowledge whatsoever as to how I could alter it to flatter my figure.

The Prince had sent many pieces of jewelry to my room as his gift to me, and I had to sort through all of them for the one that complimented my dress the most. In the end, I just chose the one that was the most dazzling. This experience almost made me cry. I was about to enter into a society about whose existence I was only dimly aware as I gazed at it from my apartment window, and I had no experience at all in assembling decent accouterments.

Now, because of my ineptness, Lord Martuzon would surely be most displeased with me. I expected even more reproof from him than that which I had already received.

When I heard the voice of the Archduke at my door, come to accompany me to the ball, my nerves were so much on edge that they were ready to explode. It would have been better to present myself to him naked, rather than to look as clumsy and unsophisticated as I did. Nana had taught me to never be embarrassed because of my body. She would tell me that clothing is merely an invention designed to separate people into social classes, according to one's means to purchase expensive finery. I certainly agreed. Tonight I was a person with no means of my own, wearing clothing that had been bought by someone else.

But the Prince smiled broadly as he glanced at my irregular attempt at being in fashion, and offered his arm. He was dressed elegantly in his red military uniform, proudly holding the handle of his gleaming sword that was swinging in its carefully polished scabbard alongside his hip.

"You look superb, Lady Safira. All the other ladies tonight will be so jealous!"

I doubted him very much, but by now I had to agree with Lord Martuzon that Prince Rudolph was a compulsive charmer. I felt weak and needy as I doted on his attention.

* * *

The ballroom was big and impressive, with massive golden walls, white marble columns, and beautifully decorated with flowers and candles on every table. Oh, and already crowded with people!

When we entered, their conversations and all other sound was immediately hushed. Everyone bowed to the Prince and stared at me, a complete stranger to all of them. I managed to keep my head high as I smiled. What a terrible feeling—not pleasure or excitement, but an uncomfortable heaviness seemed to weigh me down. I suddenly realized that I was quite uncomfortable in all this mass of people, and it was too soon for me to be exposed to such a large number at a single gathering.

Miss Flora Cristea was the first to be introduced to me. I liked her very much; she was soft spoken, intelligent, and very friendly to me. I wondered if she was the one who was loved by Lord Martuzon—if she was, I wouldn't mind.

At first, Miss Anda didn't recognize me, and when Lord Martuzon introduced me to her as his goddaughter; she was very surprised. A moment later, when a look of jealousy flashed across her face, I knew she remembered me as the girl from the third story window. After our introduction, I didn't see her for the rest of that evening.

As time passed, I became more relaxed. For the first part of the evening, Lord Martuzon kept me by his side, but as the hour grew later, he couldn't quell the Prince's desire to dance with me. I loved to dance. It was physical movement combined with grace and power, and it was something that I executed flawlessly, according to my School Master.

The Archduke and I danced numerous times that evening. My passion for dancing did not go unnoticed by him as he continued his subtle pursuit of my heart. But only my mind was open for this pursuit. My heart felt no warmth toward him whatsoever.

"I wrote to my wife yesterday," he told me during one of the dances. "If everything goes as I have planned, you can return to Wien with me in a month. Would you like that?"

"Very much", I whispered, giggling again. "But are you sure, your Highness, that I will be welcomed by the Archduchess? I am a complete stranger to her."

"I am absolutely convinced that she will find you to be a very agreeable companion. Besides, Milos and I are lifelong friends, and you are like family to him. My wife will accept you with open arms"

"Thank you so much, Your Highness. How can I ever repay you for your kindness?"

"Oh, my dear Lady, there is no need for repayment. Just adore me as I adore you."

The music had ended, but we were still standing on the dance floor. He reached out and touched my hair and my face. I did not understand the meaning of his words, but his demeanor towards me seemed to continually raise negative reactions from my protector. As a result of this, Lord Martuzon offered me his arm and escorted me away from the ball and to my apartment before the festivities had ended. This angered the Prince and I saw a strange look come over his face before I left the room.

For the first time in my life, Milos's action and attitude towards me made me lose all of my frustrations. I felt no fear of him, as I had at other times. The Prince had assured me that I could follow him to his country and into his protection, and that gave me more than enough courage to protest against this constant injustice to which I had been subjected.

"The ball is not over, my Lord! I loved my dances with the Archduke. Why did you humiliate me and rush me out of the ballroom? I am sure the others thought I had committed some terrible sin."

He didn't answer me as he walked rapidly to my quarters with me in tow. I was almost running to keep up with his long strides, especially when he took the stairs two steps at the time. As he walked into my room, he paced back and forth for a few minutes, agitated and upset.

"I was only trying to protect you! I am not deaf–I heard what the Archduke told you about becoming a companion to the Archduchess. I don't trust him! This plan of his will only come to no good, and it must be put to an end."

"What are you talking about, my Lord? I know the Prince is married, but he is only showing kindness to me. I should leave with him as soon as possible and terminate this hurtful relationship we have…"

"Is this what you think about the two of us?" As he shouted at me, spumescent saliva sprayed from his mouth.

"I did not mean to offend you," I rushed to answer, feeling more than a little fear. "It merely seems to me that I am quite a burden for you, and I am making every possible attempt to disappear from your life. My origins are a mystery, but it seems that they don't matter to the Archduke. His Highness is willing to take me as his wife's companion."

"He only wants you for himself! My God, you are so naïve!" the Governor exploded.

"And whose fault is it that I am naïve, my Lord? You have kept me in here like a bird in a cage, with absolutely no freedom…"

"I know! Please, you must forgive me…"

I couldn't believe my ears. Had Lord Martuzon just asked for my forgiveness, or was it just my imagination? He came to me, forcefully grasping my waist, and made me sit beside him on the bench.

"If your heart is set on accompanying the Archduke, I won't stop you…but…I don't want you to leave…"

"But why not, my Lord, you don't care about me…"

"You are wrong. I've known you and cared for you since you were born."

I stood there quietly, waiting for him to continue. I hoped he would tell me the one thing I had been waiting for all my life: who was I? To make me more worthy of his trust, I put my hand in his, and my bold move softened his face.

"At first, I thought you were my sister. I was ten years old when you were born. My mother died giving birth to me and Nana Saveta raised me, but there was also a very young and beautiful woman who was entrusted with my education. My father loved her very much, and so did I. She was so very good to me, and for a while I hoped my father would marry her so she would become my mother, but he didn't. She remained his mistress, and she later gave birth to you.

"I was very happy, but the truth of your lineage was revealed and I soon learned that you were not my sister. I was quite young and I didn't understand everything that had happened, but my father did, and he was devastated that your mother had a lover besides him.

"You were such a beautiful child, and it became my duty to care for you. I taught you how to walk, then to run, to pick flowers, to catch fireflies and butterflies. You can't possibly remember that — you were too small.

"The man who is your father returned a few years later to take you and your mother away. He took your mother, but in the turmoil that resulted from your father's raid on our palace, you were left behind. My father swore revenge, but he also did everything to care for you. On his deathbed, he asked me do the same thing and now I am willingly caring for you. It has definitely never been a burden for me.

"I wish I had known how to raise a girl, but I was young and stupid myself, so I relied totally on Nana Saveta. I was always afraid that someone would come to take you away from me. I am your family,

Lady Safira, the only family you have left, but I can't keep you here against your will."

"What was my mother's name?" I asked him, quite moved by his confession.

"Lady Amara. I hope she is well, wherever she is."

"She isn't dead, is she?" I dared to ask, fearful of his answer.

"Probably not, I believe."

"Thank you, my Lord, for telling me this."

I gently released my hand from his. So this is who I am: the daughter of the mistress of my protector's father, and my real father was an unknown vagabond. Why had I struggled all my life to learn the truth about myself, and now I didn't seem to want to know it?

I still had no last name, and I was not a Lady. I felt so sad.

What would become of me? Once again, I was at the mercy of Lord Martuzon. I couldn't afford to lose him or to have his anger turn against me. But what could I do? He said that he wanted to continue to have me here with him.

"My Lord, I can see now that I am an ungrateful wretch. Please forgive me. I am at your mercy again…but please don't keep me away from you…my heart longs to be near you. Please forgive me—I know it is wrong for me to ask you this—do you love someone else?"

He stood up and so did I. His hand caressed my face. His lips touched mine, but with so much restraint, like a fight that he waged with his soul.

"I love you, only you," he whispered, more to himself than to me, as he walked to the door.

15

SINCE I WAS A YOUNG girl I had wished for things and then cowardly regretted that I had pursued those wishes. Once again it was happening.

How could I not think about it? It preyed on me all night. For one moment, a week ago, I had let my guard down—and once again it happened. I treasured a memory from the past, a memory of someone who had stolen my heart and never returned it. Julian Grant's only fault was that he resembled my love from long ago and I couldn't resist him.

Now the impossible had happened—Julian had found me, he was here and I had agreed to allow him to take me to dinner. What was I hoping or wishing for?

Love? Yes, I wished to be loved and be embraced with passion but I was supposed to choose only the Immortal kind. I just couldn't allow myself, as my brother did, to find this satisfaction in the mortals I was here to protect.

*　*　*

Early the next morning Octavian took Julian's silver Camaro to the body shop. I was mad at myself knowing that I offered to fix his car for only one reason – to make him have to come back for it.

I spent quite a bit of time searching in my closet for an outfit suitable for dinner at a nice restaurant. I was the most comfortable wearing my fancy short dresses–and I own a variety of colors. If it was necessary, I could just as easily fight in a dress, as well as in my day-to-day outfit, a pair of stretch denim pants and a T-shirt. The right choice of a dress had to be something that was classic, yet elegant, perhaps the royal blue one. Then I would have to straighten my long, wild, wavy hair a little.

The gate was open and someone rang the doorbell.

"Aha", I thought, "now he knows what to do."

But it was much too early for Julian–it was only four o'clock–unless he was so eager that he just couldn't restrain himself. Octavian had already left the house for an early visit with Nelda. I could easily imagine that their kiss was only the beginning of his new unleashed appetite for a mortal's affection.

I rushed to the door, but it wasn't Julian. Instead, it was my dear neighbor, Doctor Samson, holding tight to his Rollator.

"Doctor Samson, come in. Is everything OK?"

The old man's effort to negotiate over the carpet in the long hallway was a battle he couldn't win until I helped him to sit in a chair in the family room.

Without preamble he began to speak. "I need your help, my dear. I apologize for not giving you much warning."

"It's so much of an effort for you to walk across the street. You know you can call me anytime, Doctor Samson."

"I can't talk about this situation over the phone."

I pulled my ottoman close to his chair. I looked at his small body with its fragile frame and my heart warmed to him. I was very tempted to touch him and remove all his pain—but I didn't.

"As I said before, I'm not giving you much warning here, but Ruth and I would like for you to come to dinner tonight. Actually, we really need for you to be there."

I instantly felt a sense of relief. My mind had begun to conjure many scenarios of disasters that could have happened to him or Ms. Ruth.

"Here's our dilemma," he continued. "Our granddaughter and her husband are coming for dinner. We love Carla, but we have...shall we say...a strong dislike for her husband. To be quite honest, we can't stand him. He abuses her verbally, even in our presence. Unfortunately, she can't come to dinner with us without him. This abuse has been going on for a few years now, and she's too weak to leave him. My wife and I don't have the strength to object to his abuse any more. It's so awful!"

"I am so sorry, Doctor Samson, but I don't see how I can help you."

"We're hoping that with a stranger at dinner, he will behave and we can have a decent meal together. Please come. I can't go back home without Ruth knowing we have a solution to our problem. Please, Miss Safira," he pleaded with me.

Well, the perfect date I didn't ask for and I didn't anticipate had just flown out the window. But who I was kidding? In reality I was looking forward to that dinner, and I had a gazillion questions for Julian Grant.

"Doctor Samson, don't worry, I'll be there. Let me help you get back across the street."

It was obvious that Doctor Samson needed me much more than Julian Grant. As bizarre as it was, this dinner invitation was my excuse for avoiding being face to face with a man I didn't need in my life, but who I was weak enough to want.

I helped the doctor cross the street and up the steps to his house.

"I'll be back in two hours," I told him, waving to Ms. Ruth as she looked out her living room window. But it seemed that nothing worked as it was supposed to. By the time I crossed the street, here he was, in my truck, waiting for me at the gate. He was in civilian clothes–khaki dress pants and a wine colored dress shirt. This was terrible. He was so handsome with his hair cut short. His whole appearance almost caused me to develop a nervous case of hives.

"You're…you're early," I stammered again as he followed me up the walkway to the house.

"I was afraid you would change your mind."

I turned to him and giggled nervously.

"As a matter of fact, I did. Actually, it was changed for me. My good neighbor across the street, Doctor Samson, had invited me to dinner long ago, but last night it slipped my mind. I really feel obligated to have dinner with him and his wife tonight. I'm sorry."

"Would it be alright if I came along?" he asked, quite nonchalantly.

"I don't know. I didn't ask."

By this time we had walked into the house. He walked down the long hallway and into the family room, to the detectives' favorite couch and candy bowl.

"This is a very nice house–it's huge. You can't blame me for being confused that you're living here. There's nothing I can say or do to impress you, at this point…"

He looked straight at me, like he wanted to eat me alive. But his eyes were searching and imploring, something that struck me as so unusual.

"You know, I suppose you can come with me. I really don't think the Samson's will mind having another guest for dinner at all. Wait here and I'll go upstairs to change clothes."

Was he trying to impress me? What was that all about? I had no idea, but I was happy that he went the extra mile to find me. So many emotions were rushing inside me to make me feel good, but I was confused. I certainly had planned to rid myself of him, but I really liked the idea of him lingering a bit more in my life.

When I returned, Julian Grant wasn't on the couch in the family room anymore. I found him in the library, staring at Octavian's collection of antique guns.

"Oh, wow!" he exclaimed with admiration when he saw me.

"It's my brother's collection," I said, pretending not to understand his amazement.

"I see. Your family really loves guns."

"For now, my family is only me and my younger brother, Octavian. But we do like guns. Do you have a favorite among them?"

"Yes. This M1903 Springfield. It's an American legend."

"That's a good choice. We found it in a gun shop in Missouri. This one still fires. Would you like to try it out?"

"Oh, yes, I'd love that."

"Perhaps tomorrow?"

"Tomorrow it is, then."

I giggled. I couldn't believe I had made another date with him. Now I was embarrassed.

"What are you doing in Atlanta? Are you on leave?" I mumbled, pretending not to sound too interested.

"I'm on a leave–it's for several days. I am also on a very special mission."

"Oh! I am really sorry about your car. The mechanic at the body shop said it'll be ready by Tuesday. I'm more than happy to lend you my truck until then."

"Look at this collection of swords," he said, suddenly changing the subject. 'Now, that *is* interesting. Not too many people have these kinds of primitive weapons in their collections. Do you know how to use one?"

Our swords were fierce–long and wide, with a sharp double edge, and a very bulky grip. There was nothing magical or extraordinary about them. They were made hundreds of years ago from heavy steel, for one purpose only–to cut and slice.

"How to use a sword?" I attempted to laugh, a little irritated by his interest in my abilities. "Why would I know how to use a sword? There's still some time until dinner. Would you like something to drink? We don't have anything stronger than water or a Coke, I'm afraid."

"Coke's OK, but I'd like to enjoy it in your family room."

I took a soda can from the refrigerator, popped the top, and poured the liquid over ice in a glass cup.

"How did you find me?" I asked as we walked into the family room, trying to decide if I should sit beside him on the couch, but Lord Arthur made that decision for both of us. I sat across from him on the love seat as the dog chose the couch, as always.

"Actually, I'm visiting my grandmother in Newnan," he said, avoiding my direct question again. "Surprisingly, it turns out that we're almost neighbors."

"Indeed, that is a surprise," I agreed, ironically. It was probably one in three hundred million chances that he would have a relative living close by.

"You know," he said, "I don't recall you looking like this when I first met you." Then he gasped. "Well, *that* didn't come out right. Please excuse me—you are actually very attractive…and so sexy."

"Thank you," I answered, trying not to over analyze his compliment.

"For a brief moment you made me lose my mind," continued Grant carefully. "The moment I laid my eyes on you on that day in Germany it was like you had bewitched me. I've never seen anything more amazing, like when you came out of the ashes of that barn. When I kissed you, all my will power melted. I knew then that I had to find you."

I blushed just a little, satisfied with his answer and with the fact that he didn't apologize for kissing me—a bold move on his part. Grant smiled nervously, perhaps still expecting a rebuke regarding his behavior that night. But I didn't.

"So, you aren't married?" It was my turn to gasp. *Oh, Lord! Why did I ask that?*

"No; should I be?" His eyes were completely locked on me, fascinated.

"Not necessarily," I mumbled, but I was so curious.

Just then, without warning, Lord Arthur began to growl. Dogs have a certain sense that reacts to things unseen or unheard by humans.

I stood up fast and Grant did, too. At that moment, out of the corner of my eye, I saw movement. I couldn't see clearly because Julian was blocking my view, but my instincts are always right.

Marin was up and alive again, armed with a M6 rifle that he probably found in the basement.

With my right hand I rapidly grabbed a P220 from underneath the couch pillows. I stepped on the coffee table to gain some height, and in the next second, I leaped in the air over Julian's head and the couch.

Before my feet had touched the floor, I pushed Julian down to the couch and shot the intruder. When I landed on my feet, the hybrid lay on the floor with four bullets in his forehead. Grant's astonished gaze followed me as I disarmed the hybrid.

"Who's that? You just killed him! How'd he get in your house?"

"I didn't want to kill him," I answered very calmly, "but I could see that he was armed and dangerous. He's my uninvited guest, and it's a long story that would make no sense to you."

"Jesus! We've got to call the police." Grant's forehead was sweating abundantly.

"No, there's no need for that. He doesn't look like it, but he's not entirely dead."

I picked up Marin's legs and dragged him into the kitchen. Julian followed me, moving as if he was in a trance.

"How can he not be dead?" His face looked perplexed, like that night when I came out alive from the blast. "I can see four bullet holes in his head. Safira, what's going on? What are you talking about?"

"Come here and see for yourself." I insisted, grabbing his hand and forcing him to touch the dead man. Marin was still warm to the touch, his eyes were open, and his wounds weren't bleeding.

Julian Grant was visibly shocked. I certainly had an original way of charming men!

"Oh, look at the time," I smiled, like nothing had happened as I began looking for my purse. "It's dinner time. The Samson's like to have dinner early. Their granddaughter and her husband are coming for dinner, too. Try to ignore Carla's husband. He's known to be a jerk."

16

I WAS FREE!

Free to stay or free to leave the Black Eagle Castle. I imagined myself indulging in all the wealth and accommodation that Archduke Rudolph could provide for me, but I couldn't overlook the fact that Lord Martuzon was my only family. Besides, the life I would create for myself painfully resembled the same path as my mother's relationship with Milos' father. I had learned Milos' intention towards me and I was flattered to be loved and desired by him, but I felt unsettled at the same time.

Is this how I wanted to live? What would happen to me many years from now when my youth would fade? But what other choice did I have? My mind analyzed all this as clearly and as rationally as possible.

All my life I had been sheltered from the wickedness of human nature, but my spirit was suddenly awake and aware. There was no innocence remaining in me, and the facts I had learned about myself separated me from all other girls everywhere. I was here in this palace, sheltered and protected, but my situation could have been much worse for a girl who seemed to have no future.

After Lord Martuzon left my quarters that evening, I realized that I didn't need to spy on him anymore. There was nothing else I had to know, and I was disappointed and angry with what I had learned.

Why had my parents left me behind? Why didn't my mother marry the Governor instead of choosing to have a child with a nobody? Perhaps the Governor didn't want her as wife when he learned that I was not his child. This hurtful truth made me weep in shame.

I had no other family on whom I could rely, so it was entirely up to me to make a better life for myself. I must take every opportunity to make my life as safe as possible. Milos had said that he did not want me to leave him and he appeared to be in love with me, at least on some level. I knew he would never dare to marry someone like me and destroy his reputation. I needed more than that!

I decided that I would leave with the Prince and put my embarrassing past behind me.

* * *

I must have slept for a few hours when I was awakened—being carried in someone's arms. At first I thought it was just a continuation of the dream I was having, but soon my instincts were telling me that I was fully awake. When I opened my eyes, I was indeed being carried out of the palace by way of my secret stairs.

This could not possibly be happening to me, not now, when I was finally free to leave Transylvania—and, as it turned out, the one who had held me prisoner was secretly in love with me.

I fought for release from my captor's arms, but he lowered me to my feet and he allowed me to walk. His left arm held me tight around my waist and his right hand covered my mouth so I couldn't scream. When we were outside, he lifted me up onto his horse and we disappeared into the night, without disturbing a single soul in the palace.

All this time my kidnapper's face was covered, but when I turned to face him, I saw his eyes.

I screamed with surprise. He was none other than the man who had saved me from the Gypsies, and he was also the beggar from the bridge. From that moment on I knew that my life was not in danger anymore and I become less restless.

The night was cold and windy but his arms around me kept me warm. I laid my head on his chest and felt protected by his body.

We traveled more than an hour until we were far away from the city, and my abductor never uttered a word. We finally stopped at an old building that resembled the ruins of a castle. My kidnapper helped me off of his horse very gently. I was smart enough to understand my situation: this man had kidnapped me and had taken me far from where I lived. I didn't know where I was and struggling with him would be futile. I felt no fear of him at all but I was intrigued and curious.

"What place is this? Why have you brought me here?" I asked, barely holding my tears.

He didn't answer, but he pushed me toward the castle. Its massive wood door was heavy, but he opened it with a push of his shoulder and motioned for me to enter. I wanted to resist, but everything about this man was calm and mysterious, so I obeyed.

Regardless of the rugged and decrepit appearance of the castle's exterior, the interior where I was escorted was quite nice. It was obvious that the people who had once lived there had exquisite taste; however, some of the furniture was old Victorian and had seen quite a bit of use. Not all of the candles in the room were lit, and those that were cast an eerie glow over the room. From what I had seen so far, the whole place was very disturbing.

"Why am I here? What's happening?" I asked again.

My abductor didn't respond, but he removed his face covering and his coat. His handsome face and appearance made a deep impression on me. I had never seen anybody like him before. He looked at me with blue eyes so intense that they seemed to crawl into my soul.

"Welcome to my home, Lady Safira," he said softly and his voice was so pleasant to my ears. "It may not be what you are accustomed to, but it is livable. The north side was destroyed by fire a few years ago, but everything wasn't lost."

"This is your home? Why did you bring me here" I asked, astonished.

"I brought you here because this is where you belong, or at least we believe that to be true."

"Who are you?"

"I saved your life once, remember? For now, we have to stay here and wait for the others."

"What others?" My questions to him were short and naïve.

"The others are like me and like you," he answered softly. "There is nothing to fear."

"Please, I don't understand."

"You are here to meet your real family...those who are your brothers. I am only the messenger."

I stood there quietly, trying to grasp the meaning of his words. My heart was pounding and my breathing had accelerated, but my eyes were locked on this young man and I felt that I was melting. I was not looking at a stranger anymore—he was my whole world at that moment. All others had disappeared from my memory.

He extinguished most of the candles and reclined on his back on a bench, totally ignoring me. His eyes closed, and I was standing in semi-darkness.

I had a strong wish for something extraordinary to happen to me.

"Do you mean to tell me that I have brothers? Where are they?"

"They are coming soon. I suggest that you try to get some rest. The dawn is still four hours away."

"I'm not tired or sleepy! What is your name?"

My questions seemed to irritate him and he raised his head to look at me. In the gloom, his eyes were lit like two stars. I was fascinated and delirious, but then, to my disappointment, his eyes softened to a normal sky blue.

"My name is Andreas."

Again, he laid his back on the bench in an attempt to return to rest.

"Andreas!" I called out to him.

I couldn't leave it at that. The man stood up and turned completely to me. There was something inside me that I had never experienced before, and it took over my spirit. That moment seemed to cast a spell on me.

137

His presence was disturbing and provocative to my mind and body. I felt pain and strange pressure move into my loins. The scent he was releasing in the air was taking control over my desires. It was something I had not felt before in the presence of a man.

My body refused to listen to any rationality and I removed my night dress, dropping it to the floor. He seemed to be dumbfounded seeing my naked body.

For one more moment his eyes lit up again, but then he closed his eyes.

"My dress is torn. Could I have another one, please?"

Saying these words, I moved closer to him until we were nearly touching.

"We have no clothing for females here, Lady Safira. I regret to say that you will have to continue to use your damaged one."

I did nothing to retrieve my dress from the floor, but he reached out for it. I couldn't resist him! His face leaned closer to mine and I inhaled his delicious aroma. I rose up to kiss his sensual lips, afraid that all this would disappear, as if it were just a dream. But he returned my kiss with so much passion that I could feel lust rushing through my body.

"Hurry, you must dress," he said as he stopped kissing me, listening to the sounds outside. "I think I hear the others coming." I reluctantly put on my old dress as my lips still savored the wonderful flavor of his.

* * *

Outside, the sound of the horses and the other commotion was indeed a sign of their arrival. One by one they came in the room and performed the same ritual that Andreas had done: they removed their coats and

138

uncovered their faces. And one by one, they all appeared the same. Each of them had long dark hair, blue eyes, and looked so young.

My mouth was agape and I sat there in amazement, as if I was at a magic show. I could feel all their eyes on me.

Andreas touched his forehead with the fingers of his right hand, bowed to them, and made introductions.

"Lady Safira, may I introduce to you, your brother, Serban."

Serban came directly to me and bowed.

"I am happy to have you here, my dear sister. I believe the time is right for you to join us, your family. I see you look like one of us, too. That is fascinating."

"Sir, are you truly my brother? How is that possible?" I mumbled, still afraid that all this would prove to be a mistake.

"Yes, we are actually blood siblings."

"Am I related to all of you?" I asked, terrified that I just kissed one of my brothers and revealed myself to him naked.

"Oh no," said another young man who came to bow to me. "Serban and I are your brothers—not Andreas. My name is Rares." Then he pointed to the others. "Now, meet the rest of your clan—Costan, Barbu and Razvan."

I didn't faint, but this revelation was dizzying.

17

"SAFIRA, TALK TO ME. WHAT just happened in your house? Who was that man? Are you in danger? I can protect you..."

As I rang the doorbell at Doctor Samson's home, I began to laugh. Julian's last sentence struck me as extremely funny.

"Ok," he corrected himself, "maybe I can't protect you. Obviously *you* don't need me, but can we at least talk about it?"

"There's nothing to talk about, nothing that you would understand."

"What's there to understand," he exclaimed. "You just killed a man who didn't die and you dragged him to the kitchen without calling the police."

I handed him my cell phone. "Do you want to call the police?"

There was anger and frustration in my voice, and I had to try very hard to keep my eyes under control by blinking faster so they wouldn't light up.

"No. I can't call the police—not until I can understand what's going on."

"Commander Grant, you came to my house and invited me to dinner," I said harshly. "We're here at my neighbor's house because they really *need* me to have dinner with them, so let's get it over with, OK? We'll enjoy the evening with them and then you can call the police or go on your way to your very special mission."

"I can't," he responded gently.

"You can't *what?*"

"Go on my special mission. I'm running one right now."

"I don't understand."

"My special mission is to find you. I am here only for you."

"What?"

Doctor Samson opened the door and interrupted our unsettling conversation. My dear old friend was very happy to see me. We followed him into the kitchen where Ms. Ruth was completing her preparations for dinner. She had made her famous lasagna topped with shiitake mushrooms. It was strange to combine Italian and Asian food, but it was so delicious.

She gave Commander Grant a questioning look.

"Oh, where is my dear Octavian this evening?" she asked me, smiling with her eyes. She was eighty-five, but with her beautifully coiffed hair and her slender body, she appeared to be much younger. Her navy blue apron had "Kiss The Cook" embroidered in white thread, so I did.

"He's having dinner with Nelda's parents this evening," I answered. "I hope you don't mind that I invited my friend, Julian Grant. Julian's a commander in the Navy SEALs."

"Not at all," she answered politely. "It's a pleasure to have you, Julian. Please follow me."

Carla and her husband were already seated at the dinner table. The introductions were made again and I was quite surprised to see how easy going and pleasant Julian was with the whole idea of dining with complete strangers—especially when he had just witnessed me killing a man in my living room. I was grateful for his demeanor, but I was still angry with him for his deliberate injection into my life.

I had known Carla for years. She was the Samson's only granddaughter and I remembered when she married Peter five years ago. At the time, she wasn't what one would expect a happy bride to be. It was obvious to me that there was something in her soul that was causing her to be wary about the marriage, but I didn't understand why.

I didn't know Peter very well. He was a big bear of a man, quite heavy, and with a ruddy complexion. He reminded me of someone who was always in an agitated mood, or who had drunk too much alcohol, or both.

At first he was quite civil, concentrating primarily on eating, with little talk. For a while I thought that doctor Samson's fears were exaggerated, but during dessert, he began to acknowledge me and my guest. At first he congratulated me for my beautiful home.

"Carla and I have wanted to move near here for a long time, but we've been putting it off. But we'll do it soon won't we dear?"

His wife answered with a timid smile.

"Did I tell you that Safira's friend, Commander Grant, is a Navy SEAL?" asked Miss Ruth, perhaps in a subtle attempt to change the subject.

"Oh, wow. Isn't that dangerous?" asked Peter.

"It's for a just cause," Grant responded, in good mood.

"But it also takes courage and honor," I completed his sentence.

Julian turned to me and looked me straight into my eyes, surprised by my words. I went on to say that I was quite proud of him.

"That's super. I really admire you, Grant," said Peter, with his mouth full of cake. "That's awesome. I wish I could be that good – I'd be a SEAL, too. But that didn't happen. I had to stay home to take over my father's business. You know, somebody has to make the money in the family."

Doctor Samson shook his head in disbelief. I felt the irony of Peter's words.

"Following in your father steps is the right thing to do," agreed Julian, to save the moment. "My father is a General."

"See my dear, I told you," responded Peter hitting the edge of the table with his fingers. "My wife's father is a physician, but Carla barely made it out of chiropractor school. Give me a break—that's not the way to make a decent living in this world. I'll bet the army pays an officer more than a chiropractor makes, doesn't it?"

His question was addressed to Grant, but Ms. Ruth rushed to answer differently.

"Some people love what they do regardless of the compensation."

There was an awkward silence.

"So, Safira, why're you so rich?" Peter had no restraint with his question to me.

"My grandfather was on oil tycoon. I moved here from Texas."

"I wish I could have had a grandfather like that," he rumbled cutting another big slice of cake for himself. "Carla doesn't have relatives like that. My lovely father-in-law donates most of his income to so called cancer research. So, are you two are an item?"

Peter's lack of tact knew no bounds. There was a point where he got to you, and this was it—he began to be annoying and rude. With each remark he made, he found some way to blame his wife, usually for one of his failings.

Julian didn't seem to be disturbed. He took advantage of the situation to take my hand in his and kiss it. I felt a feverish sensation on my skin where his lips touched me because it took me completely by surprise. Julian could easily provoke physical feelings in me, and for a moment, I wanted everyone to disappear–except for him.

"We're working of it," he answered, continuing to hold my hand.

"She's a nice gal," commented Peter again. "She's so pretty and skinny! You've got it made! That's how a woman should look – not like my wife. She just doesn't understand what I've been telling her for years, now. I mean, just look at her! It's embarrassing! She's a size 12!"

Indeed, Carla had inherited her father's large stature, but she definitely wasn't as disagreeable as her husband's accusation. Besides, Peter was still twice her size.

"Would you like some wine, Commander Grant?" asked Ms. Ruth, disturbed. It was obvious that Peter's ruthless remarks about his wife had escalated to a point where they were very painful for her grandparents.

Julian accepted her offer without hesitation. At that moment he sensed the tension that was building in the room, and how uncomfortable things had become.

"Carla, dear, go and bring us some wine. You're so good at choosing the best vintage."

"Sure Grandma," said Carla, standing up. She was obviously glad to get away from the table for a minute.

"She can't choose anything!" said Peter, following his wife. "I'd better go and watch out for her–she's so clumsy. She'll have wine all over the kitchen floor."

There was complete silence in the dining room, but the loud sound of voices coming from the next room made everyone alert. I couldn't stand by any longer.

"Well, it looks like it'll take the whole village to bring out the wine," I joked, as I rose from my seat, "so if you'll excuse me, I think I'll volunteer to give Carla a hand."

Julian was about to make a comment, but I pulled my hand from his and left for the kitchen. I got there just in time to see Peter pushing a bottle of wine directly into Carla's face and saying, "This is the best vintage, you stupid cow!"

He stopped when he saw me and smirked with a guilty grin. Nothing could stop me from not reacting. I went directly to him and punched his face. He backed up a few feet, in shock and in pain. The blow broke his nose and when my leg kicked in the air, it gave him another blow on the right side of his temple. I wasn't sure if he was still conscious as he doubled over, so I grabbed his arm and twisted it firmly behind his back. As I pushed him to the floor I could see that he was well aware of everything that was happening.

"Never do what you just did to your wife again," I whispered to him, as his face pressed against the floor tiles, "If you do, I swear I'll find you and break every bone in your body so you're left paralyzed from the nose down! Do you understand me?"

He didn't respond, but just lay there, gasping for air. As he turned his head I could see full blown hatred in his eyes.

"Would you like me to repeat my question and break your arm?"

Peter shook his head.

"Please," he cried, "let me go."

"With one condition: now that you're on the floor, get to your knees and ask your wife for forgiveness! Do it, right now! And remember, if you ever touch her again, I'll kill you."

He moved his bulky body and painfully rose to his knees. "Please forgive me, Carla," he whispered with tears in his eyes. He wasn't the macho man any longer.

Carla looked at us, stunned. From the other side of the kitchen, Julian watched everything without expression. I stood up, but Peter was still kneeling on the floor, unable to recover from his pain.

"I don't think we'll have any wine, Julian," I said to him with a calm voice. "Perhaps this would be a good time for us to leave."

Julian nodded in agreement, still without saying a word to me.

"Thank you for dinner," I said to my hosts, who were waiting in the dining room, frightened and unable to move. I'm sure they had heard some sort of commotion in there, but they didn't know what had happened. From their look, I think they feared the worst.

"My friend and I need to leave, now," I said smiling with guilt. "Doctor Samson, Peter is ill and he's on the kitchen floor. I think he needs your medical attention."

"Oh, dear! Was it my food?" asked Ms. Ruth. She appeared to be almost happy that Peter had been stricken with this sudden illness.

"No Ma'am," answered Julian instead. "Your food was excellent. I think Peter was just struck with a horrible migraine, combined with heartburn. Things like that happen. After all, he *is* a little overweight..."

When we left the Samson's house, Julian still appeared confused. "What was that about? Why are you always so aggressive?"

"I told you before we got to the Samson's that Peter could be very unpleasant," I said closing the gate in his face.

I was a fool to think that this could work and this man I was so attracted to, would open his mind to understand me. No mortal could accept the truth about me and it wouldn't be right to have such expectations from Grant. "Now, go on home, Julian. Dinner's over and you'll be better off to forget you ever knew me."

18

IN THE NEXT FEW DAYS, I didn't do too much. They all left me alone, perhaps aware that it was absolutely necessary for me to feel independent.

But this old palace was dreadful to me, considering how much time I had spent locked inside one, so I walked around in the gardens and the forest all day. Eventually, after an intense search, I found a woman's dress with a maroon top, cut low, and a maroon and silver striped skirt in one of the master closets. I wanted to make myself admired and desirable, and the discovery of an acceptable item in a female's wardrobe would be my tool of attraction.

During the day, Serban was always near the castle, but at night, all of them would be gone. As I watched the young men saluting and bowing to him, I deduced that Serban was their leader. That made him the Lord of this Mansion.

But who were they? Why did they all look alike, and more, why did I look like them? I loved their quiet company, though, and they treated me like a princess.

At first, Andreas deliberately ignored me, or at least, he pretended that he did. I understood that he was uncomfortably confused by my provocations the night he brought me here. I was unsettled by my own behavior, too, as I could not understand the strong attraction I felt for him. Among them all, he was the most handsome. I stared at him each time he was near me. I wished for him to talk with me, to look at me again with the same passion that he did that first night.

But his self-imposed distancing didn't last long. One morning I was visiting their rooms and making up the beds. When I got to Andreas' room he didn't leave, but he sat on a stool and watched me work.

As I pulled up the counterpane and began to fluff the pillows I suddenly felt his hot lips touching the back of my neck. I turned to him and his lips searched with hunger for mine. I trembled as a wild tension was building in my body.

His fingers made their way down to my breasts in his attempt to expose them for his mouth. My breath began to come in gasps and I wanted so badly for him to rip off my top, hoping that he would push me down to his bed. But our moment was interrupted by the noise of Serban's steps, who just happened to pass by.

Later my brother took him aside and rebuked him for the perceived indiscretion, but my desire for him grew with each passing day.

I fell in love with Andreas as I waited for the opportunity to be smothered by his kisses and lost in his arms.

*   *   *

One quiet afternoon, after I had been at the castle for more than two weeks, Serban came and sat beside me on the veranda. I told him how happy I was feeling, and how I was astonished to find myself in such fortunate circumstances. For the first time I had a real family—blood brothers, whatever that meant. Serban was so pleasant to talk with and his voice was so deep and clear.

"Are you ready to learn why you're here?" he asked me, as he gently touched my forehead with his index and middle fingers.

"I believe I am," I answered bravely, with mounting curiosity.

"We are so happy to have found you," smiled Serban. "Actually, it was Andreas who discovered your whereabouts. The attraction and the desire you feel for him is only normal for our kind."

"What do you mean?" I asked blushing that my new found brother openly talked to me about such a sensitive subject.

Serban didn't answer for a moment as his gaze focused on something in the distance that was unseen to me, but then turned to me and became more serious.

"What I am about to tell you may frighten you, but you must know the truth about us and about yourself. There is no easy way to explain our story to you, and these events are without precedent.

"You have the same trait as all of us, Safira, but it is much more pronounced. You have been named for the sapphire color of your eyes. This is why we searched for you."

"Are you telling me that I am like you? What are you?"

I still wasn't convinced, even though I remembered my strange night adventures when I could see so well in the dark. Serban continued the story.

"We are Immortal Warriors from the Kingdom of Kamara, a parallel world, but invisible to the mortal's eyes. Our earthly shelter is the Secret Mountain of Liechtenstein. We all have great skills as *warriors, but here, in this mortal realm, we can be killed. A sword can separate us from our immortality. First, however, it is time for you to know the story of us all.*

"Five thousand years ago, on the verge of a civil war, our King forced into exile to Earth three Orders of Immortal: us, the Warriors, the Defenders and the Enforcers. We crossed over here in the present land of Transylvania. After that, the portal was forever closed to us—we are never to return.

"You could only imagine the depth of our frustration and pain to find ourselves strangers in a strange place. It took us all a thousand years to acclimate to the idea that for forever, we had lost our real home and we had no other choice but to live among the mortal kind—we, the mighty Warrior Immortals. If we look up in the sky and lighten our eyes, we still can see our lost home.

"The human race was fragile and unstable, ten thousand years behind our civilization. We had the knowledge and the powers. They needed us. We had no other choice but to accept our destiny and continue our existence among a people who, if they should learn of our real abilities, would worship us as gods. Some of them did.

"We all have a Master and a Queen. The three Spirit Masters are transparent so they can be omnipresent, but at times they can take human form. They created a Council, made up from three men and three women from all three Orders, and establish new laws for our existence and survival in the mortal's land. That was when they decided to separate the Orders, instead of keeping us strong and together. Some of us cannot remember the other kind of Immortals, but I still do.

"We, the Warriors, were given three simple rules: never reveal to anyone about your true origin, never harm an innocent mortal or his property, and never interfere or fall in love with a mortal. We failed to keep the last rule, and when we started to have offspring with the mortals, we saw no danger in it.

"Later on, we came to find out how wrong we been about the ones who carry half of ours genes. To distinguish them from true Immortals, we called them Amestec. The Council punished our disobedience by ruling that it is forbidden for us to ever return to the Secret Mountain. We, the Warriors, became exiled once again.

"Gallbor, the Spirit Master, sent a few chosen Immortal Warriors to different lands to protect and fight alongside the mortals, but only to defend, never doing battle with the ones who attacked. We were accompanied by a female, the only one of her kind. Her name was Lady Amara, the Healer and our Queen.

"Immortal Warriors, males and females, had been protecting the lands of Europe for thousands of years. My father, Gavril, a Prince among the Immortals, and others, were sent to defend Valahia. I, my brother Rares, Mihnea, Andreas, Costan, Razvan and Barbu we were assigned to Transylvania.

"There came a time, one thousand years ago, when a fierce and powerful enemy from the south threatened our borders. The Prince of Transylvania at that time, Lord Fers Martuzon, made the call for us all to aid him in battle. We rose up against these mortals who attacked Lord Martuzon and we went to war. We fought well, but we were outnumbered. Some of us were wounded, but we did not feel the slash of the sword and we were not killed.

"Our kind is made of flesh, of course. Only our spirit is eternal. Our wounds seal themselves quickly, but for us to be truly healed, we still need the Healer's touch. She could erase any evidence of a wound and make any Immortal whole again. Many who were not healed by her are crippled and are lost in despair, without a meaning or a purpose.

"The Immortal Warriors are strong and mighty, but in Lady Amara's presence this is not so. She must maintain her freedom, and remain free from our love and desire for her. There are other female Immortals, but the Immortal males keep them captive for themselves;

however it is the Immortal who mates with the Healer that is granted tremendous powers—and that makes her a wanted woman.

"Gallbor intended for Lady Amara to have a master but one was never sent one for her. So, periodically she will choose a lover from among us.

"We also learned that there was one other danger for us to be near the Healer: we could no longer defend ourselves. When we are near her, we can die—we can *be killed."*

Serban stopped and took a deep breath before he continued the story.

"Lord Fers Martuzon saw the beautiful Lady Amara roaming through his palace in search of wounded Immortals to heal. He immediately fell in love with her. He tried to approach her in the very moment she found the Immortal named Mihnea, who had lost his leg.

"At the time Mihnea was loved by Lady Amara, an honor not many Immortals received from our Queen. As Lord Fers Martuzon tried to approach her, Mihnea attempted to protect her, but he was too weak. In a rage, Lord Fers Martuzon pulled his sword from its sheath and decapitated Mihnea.

"This Immortal Warrior died. When the sword cut off his head, the Healer couldn't help him because his spirit was stolen by the one who killed him.

"Unknown to us, Lord Fers Martuzon was a half-immortal, an Amestec. He knew who we truly are. Only Lady Amara knows exactly what happened next. We know that she could see the energy of life leaving Mihnea and passing into Lord Fers Martuzon. She had no choice. She accepted to be with him only because Lord Martuzon had Mihnea's eternal spirit in him.

"Lord Martuzon was immortal now. The secret of his long life was no longer a mystery. In order to maintain his immortality, he knew that his secret must be kept at all costs. Afraid that we would seek revenge and kill him, he has used his large army and the presence of Lady Amara to hunt down the rest of us.

"We fled outside the borders of our country and to the mountains; we left for Valahia to be with my father, knowing we could never to return to cities and towns in Transylvania. The Healer was heartbroken.

"And the story of an Amestec obtaining immortality by killing a true Immortal turned from a legend to a desire. Every half-immortal in the world wanted desperately to achieve immortality.

"Seven hundred years later, one of Lord Martuzon's Amestec sons, who he fathered with a Court lady, severely cut his hand. Lady Amara's instinct was to attempt to heal him. She touched his injury with her hands and a soft grayish ash covered the wound. But then she did something else—something she should not have done—something that was forbidden. She released the transforming power in her fingers and touched his heart, changing him back into an Immortal.

"Fers could see that Lady Amara had unknowingly provided him with proof that her great powers were undiminished. Lord Fers Martuzon was an impostor Immortal. His only thought was to secure his fortune and territory for his own benefit.

"Fers Martuzon was very content to live his life with Lady Amara at his side. Two hundred years later, when his first legitimate son was born from his mortal wife, Fers decided to wait until the boy became a strong young man and then have Lady Amara change him into an Immortal. Fers and his son, Milos, would create a powerful army and dominate the rest of the land."

*   *   *

I was puzzled. What I had heard made no sense to me; it all sounded like a story that had been created by a very feverish mind. But at the same time, I doubted very much that my brother was deliberately trying to confuse or deceive me into believing all this, just so I would have a plausible explanation of my existence.

"Do you mean to tell me that Lord Fers Martuzon, the governor I knew when I was a child, was Immortal, and he is Milos's father? Is Milos Martuzon an Immortal, too?"

"Fers Martuzon is the immortal father of Milos Martuzon," Serban continued, digging a small hole in the dirt with a stick. "Milos is not immortal; his mother was a mortal princess who died as she gave birth to him. Fers had married her only to secure his status and title as a Prince of Transylvania. Milos, his son is what is known as an Amestec, a Half-Immortal. He remains young in appearance, but he will eventually die from either old age or a fatal wound. He has as much power as us and our new law dictates that his life can only be ended immediately by a sword. He can receive the gift of immortality only from the Healer, and become an Immortal. Unless..."

"Unless, what?" I asked without thinking.

"Unless, he kills one of us! Amestec are the only type of mortals who know the truth about us and they are the most dangerous. Through the centuries, the Half-Immortals have been our feared enemies, and we have always been hunted by them.

"Our impulse to reproduce is twice stronger than a mortal's. We fight for the lands and seek pleasure. Immortal females are rare and most have masters and children. But mortal women are beautiful to us, so we foolishly made many of them pregnant. We kept no law in this regard. We expected the Council to punish us, but the punishment came later from our own blood and flesh.

"Our desires and lust became our curse. The children of our own kind had become our enemies, and we had to slay all of those who came after us. There was never peace between us and them. The males hunted us and the females tried to seduce us and then kill us."

"Are there any other Amestecs left beside Milos?"

"There are a few, in other lands, and Fers had other children, too. We have killed many, and a few of them have killed us. Now, our greatest enemy is Milos Martuzon."

19

SOME THINGS ARE LOGICAL, AND some are not.

To run away from Julian Grant was logical only to me. I spent the rest of the evening alone on the couch, on the very spot where he had stood earlier, as I waited for Octavian to return home from his date. I had no assurance that I wasn't acting foolishly and that I didn't risk bringing unintended consequences on myself. If I accepted Julian into my life, that would obligate me to tell him the whole truth about me, and I would knowingly break another rule.

This was my punishment for wanting a mortal's love.

My thoughts were on a carousel. I couldn't merely tell just anyone who I was. I couldn't dismiss my past and embrace my history with no suffering. I had guarded my secret for so long, and I couldn't share it with a mortal just to gain his affection and acceptance.

I saw Julian's face in my mind as it swirled with indecision. His understanding of me would be limited and my past exploits would cause him to have resentment towards me. What assurance would I have that he wouldn't be disgusted by the whole concept of an ancient, but much superior woman? The future ahead of me was very uncertain–I might not survive beyond the next battle.

I fell into a fitful sleep on the couch with Lord Arthur serving as a pillow. A noise from the kitchen awoke me. What I had heard was Octavian, dragging Marin's body back into the basement. When he returned, he opened the refrigerator and twisted the cap off of a cold bottle of water.

What a beautiful sight it was, to watch him walk around in only his dress pants, shirtless. A mortal girl could easily lose her senses under the spell of his charm.

I closed my eyes trying to suppress my own memories of my lost love. I had been going through this long life with over a century of memories–people, places, wars, plagues, wonders in the sky, history in the making. Still, there were only a few memories I held onto. A few brief moments of passion and love were all that I could conjure in the darker scenes of everyday life.

"What can we do with Marin and his twin?" asked Octavian, taking a seat beside me. "You know that he won't dry out in our presence any time soon."

"I didn't mean to kill him, but he came out of the basement with a rifle. I am not sure if he was looking to kill me or Grant."

"Well, at least we can revive both of them, now."

"For what purpose? They're not talking, not that they would say something useful to us."

"I can put a GPS signal in Marin and see where he's going. We need to find the location of their headquarters. Marin's just a foot soldier. Someone else has control over him. We need to know how many of them are out there, Amestec or Hybrids—we can't just wait for them to attack us."

"You're right," I agreed with my brother. "But we can't revive him here in the house."

"We can do it somewhere far from here. He'll need a few minutes to become completely alive. I can do this."

"No, I'll do it," I insisted. "You insert the GPS in him and I'll take him somewhere to revive him. If something goes wrong, I want him to remember me and not you."

"Wrong, Safira," argued Octavian. "You think he'll forget the way I smacked his car, threw him on the ground, beat him unconscious, and broke his neck?"

"Then we'll revive his twin. He has no memory of you."

"Yes, the only memory he has about us is fighting you with a sword."

"That's fine. I'll be the necessary information he can pass on to others." As I spoke, my voice began to tremble.

"You're so tense. What happened to you?"

I covered my face with my hands. My emotions were painful and raw, and I couldn't suppress them anymore.

"I think I finally scared Julian off. Now he's gone for good, but we had ourselves quite an evening."

"You didn't scare him hard enough," said my brother laughing. "He's still parked at the curb in the front."

"I guess he'll leave eventually," I whispered with regret.

"And what if he doesn't? Will you call him in?"

"No. I've already told him to never come back."

My answer was firm, but my heart and my resolve were weak. I thought he was stupid to not have gone home, but his stubbornness was inexplicably pleasing to me.

"Now, how was your dinner with Nelda?"

"Complicated," admitted Octavian taking a deep breath. "Nelda's parents are quite happy that I seem to be a decent guy who dresses nice, and drives a sports car–they were impressed. They have great expectations about their daughter and that sounded like a warning to me. Nelda didn't pay any attention to my conversation with her parents, though, since most times she was the instigator, crawling under my shirt."

"At least *your* dinner was a bit congenial," I said, biting my lips.

"What you mean? What else have you done besides killing Marin?"

"I roughed up Peter," I confessed embarrassed.

"Obnoxious Peter?" Octavian laughed. A bizarre image of Peter and me must have appeared in his mind.

"He infuriated me–he was so nasty to Carla. I had to do it. I couldn't let him treat her that way and do nothing.

Grant saw me in action once again. Why is he here? No one in their right mind can accept this kind of craziness from a girl and then come looking for more."

"Hey! Calm down. Safira, you cast a spell on him, remember?"

Octavian pulled me closer to him; I laid my head on his shoulder and I realized that I had become more agitated than I wanted to admit. Grant's presence, even if he was unwelcome, was fascinating me to the point that I was acting like a school girl.

I fought hard against this impulse of wishing for forbidden fruit, regardless of the price I might have to pay for it.

"This isn't right, Octavian. Why I am so tempted by him? What's wrong with me? I never acted like this before."

"The only thing wrong with you is that you don't let go of the logic and enjoy the magic of losing yourself in the arms of a fragile mortal lover. And here he is—a handsome well-built mortal soldier who wants nothing more than to have you."

"Would you tell the truth about yourself and your origin to Nelda?"

"Nelda is only eighteen, she wouldn't care. Girls don't care. But Grant is twenty-eight and he thinks differently. If you tell him things about you, and if he believes you, you at least have a friend to spend your evenings with, instead of your brother. And if he doesn't believe you, you've lost nothing. This is your best chance to be loved by a mortal, to mate with one. Yes, it's forbidden but it's fulfilling, exuberant and heavenly. This is what you need Safira, a sensitive soul in a strong man. For once, would you listen to me?"

I blushed. I playfully pushed my brother away and he kissed my forehead.

"Grant would make love with you in a hot second—and I wouldn't blame him for it," smiled my brother reading my mind. "I think he's one mortal man who could fully satisfy you."

"Oh, this conversation is insane," I said, suddenly uncomfortable, but his words had touched a sensitive matter for me. Who could measure up to Andreas? "Stop talking like this. I can't get involved with a mortal. I must belong only to my own kind."

"You're a passionate woman, Safira; don't wait another century to find a man. No one will condemn you for it—it's only natural. Our Mother had several lovers..."

"Octavian!" I said indignant. "Mother had any *Immortal* man she desired—I don't have that luxury."

"I'm just telling the truth. The love of a mortal is all we've got, Safira, and we'd better make the best of it. End of story. And until all Immortal males are at your disposal, we'll have no more debate over this subject anymore. Now, I'm going to bed," he said yawning, "I'll leave you two alone."

"I'm not letting him in this house! What if his being here has nothing to do with his feelings for me? No, I'm not going to give in."

Octavian had no answer as he shook his head. Passing by the basement door, he turned the key and locked it.

"Grant's still out there," he said as he reached the landing on the stairs. "It's close to midnight. You'd better let him in before someone calls the police or he turns into a pumpkin."

"That's not funny, Octavian."

*   *   *

I wrapped a sweater around my shoulders and I went to the gate. I didn't need to '*look*'. I could see Julian Grant's shadow in my truck. I walked across the street leaving the gate open and tapped on the window. He turned on the ignition and put the transmission into "drive".

I waved for him to come inside, so he put the truck back into "park" and got out of the truck. As he walked past me I closed the gate behind him. I paused to light up my eyes and look up and down the street. All was quiet.

Julian waited for me on the front porch. He didn't speak to me as I passed by him, pretending to be upset. I could just let him spend the night on the couch if he wished, and all this would soon be over.

He followed me inside the house and we stood in the hallway. Before I had the chance to say something, to let him know how frustrated I was that he was there, he took me in his arms and began to kiss me. His lips were pressing against mine, searching for approval–but more than that– and seeking the pleasure my kisses gave him.

Unlike my mother, Lady Amara, I was reluctant to go through this life from one lover's arms to another. But something was telling me that my days of sheltering my body and soul would be soon over.

I let myself be kissed as I felt a burning need to respond to him, to taste him—his tongue tasted like mint, as it did a week ago. He picked me up in his strong arms and carried me to the couch. He put me down on my back and gently laid down over me, his body covering mine.

"What are you doing Julian?" I asked, trying to escape him. I could hear his heart pounding, and I trembled when I felt his lips touching my neck. "I told you I didn't want to see you anymore, and I meant it."

He held me with his left arm while he continued to kiss my neck and chest, and his right hand methodically released the buttons on the front of my dress. He murmured, "I am so crazy about you."

As the dress opened, his hand began to knead my breasts and a jolt of passion shook my loins. The bottom of my dress had slid up above my waist, and I wrapped my legs around Julian's hard, muscular back.

A moment later, I felt his strong erection rubbing against my panties and my desire for him took over like fire. My brother was right—Julian Grant was one mortal quite capable of making himself equal to me and perhaps he could physically satisfy me.

Everything in me was ready to give in and make love with him, but I couldn't allow what we both wanted to happen, not now. It would be nothing more than impulsive sex with a stranger, and against my brother's advice I held back.

My body was craving satisfaction but I was hungrier for love–real love and not just lust.

"Why are you here?" I asked breathlessly, as I began to untangle myself from his arms and redressed. "You've got no right to come here and try to charm me into thinking that you're interested in me."

He stood up nervously and began to walk to the other side of the room. Secretly, I wished that he was only here for me, with no ulterior motive. My palms were sweating and my pulse rate increased, waiting for his response.

"You want to know why I'm here? It's because I wanted to know if you really do exist, that you're not just a phantom with eyes that shine in the dark who appeared in my life one night, who shot the enemy from an impossible distance and saved my men, who pointed a gun at me, who detonated bombs in the barn and came out alive, but then who disappeared from my life, leaving me behind, going crazy.

"I haven't slept except in snatches since the night I met you. I asked Pollack and the other guys if they remembered you–and of course they did. So I called the Red Cross and to find out your address. And to find out why the hell you were there. The ARC didn't send you! Anyhow, it makes no difference now.

"I wanted to find this girl was who caused me to be so agitated and who I lost sleep over. I couldn't think straight. All I could see was you pointing that gun at me and your eyes shining like stars in the dark night. I remembered touching your body, kissing you like a crazy mad man and then I hoped to find you once again. I hoped that you would not only be real, but *normal.*"

He took a deep breath. His eyes looked away from me for a moment, and then he continued, a bit more agitated than before.

"Instead, you break a car window with your bare fist, have a truck full of guns, shoot a man right between the eyes over my head, a man who doesn't die, incidentally, and to top that off, beat the hell out of the neighbor's guest. I know the jerk deserved it, but he was three times your size. That's why I am back—to find the real *you.* And obviously, I got my answer—*you are something else!*

"I've been dreaming about you every night since I met you in Germany," he continued, calming down and taking a seat back on the couch. "I wanted to find you because there's not a second that passes when you're not on my mind. Whoever you are, I don't care! I want you and I'm in love with you."

I knew then that he spoke the truth—I know when a mortal lies.

What now? I could crush his fantasy of me and tell him all about the woman from his dreams. Or I could choose to remain quiet and seek more pleasure and physical satisfaction in our relationship until one of us would drift away.

I decided to be brave and tell him everything. The chances were that he wouldn't believe my story. Or perhaps he would believe it, and he'd find the truth so fantastic that he would leave and never come back. And who could blame him for it?

"Julian, are you sure you want to know all about me?"

He nodded and quietly waited for me to continue.

"My formal name is Lady Safira. I am the Queen of Immortal Warriors."

20

"SERBAN, WHAT DID YOU SAY that I am," I asked my brother and my voice vibrated with expectations.

"You are the pure one, the daughter of the Healer and a Prince, and we took an oath to protect you," answered Serban with confidence. "Now, you are our Queen and this is the story of your making.

"When the Amestec, who she had made Immortal, realized Lady Amara's agony, he helped her to escape. Lord Fers Martuzon knew that aid had been rendered to Lady Amara and the house boy, his own son, was decapitated to pay for her freedom. This was when she sought us. She was too weak to return to Gallbor and to the Secret Mountain, so she came to Valahia to find shelter and protection. Once she joined us, she fell in love with one of us—our father, Prince Gavril. Our father was mighty, a noble Immortal, very powerful—handsome and brave, honored by Almighty Gallbor himself.

"Because of her beauty, Lady Amara would cover her face to all except our father, and he was captivated by love for her.

"*Believing that Fers Martuzon couldn't find her, she made a plan to be with us and to do her best to protect us. Everyone in the band was weak in her presence. We had no powers—the Healer had absorbed them all.*

"*One morning, nine years later when we were away hunting, Fers Martuzon found her in our castle on the mountain and took her back to his palace. Lady Amara most likely had a premonition that something ominous would happen when she sent all of us away that morning. When our father learned of her kidnapping, he was angry and devastated. We went into hiding again, this time to Moldova, because we knew that a rescue attempt would bring us near to her and we would become weak.*

"*But no one knew that at the time she was forced to return to Cluj she was pregnant with you. Lady Amara couldn't keep the secret and she told everything to Lord Martuzon. He was very angry, but at the same time, he spared the baby. She was a female with dark hair and piercing blue eyes, like her mother. He hoped that she was an Immortal Healer. It would be to his benefit to have two Healers for his army.*

"*He wanted to keep your existence a secret, but it was Andreas who sensed that another of our kind had been born and not made—one who had been born from two immortals. And that one was you, Safira.*"

"*Serban, what am I? A Healer like my mother, Lady Amara, or an Immortal Warrior like my father, Prince Gavril?*" I continued to ask, fascinated that all this could be true.

"*This, Lady Safira, we will soon learn. But to finish your story: Prince Gavril didn't know of your existence. Andreas told our father his premonition, that more than likely he had a child with Lady Amara, a daughter. Father wanted to know with certainty, but the palace in Cluj was difficult to break into. A year later, when Lord Martuzon and his household once again traveled to Oradea, he saw you in your mother's arms. He knew then that he must take both of you away from Lord Martuzon. Everyone in the band all tried and we all failed.*

"Five years later the opportunity came for us to bring you and Lady Amara home with us. Father found Lady Amara in Cluj and we all defeated her elite guards. We took her away, but unfortunately, you weren't with her as we had hoped. Fers and his men hunted father down. Lady Amara was with him when they were both captured outside of Cluj. Lord Martuzon decapitated our father, but he spared Lady Amara's life. Father's sprit passed into Fers, and the next night, Lady Amara did the unthinkable.

"She was so devastated because of Father's death that she used Fers Martuzon's own sword to cut off his head. She could only see in him the monster who took the life of her only love, the father of her child. She could not bear for Prince Gavril's spirit to remain in his killer. So my father's spirit returned to her.

"As a Healer, Amara is different than us; we have just one spirit that passes to our killer after our body dies, but Lady Amara's spirit multiplies, it is never ending.

"After she killed Fers, she had to run away and return to Gallbor. She never had the opportunity to come back for you. It's a common misconception that I killed Lord Martuzon. For her sake and to protect her, I took his death upon myself.

"Milos Martuzon, the half - immortal Amestec, learned who you are and of the potential that you have. He knew his father's story about immortality, which was told to him at your birth, but he still isn't sure exactly what role he wants you to play. At his first opportunity he will try to kill all of us and capture you, and the same old story will repeat itself.

"Andreas took you that night, fearing that Milos would make you his mistress. We returned to Transylvania only for you, to rescue you. So, here you are and this is your story. Are you overwhelmed?"

I nodded my head slowly and I continued to be deep in thought. Serban's style of telling a story was lavish, to say the least. I had no reason to doubt it, but it sounded too incredible to be the truth. Now that I knew it all, everything I had experienced – the secrets that were kept from me, the lies that were told to me, and the guards who had imprisoned me – made sense. My first reaction was to be furious with Lord Milos Martuzon for knowing all this, but pretending to be my rescuer and my family.

"This is incredible!" I whispered, holding Serban's arm.

"I know you don't want what we've told you to be the truth" he said, *"and I don't blame you. It's so senseless for us to fight for your life when yours is everlasting. But this is our way of life and this is your future."*

"I'm not a coward. I'm not afraid."

"I know."

"Serban, I want to know for sure what I am," I insisted. *"What if you're wrong? How would I know for sure? Perhaps I only inherited my parents' physical features, but not their powers..."*

"Then let's find out! Rares, come here."

We stepped out into the courtyard. It was quite dark outside, but we needed no light. Everyone's eyes were glowing, including mine. I felt the energy, and for the first time I knew how to control it. Serban passed me an old sword and Rares provoked me into a fight, but I stepped back, a bit frightened.

"I can't fight like you", I said, backing away in trepidation. *"I've never fought in my life. I can't do this!"*

"Defend yourself." Rares yelled at me, as he swung his sword in my direction.

I raised my hand that was holding the sword, trusting that my body would follow my instincts and know how to react. I was astonished! My movements were effortless, stopping every thrust from my attacker. My body floated in the air, anticipating all the moves of my opponent. I could feel a massive surge of energy course through my body, and with a force I didn't know I possessed, my sword sliced off my brother's hand at his wrist. When I saw this sight, I almost passed out.

Rares was not in pain—he just stared at his hand as it lay on the ground. Serban picked up Rares's hand and grabbed my hand, placing it on my brother's wound. Under my touch, the cut turned into gray dust, like ash. The dust changed color slowly, creating new tissue and skin. In less than a minute, when I saw that his hand had been restored, I fainted, and I had no recollection of anything else.

* * *

When I woke up, it was morning. I heard an old rooster mastering his irritating greeting and that annoyed me. Through half opened eyes, I could barely discern a shadow, a tall man who appeared to be floating to the fireplace and then quietly leaving the room after a few moments of stirring the fire.

I was cold and exhausted, thankful for the little warmth rising into the room from the burning logs. I knew I wasn't alone—other people obviously lived here as well. But where was I? Was I dreaming or was I awake?

The room was familiar, but I couldn't locate it anywhere in my clouded memories. In the back of my mind, places and people were slowly beginning to become reality, but I wasn't sure if I was remembering dreams or some past experience. Actually, I wasn't sure of my own identity at that moment.

I needed some time to understand everything. Was this reality at all plausible, or was my mind still clouded with the remnants of nightmares.

"Lady Safira. Safira!"

I didn't want to answer this summons. I only wished to be back at Black Vulture Castle, in the arms of my Nana, and for all this be just a dream. I reluctantly arose from my narrow bed.

"We need to prepare for battle, my sister! Milos Martuzon and the Archduke are on their way here."

So, it was true. My memories were now intact.

"Serban! What happened to me? What have I done? Is Rares all right?"

"Rares is fine. You did what you were born to do: heal Immortals."

My brother shook his head. I followed him out, convinced that he was not being honest with me. He was hiding something essential to protect me from the entire truth.

21

"WHERE'S GRANT?" ASKED OCTAVIAN, AS he inserted a small tracking device chip in the hybrid's head.

"He's asleep on the couch," I answered, ignoring his silly smirk.

"Why's he on the couch, when we've got four guest bedrooms?"

"I didn't want him upstairs with us. Why're you being nosy? Nothing happened last night…"

"OK, I'm not implying that anything did. I just feel a different energy in you, that's all."

"Grant kissed me," I reluctantly told him. "He kissed me and told me that I drove him crazy."

"I can't imagine any man not going crazy over you," he said, with his comment dripping with sarcasm. "Mortals cannot resist us. What else?"

"What do you mean by 'what else'?"

Octavian didn't answer me as he stood up and lifted the second hybrid's body. He placed it on the examining table and touched the hybrid's forehead.

"His brain isn't very active, now," concluded my brother, "which is why his memories about his origin have been deleted. He can be killed with intensive gunfire, so I'm sure he's just collateral."

"It makes sense—I'm certain there are more of them out there that were sent after me, and each one is probably a little better than the last."

"Exactly. So, if they're made and not born, then someone has a certain gift that lets him create these hybrids. We need to take him down."

"It's *him!*" I exclaimed with excitement as my whole body felt a rush of adrenaline. "I know who is after me. It is *him*, and no other. Octavian, think about what you just said. There's no one else in the world that could have the kind of power to transform these new creatures, except for one like me and you—not even the Immortals. The Amestec cannot create something like these. He's acquired my powers and he's used them with malice. There are many other reasons he could be looking for me, but the main one is that he thinks that I belong to him."

It was all too clear to me the identity of my hunter. I had no doubt.

"How can you be so sure?" asked my brother. "There are so many Immortals and Amestec trying their luck to find you!"

"I have no doubt about it," I said sure of myself. "His scent and his spirit are lurking over these two. He's building an army that may already be very powerful. This means that *he* has much more power than he did when I saw him last. I won't let him win, not this time. Now, this hybrid needs a name. What about Gelu?"

"What kind of name is that?" Octavian opened the hybrid's eyes and his face darkened with bitterness.

"Gelu was the name of my guard at Black Eagle Castle in Transylvania," I answered as I involuntarily glanced at the man. There wasn't a shred of resemblance between this hybrid and the guard, but the guard's name brought back intense memories of hatred. "He was the one I disliked the most–many of his teeth were missing, and those he still had in his head were decayed. But he always smiled at me. It was beyond scary!"

"Well, Gelu it is, then. Gelu is almost ready to see the world again. Are you sure you're ready for this? I don't have to bring him back to life and you don't have to confront him if you're apprehensive about it." His gentle voice softened my soul, but I understood the hint. Indeed, I was always in control of things between us and he was starting to become a little resentful.

"No, I need to do this," I said, stubbornly. "It's early Sunday morning–nobody will be in the park."

"I could come and watch from a distance. What if something goes wrong?"

"Then I'll kill him again. If I'm capable of it once, I'm capable of it again."

"Yes, you are," agreed Octavian peacefully. Then, he became more alert as I was speaking. Alarmed, I asked, "What is it?"

His eyes scanned the room from one end to the other as he became more attuned to all the different sounds.

"Your guest is awake and moving around," he said as he activated the GPS in the hybrid's head. "You might want to go upstairs."

"He's already awake? It's only five in the morning."

"So, you told him that you are an Immortal, right?" Octavian asked, pretending not to be too curious.

"Yes, I mentioned that to him, among other things. I told him that I'm an Immortal and he kissed me good night. He said he came here because he wants to know everything about me, most likely because of all the crazy things I did in Germany. Somehow, against all odds, he thinks he's in love with me."

I didn't doubt Grant's feelings, and this simple notion of his affection made me so happy. But I have been loved and happy before, and lost everything.

"What do you think about Grant now, Safira? Your judgment is always infallible."

"I think he's trying to understand if he was hit by a train or if lighting has struck him twice. I am not your regular girl next door and it's not fair for me to encourage his love—I am afraid I'll mess up his life."

"Aha! But this is you what wanted for me. You do want him. Isn't that true?" My brother's questions, like a criminal's interrogation, had started to annoy me.

"Yes, I want him. Would you just stop pressing me?"

"No, I won't stop. He kissed you and if I am right – he desires you so much that he's out of his mind. I think you should follow your own preaching. Go on upstairs, be with him and I'll take care of Gelu. "

"I can't be alone with him. This is a mortal man whose passion is as wild as the fire."

"He is not any wilder or more passionate than our kind, and you are not going to mess him up–trust me!" My brother smiled guiltily at his remark. "This could be something meaningful. Mortals like him are so rare in our life. If you want more than a passing night of passion with him, just tell him all about us, about you, about the fact that you can't grow old with him and let him choose what he wants."

Octavian shook his head and raised his eyebrows, to let me know he was serious. As I helped him put Gelu in the Land Rover, I said, "Thanks for taking him off my hands. Call me if you need my help."

* * *

I found Grant sitting on the couch, guarded by Lord Arthur. The German shepherd can be intimidating if you aren't accustomed to being followed very closely and having all your movements watched.

I had stood for a while on the basement stairs, behind the door to the kitchen, trying to think of a solution to repair the damage we both had made with each other last night. He must have thought that I was just a crazy girl who was delusional and who thought that she was some sort of supernatural being.

Oh Lord! He must have laughed at me all night. Now, at least, I was sure he was convinced that regardless of his attraction to me, I could never be believed.

I didn't know why he hadn't left when he discovered the truth about me. He was awake and dressed, but why wasn't he on his way, wherever that might be? Maybe he just wanted to see if a delusional girl looked any different in the daylight than she did in the dark.

"Good morning, Safira."

I moved with caution towards him, expecting that he would want some sort of explanation about the ridiculous events of the past few hours, but he rushed to hold me and kiss me as he had done last night.

"Julian, please. We need to talk."

He continued to embrace me with his sturdy arms, but he did momentarily stop his kisses. A few heartbeats later, I regretted that I had asked him to end them. His kisses and touches had kept me awake and thinking of him all night.

"You're right. I owe you an apology. Most of the time I'm a pretty decent guy and I don't misbehave like that."

His words did nothing but stir more confusion in my mind and send another rush of contradictions to my heart.

Was he sorry that he had kissed me and that we had almost made love? Well, Safira, you asked for it, so keep your chin up and take it. Then, I heard the garage door opening and closing as Octavian drove into the street to take Gelu's body to the park.

"What are you talking about?" I mumbled, too disappointed to say something clever or snappy.

"It was wrong for me to come here and ask you all these questions, and to demand answers. I was bold enough to tell you my feelings for you. I needed to stop there and beg you to accept me, and not act like an idiot. I'm so sorry."

This wasn't what I had expected from him, but it was all I wanted to hear. I was moving in a different direction. I wasn't sure of myself anymore, and I didn't really *want* to be sure.

Yes, I was lusting for mortal love, for mortal flesh, but I was afraid to take it and run with it. What did I really want? Did I truly want Julian or did I just want to use him as a replacement for my past love?

To do that was wrong–it wasn't fair to him. I needed to make him understand the whole truth, but it was easier for me to be in denial, telling myself that I still loved someone else.

"It's not necessary to apologize to me, Julian. I was doing my best to tell you the truth…"

"I'm not asking for it anymore," he interrupted, "it doesn't matter. What I am asking is, can you possibly feel anything for me…"

I heard the coffee maker start my morning brew. "Would you like some coffee?" I asked him quickly. "I really must have some every morning. I am addicted."

"No coffee, thanks," he answered following me in the kitchen. "I really should leave. I think I'm annoying you even more, and I don't want to do that."

He took me in his arms again. I didn't dare to raise my head. I was afraid to look in his face, into his eyes, and see something I liked and desired. But when he gently lifted my chin, and when our lips and tongues met again, it was like electricity flowing throughout my entire body.

Yes, my body reacted like that of a mortal. It was normal for me to feel and to react like wanting to make love with him.

"You still don't really know me," I whispered, trying to buy some time. "I'm carrying a long past…and I have an even more unsettled future."

"I don't have much time, Safira. I don't have any idea what's next for me. It's always like I am going into the unknown…"

This was such a letdown for me, and once again I felt like a wrestler who had been thrown to the mat.

"Julian, when you're ready to hear the truth about me, I'll be ready to tell you what I feel about you. There's no other way we can approach this."

He looked at me hesitantly.

"Then I want you to tell me…" he started to answer.

"You aren't ready for it."

"Yeah, you're right," he said sarcastically. "A girl is kissing me, turned my mind and body upside down, but she won't let me get any closer to her. She's telling me that she's an Immortal, and she's shutting me off. Safira, I don't want to lose you. After all, there's probably a good explanation for everything."

"And if there isn't?"

He took my face in his hands. His beautiful blue eyes were shining and I was falling in love with him.

"Then who the hell cares? Safira, you're the only one who can decide if we can be together or not. It's not my decision–it's only yours."

He was right. I was about to say something to him when I heard Octavian's signal in my ear.

"Safira, I followed Gelu and he's parked at an abandoned building near Newnan. It's a Save Rite on the corner of highway 34 and 154."

"How did he get there so fast?" I asked, looking at the clock on the kitchen wall.

"He had a car in the parking lot across from the park. What do you want me to do?"

"Wait there for me! I'm coming." Grant was intrigued and worried by our hurried conversation. Our magic moment was interrupted.

"I've got to go help me brother," I said to him as I grabbed my gun and sword. "You're welcome to stay here and wait for me."

"I'm going with you," he said firmly, and his eyes were fixed on my sword.

I had to reluctantly agree. It wasn't the right time to convince him that he shouldn't be involved–he was already involved–more than I would like.

We went in the truck; Octavian had used the Rover to transport the body. I let Grant drive. He was a very good driver, and he drove fast, but I could tell he wanted to impress me more than he liked to drive my truck. It took us less than fifteen minutes to get there. I spotted our Land Rover parked close to the Save Rite. We couldn't see anyone in the car, but we didn't see another car parked there.

Octavian's voice spoke in my ear. "Gelu left. I'm inside the store and it's safe. Come on in."

I crossed the long parking lot with one hand on my pistol. As Grant followed me, he checked on his gun that was underneath the shirt on his belt. The door was open. The building was rather large, but it wasn't quite empty. I could see that some activity had gone on there recently. As we entered from the front of the building there was a small office in the left corner of what would have been the show room. Octavian was at a desk that looked like it had come from a thrift store, working on an iPad.

"Gelu left this tablet behind," he said showing it to me. "I found a web site where they keep some sort of log of their activities. Look what I found on one of the links. These are the photos of the girls they kidnapped. They were attached to an e-mail address that I can't open yet. And here's one more—you're the last one in the set."

"Why is your picture here on this site?" asked Grant, extremely surprised.

I got closer and looked at my own photo. I wasn't prepared for what I saw—I was in my evening dress at the Crane Technologies corporate party in the Hilton Hotel.

"There's one more thing," said Octavian. "Look here on the live monitor at who's responding to these photographs. He's a male, but I don't recognize him. He doesn't look like anyone *we* know."

I knew the man in the image that Octavian had paused. His skin was a bit lighter and he had dark eyes. I wasn't expecting the familiar image that stared back at me from the iPad.

"I know this man. That's the guy who took my photo that we just saw!" I exclaimed, backing off with disgust.

Octavian and Grant were stunned.

"His name is Albert Solberg and I met him at a corporate party I crashed a week ago looking for Nagoshi," I explained. "He ordered his personal guards to follow me to the ladies room. I had to fight them off and run. His guards look like the ones I've already killed."

Why would this stranger have his picture and e-mail address on the iPad that belonged to the hybrid who had been sent to hunt me down? Was he looking for me, too? Who was he?

"Are you sure that is Albert Solberg?" my brother asked me.

I had little butterflies in my stomach–not produced by fear, but by unsettled emotions.

"Yes–look at the scar on his forehead. I can't forget that. And one more thing–he is from *Liechtenstein.*"

22

WE COULD SEE EVERYTHING FROM the tower of the castle. Past the old gate was a large field of wild grass, with no trees or water, allowing the castle to be vulnerable by an attack from the forest. At one time the field must have been a defense strategy for the former landlord, but in my mind it was just a dangerous setting with only one purpose—a battle.

"They're coming", said Andreas as he pressed his ear to the wall of the tower. "I can feel the vibration of the horses' hoofs. They should be here very soon."

"What are we supposed to do?" I asked Serban.

"This is not your battle, my sister. It is only for us. And we are going to fight!"

I was frightened. Clearly I could not deny that I was a Healer, but they needed a Warrior as well.

"Serban, I know Milos Martuzon very well," I pleaded with my brother. "He has been mentally unstable since he was a young man.

After his father died, he has surrounded himself with elite guards, and he has maintained his father's great army. And now, he has appropriated Prince Rudolph's private escort. He is a man of great power, and there are only seven of us."

"Six!" replied Serban. "You are a Healer, not a Warrior."

"Then why I was able to win a victory over Rares if I don't possess any of your abilities?" I snapped, frustrated at being denied.

"You sap our energy and we are weak in your presence, Lady Safira," answered Serban. "That is why you must run away from this place and hide."

"What do you mean, 'run away'? If you did not want me to be with you, why did you go to the trouble of bringing me here? Was it only to have your band hunted and killed?"

"We all needed to know," was his answer. "Rares and I needed to know that we have a sister, and that our sister was the rightful possessor of her parents' inheritance. You have no idea how important you are for us. After a thousand years there's a balance—we are seven again, the kingdom of the Transylvanian Immortals."

"There's not going to be a kingdom if you are caught and killed," I said to him, truly concerned. "If Lord Martuzon is only seeking me, perhaps it would be better for everyone if I just returned to him..."

Andreas' eyes flashed with striking blue lightning and a look of dark wrath came over his face.

"Listen to me, please," I tried to reason with them, "If I have the gifts of my mother and if I am indeed a Healer, than it only makes sense for me to return to Lord Martuzon. I can fulfill his wish to become an Immortal. This will save you from his wrathful anger. Once he is immortal, he would be under your law and you could punish him."

"*He is an Amestec–he can't be allowed to receive immortality from you. This is our law. We are the keeper of the law and you do not have the choice. When you refuse to make him transition into an Immortal, you will be in the gravest of danger,*" Serban answered me angrily.

"*She cannot be with us,*" said Rares. "*We cannot fight in her presence.*"

"*I do not agree,*" argued Andreas. "*We are strong enough to fight, even if she* is *with us. We will be seven, not six.*"

"*We cannot take her with us,*" replied Rares. "*We have found out what we needed to know about her. It's best for her, now, to go and hide somewhere.*"

"*She is your sister!*" Andreas angrily retorted. "*We need to have her with us to protect her. At least you could* pretend *to care about her–about her gifts.*"

"*I do care for her. This is why I want her away from here, so she will be free from Milos,*" Rares defended himself.

"*That's enough, you two!*"

Serban's voice was deeper than usual. "*We must think through this clearly...*"

"*There's no time for us to make a detailed plan, now,*" said Barbu, who was watching through a window on the castle's west side. "*They have arrived.*"

They were here. Lord Martuzon and his army were walking their horses directly toward us from the woods. I recognized his horse and armor, the pride of his inheritance from his father. I had not seen him in two weeks, but this man, who I once considered to be my family, felt so strange and distant to me. Now he was truly my enemy.

189

His army was not small. There were more than a hundred soldiers in formation behind him, all very well armed and very well trained. The Archduke was accompanying him and at first I did not understand why he was here. Then, behind the horsemen, I saw the Prince's personal guards, all armed with rifles. They stopped in the field, halfway to the gate.

I closed my eyes and wished I were dead–me, the Immortal!

"Safira, you must hide here in the palace. He will have to go through us to get to you. We will protect you, I swear!" Serban vowed.

"Please, let me go and talk to him. I cannot let you fight." I would rather lose my life than lose my brothers.

"They seem to want to try to negotiate. Someone is coming to the gate," announced Barbu, drawing his sword.

"Barbu! Rares! Andreas! It's time to go down," ordered Serban.

It was Milos Martuzon himself who came to the gate. Serban pushed me back on the stairs and motioned for me to go back to the tower. His hand signal clearly told me that I was not to follow him down.

"You must remain here and hide," he said. "When the battle has started, then you can go down. There is a horse ready for you in the stall. You must run away from here. I will find you again one day, I promise."

"Serban, this isn't a fight, it's a massacre," I said, trying to hold his hand. "You cannot win them over with talk. Please! Listen to me."

"I know what I'm doing. You must do what I say. Goodbye, my sister."

I ran back into the tower and knelt by the west window, hoping to learn what Serban and Lord Martuzon could possibly have in common to discuss. I couldn't see them from my vantage point, but I could hear them quite well.

"Lord Martuzon, you are not welcome on our property," I heard Serban speaking.

"This is my land," yelled Milos. "I have every right to be here. I came to take back what is mine and to kill you."

"I have nothing of yours, my Lord, and killing me won't be easy."

"I want the girl and I want you to surrender. All of you."

"My sister is no longer with us," responded Serban, and his voice sounded like thunder. "She has gone and she is far away by now. I do not recall that you were ever her rightful owner, my Lord. Go back to the city and to your palace. We will never surrender."

"We shall see about that. First I will kill you all and then I will take back my wife. Yes, you heard me—Lady Safira is my wife."

My heart was racing inside my chest. How was this possible? What kind of lies was he telling just to have me returned to him? I couldn't see my brother's face, but I was sure his face was flushed in anger as he tried to remain calm under these severe threats.

It was fortunate that it was daylight; otherwise, they would have seen his frightening eyes in the night. I supposed that Milos chose this time of day deliberately so they could see to wage the battle.

"My sister is not your wife," denied Rares. "You have absolutely no right to her."

"You are wrong. She was promised to me at her birth by my father."

"You know who she really is," replied Serban. "She has the freedom to choose whom to mate with, and she chose Andreas, who rescued her from you."

"By the laws of our land, she was in my house at age fourteen and no family came to claim her. She is mine, now," declared Lord Martuzon. "She is my wife and I have the right to take her back to my home. I will not return without her. I love her and I am ready to fight you for her."

"She does not want to return to you," responded Serban. "I will not allow you to find her. You will never put your filthy hands on her."

"Do not threaten me, boy! I am the governor of this land and I am the Prince of Transylvania. You are the murderer of my father. Did you think for a moment that I would ever forget that? I will destroy the lot of you. I promise!"

"Be careful of what you promise, Lord Martuzon, you may be embarrassed for not keeping your word."

For a moment there was quiet. Then I heard a horse galloping away from the castle toward the forest. I was numb with disbelief. So, they had kept me under guard at the Black Vulture Castle because I was Lord Martuzon's wife? He had hid it as a secret from me and from everyone else, and he had forced Nana Saveta to guard me for years in a web of lies.

Now it was clear to me why he suddenly took Nana away from my care—he had planned to creep into my room and take possession of me. Andreas had rescued me at exactly the right time.

I covered my face with my hands. I had cried many times in the past, and this time I wanted to find comfort for my pain through tears. But there was no time for that. The squealing of the gate's rusty hinges sounded an alarm, like a bugle call into battle, as the opening of the castle entrance awakened me and brought me back to reality. I struggled to lift my head and look through the window.

Outside, in plain sight, the six Warriors were lining up for battle, and the cruel vengeance of Lord Martuzon waited for them.

23

OUR BASEMENT WAS FILLED WITH guns, computers, satellite receivers, security monitors and scanners–all the equipment that Octavian needed to accomplish our search for the swords. All this high-tech array probably made Grant wonder how we had obtained them, but he didn't dare to ask. Octavian pulled up a map of Greece on one of the big TV monitors.

"His name is actually Prince Albert von Solberg," said Octavian, enlarging the Prince's image. "He's from the royal house of Liechtenstein, shunned by his family because his father didn't marry his mother. The King recognized him as a son, but denied his claim to the throne. His father gave him a very large sum of money and sent him away, but apparently he hasn't given up. Albert attempted to kill his brothers, but the plot was discovered and he was exiled. He's lived in Greece for the past seven years. Here's his location right there: Khalkidhiki–Polihrono, two kilometers inland."

The satellite was a bit unclear about showing the precise location.

"That's adjacent to a mountain area. It's not surprising to have this large dead zone area," I said, a bit disappointed.

Grant stared at Prince Albert's face. "Uh, his looks alone would cause me to exile him!"

"There's more," continued my brother. "He's believed to be responsible for the assassinations of various members of his family. We know he's murdered his uncle and his first cousin because both of them were next in line for the throne. This photo of him is recent. He didn't have that ugly scar on his forehead until ten days ago."

"So, he is not an Amestec—both of his parents are mortal."

Still, there was something about this prince that raised many warning flags in my mind, but at this moment I couldn't connect the threads of the seemingly unrelated events. I remembered him so well from the party – the creepy look in his eyes when he was watching me, the distasteful feel of his lips as he kissed my hand, and his sudden wish to take my picture as a souvenir.

There was no way this was just a coincidence, but how did everything connect? Why was the illegitimate son of a king involved in my capture?

"Did Marin and this Prince Albert meet and talk with each other before he returned to Europe?"

"It's hard to say," admitted my brother. "I can't pinpoint any time that they had a face to face meeting, but it's certainly not out of the realm of possibility. I'm still monitoring Gelu. Right now he's in Atlanta at Lenox Square Mall. It'll be interesting to know what his plans are. I am certain they don't include shopping."

"Wait," exclaimed Julian. "Who are you guys? Where did all this technology come from? Are you CIA, FBI or some other acronym I never heard of? How can you monitor somebody like that–it's illegal! And who are those guys you killed and who came back to life?"

Octavian and I looked at each other with concern. Until now, Grant had hoped that everything could be easily understood, and that every strange thing he had seen me doing was just the result of his fatigued mind. This time I ignored his outburst. The more he heard what we said and saw what we were doing, the better. He wouldn't sit quietly and listen to my story, and he wouldn't leave, so he'd have to learn by observation and participation.

"Do you think it's wise to let him go back to Newnan?" asked Octavian, as he moved his finger left and right on the touch screen to get a sharper image from the satellite. "He'll tell others about us; he'll tell about being killed by you and being brought back to life."

"I can tell you for sure that there must be only seven of them–that's the magic number. I can't hide anymore, so let them come. Seven of them aren't a challenge for us."

"Or we can find out where they are, go after them and take them down," suggested my brother. "Why wait?"

I knew that Gelu might retain some of his memories from his last moments alive. When he woke up in the early morning on the bench in the park, those memories would trigger some questions that needed some clear answers. He would know where to go immediately, but we needed to know who he communicated with.

"You're right Octavian," I said as I lowered my eyes to an old coffee table. I reached under it where a sword was hidden—it was still there. "We need to know all about Gelu's connections and locate their position; then we'll go after all of them. It is too dangerous to let them to come to us. The hunted will turn into a hunter. OK, then—that's our first engagement."

"Now you're talking. We'll get them all, Safira, that's a promise."

Octavian's enthusiasm sent the wrong signal to Grant. He started to walk back to the garage door, but he stumbled over Marin's dead body. That body was always in the way!

"Oh my GOD. This dead guy is still here in the house with you?"

"We can't bury him right now," answered Octavian as seriously as he could. "His kind is something new for us. He's a hybrid—long ago he was a mortal man, transformed by someone like us to be a ruthless soldier. Later on tonight I'll bury him in the back yard, but I've got one more experiment to do on him. I promise he won't harm you."

"Would you like some coffee?" I asked Grant, knowing that this moment was as surreal to him as possible, considering everything else that had happened to him since

Friday night when I had put a gun to his face outside my house.

His eyes shifted from me to Octavian. I don't know if it was curiosity that buoyed him or if he was just dumbfounded. Besides, how many times in a lifetime could someone be in the presence of two Immortals and be cool about it? For whatever the reason, Grant was still standing–probably because of his intense training as a SEAL.

"Perhaps we should go upstairs and let my brother work on his project," I proposed, taking his arm and leading him out of the basement. "It's time for you to go home. You need to relax."

"I *do not* need to relax," he answered me emphatically as we stepped into the kitchen. "I *can't* relax. Safira, you don't make any sense to me at all!"

"Then once and for all, *listen* to my story. But when I finish, there's no doubt that you'll think I'm a lunatic."

"I'll never think you're insane. The truth is that until right now, I thought you were involved in some sort of secret government experiment…"

I laughed–that was quite funny.

"What made you think that?"

"Just from what I've seen you do. And all that blabbering from your brother about the hybrids, I can only conclude that you are a…a…"

"A droid? Wow! I never thought of that."

"Yeah, I thought you're something like a droid. But if you're *not* a droid, if you're *not* artificial, how can I understand you? You and your brother are so beautiful–no one should look like that. It's not normal. How can you even explain what I've seen you do? How can I buy into this immortal thing?"

I poured myself some coffee, with creamer and lots of sugar, just the way I like it, and it tasted so good. I didn't ask Grant if he wanted to join me when I broke the eggs for a ham and cheese omelet–I just assumed we'd have breakfast together. He watched me in silence, but whenever I looked at him, he smiled at me. In his mind he was convinced that he finally had the answers to his questions about me, that he had found a resolution to his dilemma.

I could sense that his mind had become somewhat calmer, and that he was probably ready and willing to accept my explanations. After all, what would it take to surprise him even more? He had already accepted that I was a fighter and an elite sniper because he had seen me do these things.

With these facts in his mind, he could believe that I am a Warrior and a Healer, and it was just a small stretch for him to accept that I was an Immortal, too.

The omelet disappeared pretty quickly from his plate, and he sat there sipping his second cup of coffee as he watched me eat. He appeared to be so relieved that I actually ate food, so in his mind there was the possibility that I was really human.

"As you can see, I'm not a vampire, even though I'm originally from Transylvania. I don't drink blood–I eat food. Though, I must say, vampires are very popular these days."

"Are you making fun of me?" he asked indignantly.

"Are you telling me that would have been OK with you if I turned out to be some sort of robot or a government experiment?"

He passed the plate to me across the kitchen island, and then he held his face in his hands. During this weekend, unequal events had transpired in the life of this SEAL. One of them showed that I had the capacity for love, and one appeared to have no link in his mind with reality. That Grant could see both my tender side and my violent nature threatened his body and mind to almost spontaneously combust.

"I'm willing to accept anything you say about you and Octavian. Everything I've seen must have *some* kind of explanation."

"Are you afraid of supernatural things, Commander Grant?"

There was no humor at all in my tone of voice. Julian stared at me for a few moments trying to answer carefully.

"I don't fear anything that's physical, but I do find it hard to believe in the supernatural. In my experience, though, things that we say are supernatural always have logical explanations in the end. I accept the fact that you are better trained than me, and you can do things better than me..."

His fingers brushed and caressed my hair. I lightly touched his beautifully muscled chest with my fingers, and then I laid my head on it. He embraced me with passion and lust–I felt it and I was drowned in it.

"OK then, I'll listen very carefully. God only knows what you're about to tell me, but I'll accept anything from you. Whatever you tell me, I don't care."

At that moment Octavian hurried through the basement doorway. "Sorry for the interruption. Gelu just met with someone at the mall and the satellite image was showing both of them running to a car. They may be returning to Newnan. The audio isn't clear, but they're talking about you, Safira. The one who Gelu met is probably their leader, and he looks like one of *them, the Amestec.* I found him, Safira. I found your hunter."

Until that moment, I had hoped that everything that had happened wouldn't have this outcome, not so rapidly. But there was no more hope for peace—all my enemies were here—and I had no hope for chasing love.

It was over. Just like that.

"What does he mean?" asked Julian.

"He means that one of the hybrids he's tracking isn't a foot soldier. He's perhaps something somewhat similar to us, but not better. Keep the signal on him and get ready," I said to Octavian.

Octavian disappeared back in the basement.

"Get ready for what?" asked Grant, looking ridiculously confused.

"Ready to fight."

"Fight! Who're you battling? Look, wait, listen to me, this is insane. You two can't attack a foreign Prince. He has immunity!"

"We aren't at war with Prince Albert, even though at this moment I'm not sure about all the implications of his allegiance. Our enemy is someone else. This one is more powerful than you can imagine. Our battles with this one started long ago, and no mortal can understand."

As I spoke, I walked to the weapons collection. I returned with my sword in my hand and pointed it at Grant.

"This is what *we* fight with, Julian. This is the only weapon that can kill us."

With a calmness that I didn't think was possible, Grant took it from me and examined it.

"This is a good sword, still very sharp. I could tell from the first time I saw this weapon that you've used it recently. The metal shines differently when it's come in contact with flesh."

My eyes widened in astonishment.

"I love history and ancient weapons. You're not the only one who does. I took fencing lessons when I was very young, so I know a thing or two about these things. This sword is very old. How old is this weapon, Safira?"

"This sword is a lot older than me—about three hundred years old. I found it in a ruined castle in Transylvania and I've had it ever since. It's saved my life more than a few times."

"Oh, my God! Who are you, Safira?"

He handed the sword back to me and I put it back in its rack on the wall. "Are you really asking? Do you really want to know?"

"Yes. Tell me," His answer was definite but his attitude was tense.

"Julian, I want you to sit down on the couch. Come and sit over here."

Grant sat on the couch and looked at me in anticipation. I was smiling, so he thought it was a game—that all the talk about battles was just our way of joking.

"I want you to lie down," I continued to instruct him.

"Are you going to lie here with me?" he asked with a silly smile.

"Not right now. I'm very serious about this. Now, close your eyes. I'm going to tell you a story, but you must keep it secret until the last breath you breathe in this lifetime."

He lay down with his hands resting on his chest. My ingenious plan to spread the words of my story in the air like some dangerous germs was welcomed by my victim. Julian parted his lips, as if he was expecting all this seriousness to change into a moment of passion.

I was very tempted to become passionate with him, but I remained focused.

24

I DID NOT LISTEN TO *my brothers' warning to run away. I could not leave them, even under the threat of returning to Black Vulture Palace as the Governor's wife. How could I leave? I was the one, the only one, who was to heal them and protect them.* I could not *run away.*

The battle started.

Lord Martuzon sent his first twenty-five soldiers across the field to meet the six Immortals. With their fighting skills, they should have killed most of the Governor's twenty-five. But something was wrong. I could feel the Immortal's powers starting to diminish, and I could feel boldness and strength rise in my veins. This was a feeling I had never experienced before.

I knew then that Rares had been right—I was a menace to them. As Lady Amara had learned, I shouldn't be around them when they're fighting. When she was there, disasters had happened.

I had no hard feelings against her because she had left me behind. I know now that she didn't mean for it to happen. It was an act of courage that she risked everything to avenge the death of my father. I only wished that she had killed Lord Fers Martuzon sooner, hundreds of years sooner.

In a closet in the armor room, I found the sword I used to fight Rares, and two pistols. What I wanted at that moment was irrelevant. I fervently desired to leave Transylvania, and to never see Lord Martuzon again. The Prince would take me to serve his wife, I was sure, but the time for that had passed. I had an amazing past and legacy, more than I could ever imagine, and I had an even more disconnected future. All the dreams I had as a young girl were starting to crash around me. I could never be normal, because I never was, but I no longer felt fear or remorse.

The Immortals struggled with their fight against the last of the soldiers. Lord Martuzon brought up the Prince's guards with their rifles and the Immortals were surrounded. The guards' order was to capture the six alive, even if they were wounded, and Lord Martuzon would kill them personally. It was evident that Lord Martuzon didn't seek revenge for the death of his father by killing only Serban, but he wanted all of their lives.

I entered the field from the rear of the castle and crept through the tall grass until I was within pistol range of the soldiers. I shot some of them and some I killed with my sword. My fighting skills were good and fighting felt easy, like a dance. Although I was wearing a dress, it didn't hamper my movements at all. My brother, Serban, saw me and became very displeased.

The guards who were still in the rear aimed their rifles, preparing to fire. The six Immortals gathered around me, perhaps to protect me— but I protected them. I turned toward the soldiers, preparing myself to endure the rain of bullets when Lord Martuzon recognized me.

"Do not fire! Do not fire!" he nervously screamed at them.

"*Lady Safira, what are you doing?*" Rares *yelled at me.* "Why *are you here? I told you to leave.* Now you've killed mortals! The *balance has been upset.*"

"*We cannot fight with you here…you almost got us killed,*" *screamed Barbu.*

"*Barbu, be quiet,*" *ordered Serban.* "*Lady Safira, this is dangerous…*"

"*This is no time for preaching,*" *I shouted my brother.* "*I'm more powerful than all of you. I feel it, and you feel it too. Trust me! You must leave, run away from here. The horses are ready for you in the back. Go! Now!*"

As I said this, I started to push them back toward the gate and the castle.

"*No, we are not going,*" *said Andreas,* "*We are not going without you. Lady Safira…*"

"*I will be alright. He will not harm me, and there is no chance for you in this fight. I feel all of your powers in me. Serban! Andreas! Go! Please, I'm begging you…*"

"*What will you do?*" *asked Serban, wiping the blood off his sword.*

"*I will fight or be captured. This is my destiny—Lord Martuzon cannot change it. Besides, I am the Healer and you are bound to obey me.*"

My brother Serban nodded and bowed to me in obedience. As Andreas touched my face and kissed me, his warm lips were trembling. Behind me I could feel movement. The soldiers and Lord Martuzon were moving closer to us.

One day, I will find you again," said Andreas, as he held me closely. "I love you, Lady Safira. Don't forget me."

"I won't, I promise," I replied, as he joined the others to prepare their mounts.

I held my position between them and the army. Once they were behind the gate, I knew they would be hard to be catch. They could run swiftly, and their horses were the best. But before they disappeared from my sight through the gate, they turned again to me and touched their foreheads with their fingers, bowing in salute to me.

For just a split second I hesitated. The feeling of being left behind, again, at the hand of the same man who had been my jailer, was wearying and unpleasant. That didn't matter anymore–the Immortals were gone and they were safe for now. I did my duty. I raised my hand with my sword, prepared to fight.

"Lord Martuzon! Stop right there," I screamed at him reloading my pistol.

"Lady Safira, please don't be stubborn" he said, imploringly. "Lower your sword, and come back with me. This is a fight you cannot win."

"Try me! You lied to me–you know who I am."

"Yes, I do. I also know that unless you come back with me, I will never stop hunting your brothers."

I rapidly calculated my odds. I knew I could survive the gun fire, even though the bullets would momentarily stop me. I still would have to stretch myself more and fight fifty more soldiers. Perhaps I could take half of them–but perhaps not. I had already killed some of the soldiers, but that didn't agitate my spirit.

The sight of blood no longer frightened me, but I had to ask myself whether it was right or not to continue killing mortals. I did not believe so, but I had to learn very quickly the things I was capable of.

I dropped my sword and surrendered. Lord Martuzon came towards me with a smirk, not a smile of conquest. I immediately knew what his intentions were and I regretted giving up without a fight. My fate was sealed. His intention was to kill me, but first I must learn his reason.

"Welcome back, my dear wife. Please give me the pleasure of returning to your home. Tonight you will be mine and I will be yours, forever, as we were destined to be."

"It is too late, my Lord. I cannot be your wife because I gave myself to another man. I will never willingly make you an Immortal Warrior. The Black Vulture Palace and your guards cannot hold me prisoner anymore and you know it."

The Archduke came towards us and stopped to bow to me. I returned his salute. I couldn't help but wonder how much he knew about me and what lies Lord Martuzon had told him.

* * *

We returned to the palace in a caravan of horsemen, foot soldiers, and the Archduke's personal guards. I was taken back to my old room, and this time I was very well guarded by ten guards with rifles. I still think I could have fought them all and defeated them, but I didn't.

After I was locked in my room, I heard the sound of footsteps going back and forth in the hallway, and they often stopped in front of my door. After midnight, four of the armed guards came for me, and they took me to one of the rooms in the cellar.

Lord Martuzon waited for me there, armed with a sword. His face was pale and unreadable.

"I wish I did not have to do this, because I love you," he said, and he closed his eyes. "I watched you and I kissed you often when you were sleeping. But I must kill you, Safira. If I cannot have you, I will take away your freedom forever. You see, my father told me long ago that you can change me into an Immortal and that you and I would be together forever—but you ran away. Your immortal life is a righteous gift, if there is any truth to the legend. In a moment I will see for myself. You must die for me, but you will live inside me forever because I love you. I have always loved you, and I love you now."

I looked directly at him. My eyes shone with thunder in the dark, and I knew how to manipulate my powers. I didn't hate him at that moment. Any other mortal who could gain immortality by killing me would have done it, too.

He was the last person who deserved to inherit my immortal life, though, and that was what I really hated.

The Archduke came in the room and joined us. He didn't look well. Perhaps he was against my being killed, or perhaps he thought I deserved to die. Either way, he didn't make any effort to speak against what was about to happen.

Milos made an attempt to kiss me, but I turned my head. His face wasn't the last memory I wanted to have in this short life. This day was my birthday—I was just turning twenty, I think—but I had stopped aging long ago. Now I would be forever young—in death. And my end was in the cold cellars of Black Eagle Palace.

Milos Martuzon did not waste any time. He raised his sword and with a swift downward chop, cut off my head.

It was fast and I felt no pain

209

25

"WAIT A MINUTE, WAIT A minute!" screamed Grant breathlessly as he got off the couch. "This is really hard to swallow. You need to stick to something more realistic, like some creepy immortals, but not this. You can't say that last thing. You just can't sit there and tell me that you've been decapitated, and yet, here you are, living and breathing in front of me. Come on!"

"Do you want to hear this or not?" I threatened him.

"Of course I do. This is fascinating, and I'm hooked. I've *got* to hear the rest of it."

I paused before resuming my story to have a sip of coffee, and his cell phone rang.

"Grandma!" Julian exclaimed. He seemed to be truly surprised by her call. "What time is it? Is it already nine o'clock? Right, I'm on my way."

He sighed as he ended the call, obviously quite disappointed.

"I've got to go. I forgot that I promised my grandmother that I'd go to church with her. Will you give me a ride home? Maybe you can finish your story on the way."

"You're welcome to use my truck," I offered him. "It'll be good for both of us to be apart for a while. You've been here at my house for the last two days, and you've seen and heard so much. I think you need to think about what I've told you and clear your mind before I finish the story."

"Everything's so jumbled now—I'm not sure I can do that. But I really do need to go. May I come by later?"

"Sure." I agreed, but I doubted that it would happen. I was sure he would run for the hills and avoid me for the rest of his life.

He left the house without speaking. I followed him to the truck and I removed all the guns. He shook his head like he was trying to wake up from a bad dream, but he still didn't say anything. By the time I reached the remote control to open the gate, he had started the truck. He immediately slipped the gear shift into "drive" and sped off down the street, seemingly relieved to regain his freedom.

* * *

My brother signaled me from the basement. He had been down there for quite a long time.

"Octavian, what's going on?"

"Has your mortal boyfriend gone?" he chuckled.

211

"Yes, he has, and he seemed quite happy to get away. Why?" I asked as I took the steps down to the basement.

"I think we have some uninvited guests. Come and look."

"Is it Gelu? Did you lose his signal?" I asked as I looked over my brother's head.

"It's not Gelu. I'm still getting a signal from him. He's with the Half-Immortal, and they've gone back to the Save Rite."

A dark colored Ford Expedition, similar to the one Marin was driving that day at the academy, was parked in front of Doctor Samson's house. Our camera's angle could only photograph half of the vehicle, but that was enough to raise red flags in our minds.

"I told you there must be more like them, Safira, and they are here. This isn't going well at all."

We were both taken by surprise to see two young men and two girls with long blonde hair getting out of the car and walking up the sidewalk toward our neighbor's front door. Alarmed, it took us only a few seconds to grab our pistols and exit from the lower level of our house into the back yard.

"I'll take the front," I motioned to my brother, "you go to the back patio door."

We started to run in the different directions. Our fence was low enough to be able to hurdle it without any effort. I didn't see anyone at the front door, but the door was wide open. I tried to *look* but because it was daylight, my vision wasn't able to capture what was going on inside.

Beads of sweat were beginning to slither down my forehead–they were intruding at the wrong house, and my senses were telling me that the Samson's were in eminent danger. I ran through the door with a gun in my right hand.

I had visited the house many times and I knew its layout well. I spotted one girl in the living room area and I shot her in the back, but there was no blood from her wound.

She turned her gun on me and responded with rapid fire. I leaned over backwards, away from the path of the bullets and seven 35mm rounds flew over my torso. I quickly got to my feet and shot her in the forehead.

A hole appeared in her forehead and exited through the back of her skull. It looked like a simple through-and-through shot. The bullet scarred the wall as it passed through her head, but there was no blood or brains from the wound.

The other girl came out of the kitchen, firing randomly and aiming at nothing in particular, just hoping that she might hit somebody. I leaped from behind the stairs with both of my feet kicking her back. She fell to the floor with her face sliding across the carpet, rolled over, and started to fire her weapon.

I backed away, hiding behind the china cabinet. Octavian was inside the living area by then and his shot was deadly. A hole opened in her forehead, but like the other girl, the shot passed directly through her skull with no gore from her wound.

I ran up the stairs, thinking that Ms. Ruth and Doctor Samson had probably been in their bedroom, dressing for church. As I turned on the landing halfway up the stairs, a man started shooting at me from the upstairs hallway.

I let him empty his magazine. The wall behind me was heavily damaged from his bullets and the paintings that were hanging there were ripped apart and falling out of their frames. As his pistol ran out of ammunition, he reached for his rifle.

With one foot on the wall I propelled myself at him, and my other foot hit him hard in the jaw. He fell from the hallway over the banister and landed hard on his head in the living area. Octavian was waiting for him and he met the same fate as his female cohorts.

There was one more intruder remaining. The other three had been eliminated in less than a minute.

I heard a scream coming from the master bedroom. The door was shut, but I kicked it in and stepped into the room. As the door slammed into the wall, someone jumped through the second floor window and landed in the back yard. Octavian ran past me and leaped through the window to chase him.

I wanted to follow Octavian, but what I saw next made me completely immobile. Doctor Samson lay motionless on the floor, halfway in the bedroom and halfway in the bathroom. Ms. Ruth hovered over his body, crying, and calling his name.

My immediate reaction was to go to him and check his pulse. I felt his wrist, but there was nothing there. He hadn't been shot, but all the shooting that had taken place and the apparition of an armed man in his bedroom was enough to frighten this fragile elderly mortal, and his heart gave out. I wanted to touch his heart, but an invisible power stopped me from doing it.

I stood there, feeling powerless and helpless, looking into Ms. Ruth's red rimmed eyes while she was telling me that he was gone.

"Octavian," I signaled my brother, "Doctor Samson is dead."

A strange noise came in response from my brother's phone. He ground his teeth together, and I knew he was devastated and furious at the same time.

"I'm on him, Safira! He's in the Expedition and I'm following him. When I catch him I'll kill him, I swear!"

"No! I need him alive. Can you do that?"

"Only if I have to! Keep communications open."

I helped Ms. Ruth get to her feet and to lie down on her bed. I couldn't hide this scene. I couldn't even manipulate Ms. Ruth's mind into believing that Doctor Samson had just fallen on the bathroom floor and died. There was no way I could explain away the bullet holes in the walls and the strange dead people scattered around on the first floor.

I called William, the Samson's son who was also a physician, and explained him half of the situation. As quickly as I could, I pulled the three bodies to the back shed, one by one, and hid them.

I was definitely tired of dealing with these hybrids!

I dialed 911 from the Samson's bedroom phone after I had hid the bodies. I didn't try to hide the bullet casings, and there was no way to hide the bullet holes and the total disarray in the house. The invaders had been armed and they used their guns to frighten the Samson's. They all wore latex gloves, of course, so there were no fingerprints. Yes, this could be a case of a robbery gone bad. I just had to convince the police of this lie.

When I returned to check on Ms. Ruth, she ran weeping into my arms. I had maintained my composure this long because I had to take care of the crime scene, but seeing Doctor's Samson's lifeless body again brought me to tears. Ms. Ruth asked me continuously why this had to happen, and at the same time, she was praising me for saving her life. I denied this notion, but I wondered if the hybrids would have spared their lives after they realized that they were in the wrong house.

Probably not.

I touched Ms. Ruth's forehead with my fingers and her breathing became calmer. All this had happened because of me – they were looking for *me*. There was no doubt in my mind about this, and the Sampson's had paid for the intruder's mistake.

* * *

Dr. William Samson's home was just a few blocks over from his parents. He arrived at the same time as the police and the ambulance. I had told the 911 operator that one person was dead and that shots had been fired, so they sent quite a fleet of patrol cars to the house.

Among them were two detectives who I already knew: Morris and Gibb. They looked at me only a little surprised– I think they were expecting to see me there.

Detective John Morris was perhaps in his late thirties, just as tall as I was and with blonde short hair. His face had a distinctive look and certain intensity coming through his blue eyes. He was very anxious to talk to me, but he deferred to Detective Gibb's seniority. It made no difference to me, but it was more than fifteen minutes before I spoke with Detective Morris.

"Well, it's nice to see you again, Miss Tash," he said, and his open smile was quite a surprise for me. "I hope you remember my partner and me. We were at your house not too long ago…"

I nodded, but I was determined to be cautious about how much information I would make available to them.

"It looks like this was an attempted robbery, but we need your version of what happened. As you said before, you were the one who discovered the victim…"

"Actually, it happened right after my brother left for Sunday school at church when I heard gunfire and Ms. Ruth screaming. I saw a car parked in the street, and when I approached the front door, two guys were running out of the back yard. They got in the car and drove off in a hurry. I ran upstairs and found Doctor Samson dead. That's when I called the police."

My story was somewhat disjointed and it sounded a little ridiculous, but I was trying to take my brother out of the picture and avoid some awkward questions. Nevertheless, the questions came.

"Wow, what you did showed a lot of courage, Miss Tash. I would probably think twice before I went into a situation like that. Describe those two guys for me."

"Oh, let me think," I said, pretending to search my memory. "It all happened so fast. All I can tell you is that they were white, tall, and they had long hair. From the glimpse I had of them, I think they were blonde."

John raised his head from his notebook and he walked towards me, looking straight into my eyes. What he had on his mind wasn't exactly what I expected, but he was clever.

"Miss Tash, do you wear contact lens?"

I knew where his question was leading.

"No, I don't wear blue lens, and this is my natural hair color."

Our eyes met again and he tried very hard not to smile.

"Stay here, Miss Tash. I'll be right back. I just need to check out something with my partner."

John pulled Gibb aside, thinking they were a safe distance from me, but I could hear them talking to each other.

"Bob, look at this girl. The intruders she described are exactly like the ones who were involved in kidnapping the girls in our case, and they're the ones who shot the police officer, too. She fits the profile of what the kidnappers were looking for: young, blue eyes, dark hair. And she lives across the street from the crime scene. I think what we're looking at is just a terrible mistake."

"You think they were after her?" asked the other detective.

"They had to be! What kind of burglary is committed on a Sunday at ten in the morning?" insisted John.

"It's happened before," commented Gibb, shaking his head.

"Listen. They were armed and they didn't hesitate to shoot. If their target was really those two seniors, they would have traveled light. And they ran away without stealing anything."

"OK. So your theory is that they were after her. But why?"

"She's very rich. They could have held her for a good ransom. She lives with just her brother. These guys, whoever they are, are getting very aggressive and dangerous. We need to protect her, Bob. I leave close by, on Crescent Street, so I could stand guard for the next few days…"

"Are you serious? Those guys aren't coming back here. Did you see the alarm system in their house? They don't need us! That system is better than the one at the White House. Money can buy everything these days."

Detective Gibb seemed unconvinced that everything was as clear as Morris claimed it was. He looked in my direction as I sat quietly on a kitchen chair.

Another man, probably a crime scene investigator, came downstairs to talk with the detectives.

"I recovered two guns, but they may have had others," he said. "There was a lot of shooting. Some things got destroyed, but there's no trace of blood anywhere. Doctor Samson wasn't shot—they just scared him—but it was enough to cause his heart to give out. They exited from the master bedroom window. You need to check all the hospitals in the area. They probably got hurt, jumping from that height."

"My God!" exclaimed Gibb. "So, nothing is missing? Why did they have to shoot?"

John Morris came towards me slowly, still writing in his notebook.

"Octavian!" I whispered into my brother's open line phone. "Where are you?"

"I managed get behind him and I caught up with him on Highway 74," answered my brother. "For a while I was right on his tail until he got on Interstate 85. He saw me and started to drive faster, trying to lose me. Two exits before the airport he was trying to watch me in his rearview mirror and he wasn't paying attention. He crashed his car into a median wall. I stopped right behind him, snatched him out of the car, and put him in my trunk. When the cops get here, they'll think he ran away because he didn't have a driver's license."

"Do you mean to tell me that you've got him alive?" I couldn't believe my ears.

"Yes. I've got him," Octavian confirmed. I could tell that his breathing was heavy because of a rush of adrenaline.

"Be careful when you come home. The street's full of police and they may have it blocked off by now. When you show up, pretend you were at Sunday school."

"Yeah, I know what to say. I had left for church before the incident–I don't know anything."

I stood up and turned to Detective Morris. "I need to go back home and wait for my brother. He'll be devastated by Doctor Samson's passing–they were very close. I'd rather give him the news myself."

"Right." The detective answered, massaging the bridge of his nose. "I'm sorry for what happened, Miss Tash. Please make yourself available for the next few days. We may need to talk with you soon. By the way, we'll need to get a technician out here to check your security cameras."

"I understand. Am I in any danger, sir?"

"I don't think so. Besides, I'll keep an eye on you, I am your neighbor–I live at the first house on the next street. We'll get them soon! I can assure you of that."

In the meantime, Octavian came home and drove his Jaguar straight into our garage. The police at the entrance to our cul-de-sac had questioned him, but they let him pass. He drove past the seven homes on our street and he wasn't questioned again. I ran over to him, afraid that police might gain access to our house before Octavian could remove any incriminating evidence of our intervention.

I laid my head on my brother's shoulder. We were both shaken by Doctor Samson's passing.

"Octavian, go inside and check the security cameras."

"I heard what Morris said," answered my brother. "I'll take care of it. You stay out here and keep an eye on the detectives."

"It happened again," I cried. "The collateral for my safety was our mortal friend."

"Talking about mortal friends, look who's here," said Octavian pointing to the street.

I turned my head to the entrance of the cul-de-sac. Julian Grant and Nelda were at the barricade requesting permission to pass. My brother waved to them.

"I'll take care of Nelda," he said to me. "I'll send her back to her home. You'll have to deal with Grant, fast—we've got work to do."

I nodded. I couldn't understand this mortal at all. He was back again—back for me.

Octavian walked up to the end of the street to talk with Nelda, to convince her to go home. He hugged the girl and kissed her. That short, affectionate moment was like medicine for him. A moment later, Nelda left, and my brother came back to the house and went to our basement.

As soon the police cleared him, Grant rushed toward me. He ran down the street and took me in his arms, holding me tight.

I'm an immortal who doesn't fear any danger, but I'm also an immortal who fears a mortal's love.

"I'm sorry," he whispered to me, "I'm so sorry. I heard it on the radio news when I got out of church. It said that there was an attempted burglary that had been interrupted by the next door neighbor. I knew it was you, from the address. Are you OK?"

His voice was soft and loving, and I held him tightly, too.

"Come on, let's go inside."

At that moment the front door of Doctor Samson's house opened. The EMTs had covered Doctor Samson's lifeless body with a sheet and placed it on a rolling stretcher, removing it from the house. As the stretcher bumped its way down the front steps, the sheet slipped a little and I saw his white face, with no spirit or consciousness remaining in it. The realization that he was really gone hit me hard.

Julian bent his face to my ear and whispered, "What happened when *you* died, Safira?"

26

I FELT MY LIFE *AND the life of my immortal brothers leaving my body. Then, I felt nothing.*

Death was quiet and peaceful, like an interruption of thinking. In those moments when your mind is empty—you don't seem to exist. It's like you're in a deep sleep, one of those without dreams.

My spirit left my body and remained hovering in the air, above the room. My spiritual eyes were seeing everything. Lord Martuzon's soul was very much tormented, but the murder he had just committed left little impression on his demeanor.

"I cannot believe you killed her!" exclaimed the Archduke, and I saw that he was weeping. "She was so young and beautiful. Why did you keep it a secret from me that she was your wife? It was wrong— I was in love with her. She was to follow me to Vienna."

"Please forgive me, my Lord," murmured Lord Martuzon, "but she was not told about her situation either; our marriage wasn't consummated. This is why I hid it from her, so she would not try to run away from me. I will hunt down and kill all of those who took her

away from me. But she deserted me—she deserted you too. Her heart was turned away from me. The punishment she received was right. I could not let her go—now she is mine forever."

I was dead, left there lying on the cold floor.

Soon, a deep darkness covered the room, and I could see or hear nothing. I don't know how long I was in complete darkness. My eyes were open but I couldn't see. The next thing I remember was taking a deep breath. Someone was softly touching my heart and my forehead.

* * *

When I opened my eyes, light was surrounding me. I was lying in a room with many windows and the sun was bright and gorgeous in here. Someone was singing a song, a beautiful song that I remembered from long ago.

My mother would sing it to me when I was a child, and the singing was similar to what I remembered from my childhood. Suddenly, I lifted my head and I remembered that not very long ago I had no head—but now I did.

I remembered that as a child my mother would glide softly into my room in the early mornings, trying not to awaken me. Her silhouette was so graceful as she moved from window to window to open each of them wide. Then she would sing, just as she was singing now. My mother, Lady Amara, was there singing to me. If this was the heaven for Immortals, it was a wonderful and magical place.

I hoped and prayed, now, that this place I was in was real, and that I wouldn't wake up in some ordinary, dreary place.

I closed my eyes again, trying to prolong the moment, but just as I closed my eyes I glimpsed two figures passing by my bed. One of the figures was a young man, perhaps sixteen, with the same facial features as mine, with eyes and hair like mine–and a woman.

"Mother!" I called to the female.

"Welcome back to life, my daughter."

She came into my field of vision and held me close to her breast. I immediately touched her face to be sure this wasn't a figment of my imagination. But it was her, my beloved mother. I hadn't seen her in fifteen years, but she had not changed a bit. Now that I had grown to be a young woman, I realized that amazingly I looked exactly like her.

"Mother, have I been dead? What happened to me? Am I really alive once more? How is this possible?"

"Yes, my dear, you were truly dead, but your brother brought you back to life."

`"My brother? Mother, I'm afraid that Serban and Rares are not near here anymore…"

` I started to weep, because my memories of them and of Andreas, who I loved, were overwhelming.

"I am referring to your brother, Octavian," she answered pointing with her head towards the boy who was still leaning against the window. "He brought your spirit back into your body."

I turned to look at the youth.

If I had previously thought that my existence was a great deal like a tale of vivid imagination, the appearance of this new brother with such extraordinary powers seemed almost impossible.

"Octavian is your brother, too," Mother continued, undisturbed by my amazed appearance. "Although he is not a Healer

like you, he can bring back the spirit of all the slain Immortals. That is a gift that only the mighty Gallbor has. You can do the same thing as well."

I touched the skin on my neck where Milos' sword had severed my head. There was no scar there, nor any indication that I had ever been injured. Still, it was extremely difficult for me to comprehend what I was hearing and feeling.

"As your mother, I saw in my spirit's vision what had happened," continued my mother with her soft spoken voice. "Octavian and I rode our horses for three days until we arrived to Oradea, on the day of your burial. Octavian killed Lord Martuzon's soldiers who were assigned as your funeral detail and we rode back here with your body. You see, once Immortals are slain, our bodies will disintegrate into dust after seven days.

"When I killed Fers Martuzon, I ran away to hide. I could not come back for you. Can you ever forgive me for my absence?"

"I have always waited for your return, Mother," I responded with happy tears, "and indeed, you came back for me. Everything is good, now. But what can you tell about my other brothers?"

"Gallbor called them to a higher cause," answered Octavian coming closer to me.

"But this is their land to protect."

"From now on, their mission is to hunt the impostors Immortals," answered my mother. "Now, you need to go as far away from here as possible. Lord Martuzon is immortal now and he's dangerous. He didn't change his appearance—Amestec do not change when they kill us, but they do inherit some of our gifts. He will seek you out soon enough, once he learns you are no longer dead—not only him, but all other remaining Amestec."

"Then we must stay here and seek revenge, Mother, because he killed me." I felt strong desire to fight and a new kind of energy rushed through my body—surely I was renewed as a Warrior.

"Revenge is for later!" interjected Octavian. "Lord Martuzon has inherited your powers and has an army. We are alone and we cannot win — not this time. We must leave until the time is right. Then we will do our duty and fight the Amestec."

"How old are you?" I asked, intrigued. I was already starting to feel a strong attachment for him.

"A little younger then you," the young man answered with dignity. "What difference does it make?"

"Then you are my younger brother and you must listen to me."

My protective instincts for this new and younger brother were overwhelming.

"Mother!" I implored her to defend me.

Lady Amara smiled. She understood me very well.

"You are to listen to your sister, Octavian. Remember, your duty is to protect her. Now, I need to say goodbye to Safira. Wait out in the hallway."

Octavian bowed to me and left the room obediently.

"Where are we now, Mother?" I asked finding refuge in her arms.

"We are in Alba Iulia, at the Three Horses Inn," she said holding me closer to her chest. "I must say goodbye again. You and your brother must also leave Transylvania and I must return to the Secret Mountain—our shelter, and serve in the Council since there are a few inactive Warriors left in the City. I ceased to be a Healer the

moment you were born. All of my powers were transferred to you. Now I am only a Watcher and I foresee the future. I suppose you have many questions you need answered."

"Perhaps just one. Am I like you Mother?"

"As you are aware by now, our true origins are not from this world. You are Healer and Warrior, like none other before you. You and Octavian are my only children. Your bodies are indestructible. They heal by themselves, unlike the bodies of the older Immortals. It was a gift given to you and Octavian by Gallbor's spirit. But be forewarned: the blade of a sword can kill you again.

"Your new mission from Gallbor, our Master, is to find the magical Fire Sword and the Silver Sword. They disappeared from my master's palace one thousand years ago. Both must be brought back into your control before the Amestec finds them and use them against us. Find these swords Safira, for they are dangerous.

"The Fire Sword can destroy your body. The wound it would inflict would not heal. If the Fire Sword cuts off your head, it cannot be reattached to your body, so your spirit would have to linger in exile and despair.

"The blade of the Silver Sword turns invisible—this is the one sword that can rip your spirit—yours, your brother's and that of any other Immortal—into nothingness. When this happens, no one can revive you, not even Gallbor. You cease to exist."

"Why is it left to me to accomplish all these things, and to no other Warriors?" I asked, worried that this task was too overwhelming for me and I was unprepared for it.

"The world has changed. Our old order of Immortal Warriors is weak. It cannot protect itself or the mortal kind. Only a few of us are left alive and we lost our dignity as an Order. The Council decided to have the active Warriors find a new shelter and wait for a new future to unfold. But the ones who stay behind will come looking for you, driven by a wild and supreme purpose, to mate with you and be your master. They will all look for you in Transylvania, so you must leave this place.

"Lust, our greatest weakness, will overpower many of the Immortals—they will mate with mortal females again. The Amestec will seek you, generation after generation.

"But don't let your guard down. The old enemies that our kind has fought for centuries, and the ones we created ourselves, will hunt you always. One day, a new war will start, and your new battles will begin. A hundred years from now, a new rise of the half-immortal Amestec will evolve and they will discover your existence.

"Your oath is to protect humans but remain in the shadows. No mortals will perish at your hand, but be careful—your gift should never be used to revive one of them. Not being obedient could destroy you."

"What about Octavian?"

"You must keep his existence a secret at all costs. His brings back to life the spirit to the fallen one. That makes Octavian the most powerful Immortal after you and Gallbor. Keep him a secret until the time is right—then he will rise—but for a higher purpose that is not to be made known to you at this time. He was made aware of that. But he will fight with you; he will be your Warrior until one day, when all the Immortals will unite and will be powerful again.

"As I did many times in my long life, you are also free to find pleasure and love within your kind. But only one can be your Master. He is the one who can defeat you in battle and he will be powerful enough to protect you. You are the only female Healer, you are now the Queen. Be ready at all times."

"Will I see you again Mother?"

"I will always see you, and you will always be aware of me. The Black Eagle Palace cannot harm you anymore, but your legend will remain with it."

* * *

I said goodbye to Lady Amara, and the next day Octavian and I left for Oradea. I had an intense desire to return to the Black Vulture Palace and kill Lord Martuzon. I knew I was strong enough to do it, but the time was not yet right.

We left Transylvania after a month. Before we left, I had the pleasure of seeing Lord Martuzon marry Miss Anda Kovack. I could only imagine what terrible children they would produce. They all would be Amestec—my future enemies. Some of them may be alive today, but I have not encountered one so far.

After we left Oradea, our next place to hide was Vienna.

In 1889, I saw the Archduke Rudolph again before his death. His young mistress wanted to leave him, and the prince couldn't bear to let her go, so he killed her and then he committed suicide. It was such a disappointing end for this very flamboyant but impressionable prince.

He learned a terrible lesson from Lord Martuzon when he witnessed my slaying.

For a few years we lived in Frankfurt, then in Paris, and later in London. I searched for the magic swords in every place. In 1909 we crossed the Atlantic and we came to America. As my enemies have found me, the swords will too.

Is been said that the Black Eagle Palace still stands today in all its grandeur in the downtown of the city of Oradea—waiting for my return. We both survived.

27

"SOME PEOPLE TELL A STORY about an Immortal slain in a dungeon there, but it has become only an urban legend."

Julian Grant stood beside me in silence. My story was certainly not easy to believe. After hearing it, a person's sanity would be in question, not to mention that of the one who told the story.

"We were forbidden to tell our friends the truth about us; we told everyone the same story—that we had a rare disease, untreatable, which always condemns us to loneliness and appearing to be young.

"One evening, forty years ago, when we lived in Arizona, Octavian and I went to a movie. While we were out, our adopted parents were attacked in their own home, like the Samson's, and they were murdered by Amestec. Octavian and I realized that we needed to have all the means possible to protect our mortal friends.

"We were Warriors without weapons, so we bought guns. Also, we are savants–our natural knowledge is thousands of years ahead of the mortals."

Grant nodded a few times, perhaps now having a better understanding of all our skills and actions, and our basement was not a mystery anymore.

"I have always been hunted by Amestec but this time it's different," I continued determined to bring my story to an end. "Someone has created a private army of hybrids and they're searching for me. Innocent people, like these young people who invaded the Samson home, have been made into hybrids. I firmly believe that Milos Martuzon is the only one who could be behind all this. He made the hybrids, or at least, caused them to be made, and sent them after me."

"But how could he even know you're alive? He's the one who killed you!"

"That's right. But three days after I was buried, he found his soldiers dead near an empty grave, and he uncovered evidence that my mother had been in Transylvania. He's assuming that either she helped me, or my powers are greater that he thought. Still, it was my death that gave him everlasting life. I'm afraid that he may have acquired my spirit along with my powers, and my powers have become menacing in his hands."

"How is that even possible? I am sorry for these stupid questions, but I need to understand."

"My spirit multiples because I am a Healer. Julian, Milos Martuzon will do anything to capture me again because it's in his instinct, and because he thinks I'm his wife. Besides, anyone who will manage to kill me will inherit all my powers."

I looked away, but Grant took my hand into his.

"I'll protect you–at least I'll try. I've got skills, too."

"You're not listening again!" I found myself gasping for air as I realized that I must push Grant out of my life forever. "I risked everything by telling you who I am, so you could understand what's been going on and why I'm doing these unusual things. Tell me, what exactly have you thought about during the three hours you were away from me? Do you wish now you would never have come looking for me? And be honest."

"I *will* be honest," he responded with a guilty face. "I believed your story. Then I thought about what you had told me–that you're married, and I was about to start an affair with a married woman."

"What? Is this what you thought about while you were supposed to be paying attention to the sermon in church?" I asked, making every effort not to smile.

"You *are* married, right? To which one? Milos Martuzon or Andreas?"

He was right. My past marital situation was still unsettled, and this brought a new perspective to my present status. I was free to choose a lover, but only one of my kind. With none of them around me, my weakness for Julian felt indeed like a forbidden affair.

"I don't know. One who said he loved me also killed me. The other one who said he loved me never returned to me. I don't seem to have a very good track record when it comes to love, do I?"

"Let me love you, Safira. Let me make love with you and make you lose yourself into my arms. I know you want me, too…"

"I can't." I knew I must let him go before it was too late and I would give in to temptation and make things more complicated for both of us. I needed to stay focused on my war ahead and not act on my weakness. Our love was doomed even before it started.

"Why? Because I'm mortal and I'm not like you?" Grant lifted my face and searched for a different answer in my eyes.

"It's because of what *I* am and what *I* must do."

He touched my chin as he lowered his lips to kiss me when my brother cleared his throat behind us.

"Julian, please leave," I implored him. "Everything's hopeless, now. You should not even be in my life. Things have changed overnight. With all the turmoil that's going on right now, there's no time for us. I have to fight my battles and mortals have no place in it."

My brother waited for me, but I motioned for him to leave. Grant didn't show any sign of leaving and I couldn't look him in his eyes.

If I had, I would never have been able to resist him.

"I asked something of you," he said, grabbing the keys to the truck from the coffee table. "Please, don't push me away. I want to be with you! We've gone too far to stop, now."

"Now things are different. I can't risk putting your life in danger. Love and war is a volatile mix, and this is something I must do alone."

"So, this is it? After you tell me all about your past, is there nothing for me in your future? Will you still say that all is lost between us?"

"I am not certain of anything," I answered, restraining my tears.

"You're right, I'd better leave. It'll be up to you if you want to see me again. Good bye, Safira"

* * *

I should have followed him to the garage and tried to say something more promising to him–that this situation might just be temporary–but I let him leave. Everything that had escalated around me from the moment I discovered the evidence of an Amestec on my trail was clashing with any possibility that I would ever taste a sweet moment of love peacefully.

If my enemies found out about Grant, they would use him against me.

Octavian put his arm around my shoulders and we made our way into our den. He sat beside me on the couch, quietly studying me. My face was a portrait of my thoughts, and it spoke volumes with no control from me. I was bitter and sad, with feelings of utmost frustration, and it was difficult for me to conceal my growing pain and fear of losing Julian and his love, but still it was me pushing him out of my life. But not out of my heart.

"The security tapes have been altered," Octavian said, still staring at me. "The hybrid is in the closet with Marin. He's hurt pretty bad, but he's still alive. I'll bring the other three home tonight and we'll bury them as soon as we can. You had a pretty intense moment there with Grant. Are you OK?"

"Yes, I think I am," I whispered. "I had to let Grant go, for his sake."

"Safira, why are you tormenting yourself and him? You're running in a circle."

"I don't know how to keep him, fight a war, and be a warrior and a lover."

"Then you must get him back, let him help you with that. You don't have to control everything."

"Do you remember Mr. Scott? He lived across from us in Glendale."

"Yes. What about him?"

"Mr. Scott would go the city homeless shelter every morning to find somebody he could help. People took advantage of him a lot, but he didn't care. When he died, he was alone and forgotten."

"That's really a sad story." My brother waited for me to continue, puzzled over my change of subject.

"What drives mortals to do what they do? Is it passion? Love? Endurance and fulfillment? Even without a reward,

Mr. Scott was happy. He was happy to do what he did without any expectations. His story isn't sad, not for him. The sad ones are the people who he helped and they didn't pay it forward. *I* didn't pay it forward."

"Those are deep thoughts. How do they relate to this situation?" Octavian softly asked sensing my deep sadness.

"Why can't someone like Mr. Scott receive my gift? What about Doctor Samson, Paul and Julia, and kind Mr. Benson? Why do I have this gift if I can't save the people I care about? I just don't want to lose Grant like that."

"I understand your pain, but mortals cannot taste immortality—we can't interfere in their destiny."

"Too late for that, isn't it? We already did—that's why we have the Amestec. Now we need to eliminate the particular Amestec who sent the hybrids to attacked Doctor Simpson, than find and kill Milos Martuzon. He's mine to kill. Octavian, promise me this—I'm strong enough to kill him myself, aren't I?"

"Yes you are, Safira," agreed my brother, "you are one feisty, incredible powerful warrior. Immortal and Amestec—they all know that."

My brother stood up and took a Wilson SDS and a CQB out of the waist band of his pants, placing his favorite guns on the coffee table, but hiding the sword under it. "Safira, do you think Lord Martuzon is here, in Atlanta?"

"I don't sense his physical presence around me—I just sense his soldiers. I can only assume by the nationality of his men that he's in Transylvania or Romania. At least we can start there. Start searching–we may need to leave the country."

I was sure that his villainous and dark presence was nowhere near me.

"Octavian, other Immortals are being hunted down and slain–I feel it in my spirit. It's happening everywhere."

28

THE BITTER TASTE IN MY mouth didn't disappear. I couldn't forgive the death of Doctor Samson and I struggled with the need for revenge. I felt ready for a fight.

Lord Martuzon had killed me once, and also my mortal friends, and he stopped me twice from loving the ones who I desired the most: first, Andreas and now, Grant. That was too much disappointment for me to take, too much to allow to go unpunished. I was ready to fight him and I felt powerful enough to kill him.

The sound of the doorbell startled me. Lord Arthur ran to the door, barking bravely and warning of uninvited guests. For a split second I wanted it to be Julian, but it was Detective Morris.

I handed him the security tapes and he thanked me for them. He handed me his business card and promised to call and keep me informed. He seemed reluctant to leave, but he couldn't seem to think of another reason to stay, and I was more anxious to have a conversation with the new hybrid.

He was laid out in the basement's hidden closet, on the cold cement beside Marin. I dragged him out into the hallway by his legs. The impact of the accident had broken four of his ribs, his right leg in two places, and his right shoulder. His right lung was punctured and his liver was lacerated.

A mortal wouldn't have survived those wounds for as long as this hybrid had. He didn't have a pulse, but I knew he was still alive. I lifted his head and propped him up against the wall.

"What's your name?" I asked, as I touched his forehead to awaken him. I was determined to force him to tell me everything he knew about Lord Martuzon. He didn't answer, so I decided that he didn't speak English. I repeated the question in Romanian.

"*Cum te chiama?* (What's your name?)"

"Mircea," he answered in his native language. "Are you going to heal me?"

His dark eyes were imploring.

"How do you know I can do that?"

"I was told that an Immortal called the Healer can do this for us," he answered obediently, taking long pauses between his words. "I was told that if we are wounded and she touches us, we will receive healing and true immortality."

I stood over him as he tried to reach for me with his left hand.

"Who told you this, Mircea?"

"*She* did…"

A chill spread through my entire body. I thought that he was still delirious and not able to comprehend my question, so when I repeated the question, I received an identical answer.

"Who is she, Mircea? What's *her* name?"

Mircea couldn't respond. Darkness absorbed his mind for another moment.

"Does she look like me?" I asked, with much more firmness in my voice.

"Not at all. My commander calls her 'Mother'. *She* sent him to find you because he could trace your scent."

I was completely surprised and unprepared for his answer. I rose and walked away from him for a moment. If you know your enemy, he is easy to defeat, but if you have no knowledge of his existence, ignorance will bring you down. At that moment I couldn't comprehend what I had just heard. I signaled for my brother to listen to our conversation, and I powered up the camera and the monitor.

"What is your story, Mircea?"

He answered me with another silence.

"If you want me to heal you, I expect a little cooperation from you."

He lay there, inert, for almost five minutes. I thought he had drifted into unconsciousness again, but he began to speak.

"A few days after I got out of the army in Romania, a nice lady who appeared to be very wealthy came to me and offered me a lot of money to work for her. I was poor and my family was poor. She promised me and the others in my squadron a long life. I believed her, and it has been more than a year since she transformed me into her soldier.

"My brother is waiting at home in Oradea to join me here. She brings more and more of us here each year. She told us that you are even more powerful than she is, and that you do not die, even if we harm you. She needs you for *them*."

"Them? Who's the 'them', Mircea?"

"They are just a few in number, but they are her real children, especially *one* that she favors. Some of them were wounded and they died. She tried to heal them, but she cannot do that, so that is why she is hunting you. But what they really want with the soldiers is to go to war and take over Lichtenstein, and eventually build a superpower with more of them becoming Immortals. Only six of us and one of them were sent to find you and take you to Greece."

"To Greece? Is the man in charge of your army tall and swarthy, with long brown hair and green eyes?"

Mircea shook his head.

"No, his skin is very fair, his hair is a dirty blonde color, and he's very wealthy."

243

Could I be wrong about all this? Lord Martuzon and his army of hybrids weren't in Transylvania, but in Greece, and Prince Albert was in charge of them. Perhaps the Prince was helping Milos to search for me, while they plotted to start a war against Lichtenstein and his father. That was quite plausible.

But who was *she*, the female hybrid maker?

"I am telling the truth," continued Mircea. "My commander, Marcu, is at the Save Rite warehouse; he detected your scent in this town."

"Where's your home in Greece?"

"Polihrono. I do not want to be like this any longer," pleaded Mircea. "I am losing all the memory I ever had of my family. Can you make me like I was before? Please, I just want to be healed and transformed to my old self."

"This is terrible, Safira," said my brother who came down in the basement to join me. "He's not a mortal any longer and you can't bring him back to real life."

That was true. Perhaps because he was newly transformed, he still desired to be the way he was before. But I remembered how disconnected from humanity Gelu and Marin were, and I knew that my brother was right.

"I'm sorry, Mircea, but I can't make you mortal again, but I will give you immortality."

The young man smiled at me. Death is not always eternal–not around me. Soon, more will join him. Our enemies just multiplied. But mortal or not, we must take them all down.

"Did you hear Mircea," I said as I slammed the computer desk forcefully with my fists. "A female, possibly an Amestec with forbidden gifts, made the hybrids that Prince Albert commands. It drives me crazy that I can't determine who she is."

"At this point in time it's not relevant," replied my brother as he tried to calm me down. "It could be a diversion to throw you off."

"The only other explanation is that perhaps the female is Lord Martuzon's daughter–she could have inherited some of his powers. It's possible that she lured Prince Albert, who has the money, to help them capture me in exchange for an army, revenge and immortality–everybody wants immortality. Besides, Mircea just confirmed to me that Marcu, one of her offspring, is his commander, and my hunter."

"Damn, Amestec," exploded Octavian, extremely furious.

"Octavian, we need to get ready immediately," I interrupted him, a bit nervous. "If they want to invade Liechtenstein, we must stop that at any cost. Serban told me long ago that the Secret Mountain is there, where all the other Immortals found shelter and Warriors are among them. We can't allow Lord Martuzon with his Amestec offspring, Prince Albert, and his army to gain access to them–they will take them down. This army is not about capturing me; it's about hunting all of us. Our war just got a little wider."

"Are you going to defend a place that exiled the Warriors for the second time?" asked Octavian sarcastic.

"We were at fault. We are leaving tomorrow morning."

I left the basement in a hurry with my brother following me. We were both angry because we felt betrayed and weakened before the real battle started. It gave me no satisfaction to admit that I might have to shed some of my dignity as a proud warrior and play tricks if I wanted to be a winner.

"Octavian! How would you feel about a major makeover?" I asked him abruptly.

"What are you talking about?" Octavian's expression changed and he began to look worried.

You need to get ready for the summer with some highlights in your hair." I said softly and waiting for his negative reaction.

"This is crazy," my brother exclaimed indignantly. "What's this about? I can't color my hair. It's ridiculous!"

"You can't go into the snake's pit looking like an Immortal," I stood my ground. "Our look is giving us away. I need your help, Octavian, and I need for you to be alive. Looking like you do now, you're a very visible target and all the Half-Immortals will try to kill you. You're the only one who can bring me back to life if I'm killed again. So please, humor me with this small favor."

My brother put his hand on my shoulder, and then he touched my forehead with his two fingers, the way I would do with him.

It was the old symbol for calming and healing the spirit.

"I must see Julian Grant," I said to him. I got in the Land Rover and drove away. There was no book of wisdom in existence for an Immortal to follow. I had rules for my life, but no spiritual strength to stop the path to a relationship with a mortal. We, of all people, should be wise and self-controlled. Were we? Not hardly.

Now I was Eve, looking at the beautiful apple with lust, and my hand was in the air, ready to touch it and claim possession of it.

29

JULIAN'S GRANDMOTHER CAME TO THE door with a wooden spoon in her hand. The bowl of the spoon was red, with bits of mushrooms sticking to it, so it was obvious that she was making spaghetti sauce. I tried to introduce myself but she took me by the arm and led me inside the house as soon as she saw me. Contrary to my expectations she was also tall for a lady of seventy years, but she was still very slim, with naturally blonde hair and hazel eyes.

"Hello Safira, please make yourself at home! Julian is outside working in the back yard..."

"How do you know who I am?" I asked her, sincerely surprised.

"How do you think?" she answered, motioning for me to follow her into the kitchen. "He can't stop talking about you since he came to visit me. It's so wonderful to have him here with me—he's gone so much, I only get to see him once a year. I think he came back home just for you, but I'm so grateful for that."

"Oh, I am sure he enjoys being with you…"

"Well, my dear, Julian's my only grandson, and no matter how old he gets, I'll always think of him as 'my grandchild'. But don't tell him I said that. I'll go outside and let him know you're here. He's repairing my fence. The boy who cuts my grass always manages to break something."

"That's all right," I said quickly. "If you don't mind, I'll just go on out to see him."

I loved to be outside. It was my favorite place to be, because I was kept as a prisoner by Lord Martuzon for so long. I love the fresh air and the sound of the wind. The wind has its own language, one I can understand. There are sounds and whispers that every current of air makes, and each one has a particular meaning—sometimes danger or sometimes peacefulness. The wind has its own way of telling the future.

I sat on the top step of the porch, watching Julian repairing the fence. He was an excellent carpenter and he knew exactly what he was doing. He was quite handsome in his jeans and a t-shirt that was too tight for his abundant muscles. His arms and his chest were muscular without being overwhelming.

What plausible pretext could I find to not love this man or to turn his heart away from me? Was I here just to convince myself that I had made a mistake? I encouraged my brother to fall in love with a mortal and he was bold enough to accept it.

Me—I was running in circles!

A wonderful breeze flirted with my face and body. I closed my eyes.

The sun of that late April afternoon was quite perfect in warming me. At that moment, a vivid memory from my past made me smile—the first time I was freed from Milos's palace and I was with my brothers. I spent that whole day outside lying in the grass and smiling at the sun. It felt so wonderful. The wind had rumpled my hair, but I really wasn't worried about how that made me look.

I loved for the wind to caress my hair—but maybe it wasn't the wind I was feeling.

Through my half opened eyes I saw Andreas standing over me. His face was so close to mine, and I could smell a strong scent of lilac flowers on his skin. This is the scent of Immortals. We were alone for the very first time, without Serban's watchful presence to protect me from his love.

The spell that I felt the first night we met produced a strong and almost painful desire for him. He gently stroked my face and my breasts; and his beautiful lips were searching for mine, just as mine searched for his.

My whole body trembled wanting him, and when Andreas removed my dress I wanted him to possess me totally and completely. I opened my eyes widely to see his face radiating with passion.

But it wasn't Andreas I was seeing—it was Julian. My memory of Andreas brought as much pain as it did pleasure. I wished I could hide the tears that escaped my eyes without restraint.

"Safira!" Julian voice was a soft whisper of love.

I could distinguish one man from the other, but I couldn't separate my love for them. I took Julian's face in my hands and kissed him. I kissed the man I love now like I kissed the man I loved once, long ago. It really didn't matter that one man was exchanged for another in my mind.

"I'm so happy you came to see me. I thought I had lost you..."

"I came to see you, because I owe you an apology," I said as I stood up. "I wish I knew what to do about us, but I don't. The truth is that I shouldn't even be here with you. Pretty much everything is against us being together."

"That's not true. Safira, I'm in your life for a reason and for a time like this. You can't get rid of me."

"I also came to say good bye. Tomorrow I'll be flying to Greece with Octavian. We don't have any time to waste—things will escalate and get worse the longer we wait. I know what they're planning to do, and if they succeed, it'll be a disaster for everyone in Liechtenstein."

Julian backed up, a bit puzzled by my change of attitude.

"I'm coming with you. Safira, please, let me call in some of my men. They're extremely loyal and they love to fight. I can get you some help, at least to fight the hybrids—we can easily do that."

"Julian, I can't allow mortals to be involved in this. I'm sorry."

"You can, but you don't want to. Isn't that it?"

Another quiet moment was interrupted by his grandmother, who opened the sliding glass door.

251

"Safira, would you like to stay for dinner? My spaghetti sauce is the best in the south."

"I believe it is, Mrs. Grant, but I really must go. Can I get a rain check? I do love spaghetti and any other Italian dish…"

"Sure, you're welcome here anytime," she said, satisfied by this little victory.

"Please, give me one more chance," asked Julian softly. "Let me drive you home."

I followed him outside to my truck parked on the side of the house. He barely waited for me to get seated before he turned the ignition key. His muscles were tense and his face was sweaty.

"Safira, are you all right?"

"Yes, I am. It's the calm before the storm, or in my case it's the calm before the war."

"There's nothing calm about it," he exploded. "Why are you doing this? Why are you going there? It looks to me like Lord Martuzon's luring you into a trap so he can snatch you again."

"This is what I do," I said without looking at him. "They want to attack and take over Liechtenstein, the secret shelter of the order of Immortals. They want to hunt them down and in the process more innocent mortals are going to die."

"I just want to understand…" Grant's voice diminished in power as he could not ask any more questions.

"This moment in time was long ago predicted for me—my mother warned me about it," I stubbornly continued. "These people have powers that mortals can't defeat. Through my birth, I'm indestructible and born to stand against them. You took an oath once to protect your country and its freedom. I am a soldier too, and my oath is to protect mankind. I must make a stand against this enormity. There's no one else who can. I am a Warrior, Julian."

"Now I understand," he answered plainly.

"You do?"

* * *

In spite of the heavy traffic and the distance between our homes, we arrived at my driveway too quickly. I wanted our time together to last as long as possible. I quickly glanced at Doctor Samson's house, now abandoned by all the living. The curtains had been closed and all the doors were locked indefinitely. A for sale sign had appeared in the front yard already.

When I turned my head in the other direction, Grant took my hand in his and kissed it.

"This is what a gentleman would do with a lady in your time, isn't it? You were in the company of prince and kings, and you still look as if you belong to those times. Safira, you told me your story, even though it was hard for me to understand. I thought to myself then that there must be a reason you wanted me to know who you really are, even though you keep pushing me away.

"It was strange that we met that day in Germany. I felt so stupid then, and I know I'm still stupid now—who am I to be loved by you? When you came to my house today, I felt like a miracle had happened. Then, when you kissed me, I was sure you were thinking of Andreas, but you definitely kissed *me*! So, this is my declaration—I will fight *with* you and I will fight *for* you..."

"Julian..." I struggled to say something less encouraging.

"I could have died a million times, already. I'm a Navy SEAL, specially trained for danger. You don't have to push me away or keep me away from danger, just to protect me. We die, Safira, all people die in the end..."

"And I am to stay alive and suffer when you die? I do have feelings, Julian. I'm not an inhuman droid."

"What are your feelings for me right now? Please tell me!"

As I was about to answer him, Octavian returned home with Nelda following him in her white Acura convertible. The highlights in his hair changed him completely, giving him a more popular and softer look. He was not all that striking anymore and his blue eyes were less intense. I knew this was a good transformation, but I knew he didn't like it.

He jumped out of the Jaguar and helped the girl to get out. Nelda went into his arms immediately.

Julian and I watched them in silence. Perhaps they weren't aware of us sitting in the truck, but knowing my brother, I'm sure he knew that we were there. They didn't care. It was a beautiful scene to see them together in the dimming light.

Octavian bent her gently against the car and their two bodies touched and connected, almost as if they were just one. Their lips crushed against each other's in an exuberant movement, restless and hungry for more. I knew immediately that my brother had not behaved himself and most likely they just had made love.

Yes, this was the calm before the storm, the love before the war.

"She's quite young," said Julian, still holding my hand in his.

"And he's very old," I answered, trying to smile. "This is not an ordinary matter. I don't think we feel love any differently—in a way, we were made to love mortals."

"I highly recommend you using me as an experiment," offered Julian, caressing my hair.

"I might consider your offer, after I return from Greece," I answered, knowing that my return might not happen.

"This means you're going to make love with me?" Grant's body tensed for a moment under the influence of such desirable suggestion. "Why wait that long? You know, in my world, the tradition is that we are supposed to make love after a fight."

"We did not fight. Is this all you think about and all you want from me?"

"Safira, you know that I want a lot more from you. Obviously you put passion in everything you do. I want to be your man, to be loved by you even for a day. I know that I may not have too much time left since you must choose someone of your kind, but now, here, this is my moment and I don't want to waste it. Please, let me come with you."

"No. I won't let you see me fighting like that. You've already seen me doing horrible things, but nothing like this. Our swords do one thing only–behead–and that's not pretty. Julian, I can't endanger your life."

"If this is what you want," he answered, sounding extremely disappointed. "But I can get you some help – you can't fight and win this war by yourself."

Of course I could–I didn't need anyone's help–but there was no way I could convince Julian otherwise.

Julian kissed my hand again. I got out of the truck feeling that my body was unattached to my spirit. I wanted him so badly that I made him a promise I couldn't keep.

30

THE ENTIRE BAG OF POPCORN was empty. I had eaten it all, and I didn't offer to share it with either Julian or Octavian, like I had done before.

I got a glimpse of Julian, who was sitting beside Lord Arthur on the patio and talking intensely into his cell phone.

"It's settled, I'm coming with you," he said, closing the patio door behind Lord Arthur. "I called three of my men—Pollack, Conrad and Hamilton. I told them about the villain Prince Albert, and about his imminent intent to attack his former country. They all agreed to join me and you, to eliminate him. I told them that you are some sort of government experiment, a super fighter—that's something appealing to them."

"Julian, this is not a joke! You could be court martialed."

"Yes, I know. Now, it all depends if you succeed. Also, one of our bases is in St. Nikolaos, Greece; we could get passes to cover ourselves."

"Wait! Why do you think your men will do this?"

"You know, we the mortals have honor and courage too. Well, I guess I've got to go and pack my things," he said, getting ready to leave.

"Please, Julian, reconsider," I begged as I followed him to the garage door. "This is a very dangerous mission."

"I'll be here at 0600!" he said, before the door slammed. I was still speaking as I heard him speed off in my truck.

"He'll be here in the morning," conformed my brother, as he opened a big plastic container of rifles for me.

"This is a mistake for Julian to come with me," I said and the frustration almost made me cry.

"Let him be, he's right," responded my brother, unsympathetic to my whining. "I located Prince Albert's mother. You are not going to like this. Her name is Anna Martuzon, she was born in Transylvania and she's from a royal family. Can you believe it?"

"Of course," I murmured thoughtfully. My hands shook for a moment and I put down the gun I was inspecting. "I am not surprised at all to hear that. If she's Milos's half- immortal daughter, I am certain she had an affair with an Immortal. After they fell in love, she had only one thing in mind – to kill him and gain full immortality."

"This means that Albert ..."

"... is half-immortal," I finished my brother's sentence. "He is Amestec, and he is Lord Martuzon's grandson. Now it's all clear. This is how they're all connected—they are a big happy family. The mystery is solved. All the signs were there for me to be suspicious of him. How could I have been so blind and not to have seen him for what he was?"

"Are you certain?" Octavian shook his head, wanting to dismiss my findings.

"Yes, I am certain—I met this man face to face. That explains why the Prince is planning a war against his father, the King of Lichtenstein. Not only for revenge, but to hunt the Immortals. His mother's hiring former soldiers from her country, Transylvania, and they're being made into hybrids. If I am not mistaken, he's also looking for the lost swords.

"Having the swords will give him unlimited power over all Immortals. All will fear him and surrender to him. His mother has a few more children that are looking for immortality and even if they acquire it by killing the old ones, they still need me, the only Healer. And of course, Milos just wants me back to be his wife.

"Octavian, go ahead and move the plane—we're flying out from Newnan airport, so make sure we're loaded."

I went upstairs to my bedroom, trying to calm my body and my spirit from the tension of this revelation about Prince Albert as a dangerous half-immortal and his immortal mother. Everything made sense, now. They were related to Lord Martuzon, so they were the very first to learn about my existence and hunt me down.

I remembered then that I must go and capture Marcu. If I was right about his mother, then he is also Lord Martuzon's grandson. I changed clothes and put on my red dress.

Before I got into the Jaguar, I grabbed a long cylindrical hard paper tube with my sword hidden inside.

* * *

Thomas Crossroads, between Peachtree City and Newnan, is a strange intersection, with three gas stations, three banks and three pharmacies on the four corners. One of the pharmacies, a Save Rite, was abandoned and was now being used by Marcu. The abandoned Save Rite is behind one of the banks that had a real estate office and a car wash attached to it.

I parked the car away from the security light and I merged into the shadows, walking slowly to the building. There was a little light coming from a low watt bulb in a fixture in the back of the store, but it wasn't strong enough to show any activity on inside. But I don't need light to function.

I sensed some movement in the building as I stood in the driveway. Perhaps Gelu was still with Marcu. The door was unlocked, so I knew they were waiting for me. I walked inside, laid my sword by the door, and walked toward one of the cubicles on my right, but I didn't sense any eminent danger.

Marcu was seated in a chair that he had pulled up to a small table, with a booted up laptop's light reflecting off his face. He was looking at the screen showing all the kidnapped girls' pictures, including mine.

He had fair skin and long, shoulder length curly blonde hair. He was quite handsome, slim, and with a clear face—he was only seventeen years old—but his eyes were deep and lifeless. He didn't blink and he didn't have the mark on his neck.

This time I could sense that he was an Amestec—one of *hers*.

"I should have known better," he said, as I approached him. "All these girls were missing your 'scent', even though they all met your description. It confused me. Then, we went to the wrong house because that stupid Manea couldn't remember where he'd been stored for almost a week. And now, here you are.

"We've been looking for you for more than fifty years, tracking down the rumors that you really did exist. Some of the older Amestec from Germany and Austria said they had even seen you in the flesh, but they lost your trail after a while. In time, we viewed these sightings as "old man visions". The Irish Amestec didn't care about you very much. They had their hands full, hunting and killing Immortals on their land."

"Why are *you* looking for me?" I asked, standing firm in front of him.

The question was tricky and I wasn't expecting an answer from him, but I got one, anyway.

"We have searched for you since the first one of us died. In spite of us being half-immortal, we still die like any other mortals. We have the gift of staying young, which would be extraordinary if we were females, but as males, we want to live long, be strong, and have the whole world at our feet. Each of us wants to rule a country of our own. We are about to become a new force in the world. These are our desires…"

"All right, I've got the picture," I interrupted him annoyed.

"...and to have a beautiful woman at our side," he continued calmly. "None of us want just any kind of woman; we all want the only one in the world, the Immortal Healer. All of us have our dream of finding her."

"Apparently you're the lucky one. Who's your father?"

"He's not who you think. My father was a plain Greek mortal with a good material situation, and my mother has had several husbands. I have many half-brothers and sisters, and I'm the youngest."

"Then, how's your mother making these hybrids?" I asked, a little puzzled about his easiness in conversing with me.

"It has been said that my mother was once married to an Immortal and she killed him—at least, that's how I remember the story. Now she's immortal and she has some powers, but they're not nearly like yours." So, I was right about her, and how she became a hybrid maker.

"You are the only Immortal Healer," continued Marcu, quite confident. "Can you imagine having somebody under your control who can heal any kind of wound and resist fire, bullets, and explosions? The possibilities would be limitless, and having you near us would be priceless."

"What if they lied to you?"

I felt a little thrill in starting to play my game with him. He was also playful and lively. Unfortunately, in a few minutes, one of us would be no more.

"Well, I am sure they did lie a little to me, but I'm willing to take my chances with you." His friendly posture was a reflection of his real feelings of happiness and the sensual pleasure he received just from looking at me.

"Immortality comes in two ways," I said impatiently. I felt a strange sympathy for this young man and I needed to remain calm. "You can either kill me or I can kill you and bring you back as a true immortal. But before you decide what you want to do about that, tell me—what about your oath? What if your mother and your siblings hunt you down because you didn't bring me back to them?"

"Safira, what are you doing? This isn't part of the plan!" I heard my brother's frantic comments in my ear. "I'm on my way to the warehouse. Finish him fast!"

"I suppose the chances are that they will hunt me down, but I have you, don't I?" Marcu's face suddenly became radiant.

"Still," I said, "there are too many to battle when they become your enemy—plus your mother, Prince Albert, and your grandfather, Milos Martuzon. What will you do?"

Marcu became visibly angered and the mention of Albert's name made him tremble. Now I knew about him with certainty. The prince was the one who was most powerful and who was most feared by all. But Marcu didn't seem to know too much about Lord Martuzon.

"I know what you're trying to do," he said. "You want to test my loyalty to them and you think I'll fail that test."

"I'm not worried about them. I'm testing your loyalty to me."

"Did I fail the test?"

I nodded, so he reached under his chair for a hidden pistol. He got up, passed by me and before I could *look*, I heard shots fired in the next cubical. Marcu had shot Gelu (Manea was his real name), but the hybrid got up from the floor with his chest full of bullets and picked up a sword, the same one he used with me in the park, and attacked Marcu.

The Amestec grabbed his own sword that he had at the ready and they fought. Judging by the look of their weapons, they seemed to be more recent copies of my own sword. It took just a few minutes of fighting before Marcu swung his sword in its fatal arc and Gelu's head dropped to the floor.

I wasn't wrong–Gelu was harder to kill this time, after we had revived him. During the fight I observed Marcu's fighting skills, and I analyzed his style and weaknesses. I saw that when he was fighting, he frequently looked at me and he lost focus. His eyes had changed color and they were green again.

"I hated him, anyway," he said, returning to me.

I looked into Marcu's eyes, trying to read his emotions. I had known for so long that an instable soul has no wish for the good of others–only for itself.

He was lusting for me and lusting for the gift of having me exclusively, regardless of the oath he took. Perhaps I shouldn't be so harsh with him. He was so young. But why had they sent him? Perhaps it was because he wasn't as desperate as the others. They had sent him as collateral, an easy target and bait for me to follow his story back to them.

"What have you decided?" I asked, as I pulled up my dress a few more inches.

He came even closer to me and annoyingly inhaled my scent—lilac flowers that had freshly bloomed in the spring. I felt that if I wasn't so threatening to him, he would most likely attempt to make love to me.

"I will allow you to choose, my Lady!"

I grabbed his pistol and shot out all the lights. The Save Rite wasn't completely dark. A bit of light was coming from the exit sign. I rapidly ran towards the door to retrieve my sword. My shoes fell from my feet as I leaped into the air and over Marcu's head.

He was right behind me, attacking my back with his sword with a remarkable capability of fighting in the dark. He positioned himself between me and the door, swinging the sword towards my head as I defended myself, unarmed.

My eyes were adjusting to the gloom, allowing me to see him and his position in the room. Four more times his sword tried to reach me with an incredible slicing power, forcing me to stay ahead of his movements. It was imperative that I get to my weapon, and I needed to disarm him of his by distracting his attention.

His hands were maneuvering his sword with a swiftness that belied his age. I could hear the sound of the blade whistling through the air. It missed me because I floated in the air, from one wall to the other. I avoided his wrath by defying gravity, but when my eyes were totally lit, he lowered his sword for a second to stare at me.

"So amazing!" he exclaimed in awe. "I want those eyes."

"Then I will give them to you."

But before he could respond, my body flew into the air again. My right foot smashed into the hand that was holding his weapon. As I grabbed his sword, I rotated my body to gain more leverage. Arching my sword horizontally, I terminated him by decapitation. When his head rolled across the floor there was no blood.

I immediately got on my knees and grabbed the head by its hair. I attached it to his neck and I touched the cut with my finger as I seen Octavian doing it before. His skin reattached itself without a trace.

He still had that bemused expression on his face, as if his eyes were still seeing me freshly, beyond death.

"He made his choice," I said to my brother, who came inside the Save Rite a few minutes later and found me still on the floor. His eyes had lit, too, and he was holding my sword. "This was too easy", I said. "He was good, but too inexperienced."

"It wasn't easy, Safira—you fought him unarmed! I see you got my healing skill, but now we need to take him home. I heard a gun being fired a couple of times."

"He shot Gelu and then killed him with his sword. I was right, Octavian—the Amestec don't show loyalty to anybody. They don't have any dignity—he attacked me from behind! There are fourteen of them left, and Prince Albert is their mighty Amestec ruler."

"Hurry Safira," my brother said as he lifted Marcu's body to his shoulder. "Find your shoes and take care of

Gelu. We need to leave immediately. There's always a police car watching this intersection."

31

JULIAN GRANT STOPPED IN FRONT of our house half an hour early. He must have had an anxious night following his conversation with his guys and he probably didn't get very much sleep. He rang the bell at the gate and when I opened it to let him in he parked my truck in the garage, got out, and waited for us there.

"This will be a fun ride," said Octavian, getting into the driver's seat of the truck.

Grant and I got in the Hummer with me behind the wheel. Mircea and Gelu were in the back seat with us, and the other four hybrids were in the truck with Octavian. Grant raised his index and middle fingers to his forehead in a salute, but he said nothing. The sight of the people that he knew were dead and now were alive again seemed to take him aback, and he was deep in thought.

It was a quiet drive to the Newnan airport, twenty minutes to the south of Peachtree City. I didn't attempt to start a conversation—I had more urgent thoughts on my mind than to start explaining to Grant my plans for this mission, so I left him in peace.

On the night before, we put the hybrids who had invaded the Samson house and the Amestec in our closet. The necks of the hybrids had been engraved with the same letter A, the sign of their transformation and most likely a mark that they belong to Prince Albert.

My night was restless and I had slept poorly. Marcu was not the first half-immortal I had ever killed, but doing that was very different from killing hybrids.

I felt that I had a stronger connection with Marcu than with the hybrids because he attached himself to me so easily. The hybrids were cold and unfeeling, but the Amestec was more emotional–uncommitted, but ready to experience the great mystery ahead of him. I had expected that killing him would bring a sense of relief to me, but I came home without the feeling of gratifying achievement.

"Are we doomed?" I had asked my brother while we were trying to decide how to dispose of their bodies. "We're going to engage in a war that was prophesied to us so long ago, and we have no more of an army than we had in 1885. Even Grant would call this a suicide mission."

"We can revive the hybrids and use them as our own soldiers," suggested Octavian. "They'll be loyal to you forever. Gelu was loyal in his own strange way, even if the consequences were terrible. I'm sure he deliberately gave them wrong information when they went to the Samson's house."

Uppermost in my mind was the thought that a mysterious Healer was an imposter and that made me angry and anxious, too. I didn't care who *she* was, but she and her wicked sons must be terminated without a trace. She gradually faded from my thoughts as I devised my battle strategy.

Indeed, it was sad to have killed Marcu, but I had become accustomed to terminating Amestec, like everything else I had been dealing with over the years, even losing my dear mortal friends. The suffering and pain that came from those experiences helped me to remain human in my immortality.

My long life was filled with events, ordinary and extraordinary, and those matters were related to my skills. My mission was what defined me, and it should always be for the good of others. That was my own war, a new kind of war.

"Revive them all except Marcu," I said, approving of my brother's suggestion. "Later we'll see about their loyalty. Cut their hair short so we can easily identify them. And we must be sure that none of them remain alive after we use them."

"The girls, too?" he asked. "Those girls are so pretty. What a pity!"

"I'll revive the girls and Gelu. This will be his second revival. Yes, the girls' hair will have to be bobbed, too."

Until yesterday, I thought that it was only Milos Martuzon's plot to capture me again and hold me hostage for his own benefit or for the benefit of his offspring.

Now, nothing was as it appeared to be—nothing!

* * *

It was daylight, now, and I drove the Land Rover directly to our jet. Octavian had made arrangements the previous night to have it fueled up and ready for us early this morning.

"What are you doing?" asked Julian, observing my maneuvering to drive the vehicle into the back of our jet. The others were using the stair on the side. "This is a BBJ."

"Yeah, it's a BBJ transformed to take cargo," I responded. "We can land this plane at the city airport, and we're taking the Rover with us. I had this vehicle in Germany, remember? It's loaded with weapons and it's armored."

"How do you plan to get into a foreign country with all this containers full of rifles?"

"Well, we are just going to drop them there—from the air."

As the rear of the plane was closing behind us, we got out of the car and made our way to the cabin. I sat down in one of the leather chairs next to the cockpit and put my purse beside me.

Octavian stepped into the cockpit, sat down in the captain's chair and started the engines, while the hybrids were taking their seats behind me. Julian remained standing, like he was waiting for something.

"You'd better sit down and buckle your seat belt, Grant," said Octavian, "I'll be taking off in two minutes."

"Who's flying this plane? Don't we need some pilots?"

"Relax, Commander," smiled my brother. "I've been flying since 1932. Don't worry–this one almost flies by itself, anyway."

Julian took a seat across from me. We buckled our seat belts, but we still didn't talk. We had seven hours to fly before we arrived at our destination, and I could feel that his mind was still a bit unsettled. For the first thirty minutes he tried hard to stay quiet. We glanced at each other from time to time out of the corners of our eyes, and I could easily guess that he was either terrified of my brother flying the plane or because the hybrids were in the back.

After a smooth take off we reached cruising altitude, and he started to relax–maybe a little too much. He was asleep on and off for the next seven hours.

* * *

"We're here!" said Octavian as he left the cockpit. "We are over Polihrono. Safira, I think you need to come down to just four thousand feet. That'll still give you enough air speed to land in Thessaloniki."

I exchanged places with my brother. The local time was shortly after nine in the evening. It was dark and slightly overcast, perfect for our little intrusion from the sky.

"Grant I need you in here with me. Octavian and the hybrids are going to parachute with the ammunitions and do surveillance."

"Can you jump from this altitude?" asked Grant, a bit distracted.

"Yes, even you could, too", said my brother, impatient. "Now, please step inside the cockpit – Safira needs to open the hatch. It's automatic and you don't want to get sucked out with us."

Julian came into the cockpit and took the co-pilots seat. He seemed to have that hostile attitude on his face again. I opened the hatch for the hybrids and my brother, and they sailed out in the direction of Prince Albert's compound. Octavian would use his natural powers and his glowing eyes to see all the details and find the precise location of the prince's army, as Mircea had briefed us.

I suspected that the headquarters in the mountains was camouflaging interior tunnels and rooms that we couldn't see. Octavian and the hybrids would wait for us at the established location in town, once this part of the mission was complete.

"We're dropping well," said my brother. "Our cargo is safe." I rolled the plane to the right and headed to Thessaloniki. Thirty minutes later we received permission to land on a private runaway, about nine kilometers from the Macedonia airport.

Grant was quiet, watching me maneuver for a landing. I couldn't tell if there was admiration in his eyes because of my piloting skills, or caution and fear that he might have to take over control of the plane if I botched the job. By the time I powered down the jets, he had made his way to the cargo hold and was already behind the wheel of the Hummer.

I let him drive.

* * *

After we had presented our passports to the local authorities, they checked our car and let us pass.

"Where now?" Julian asked, a little sarcastically.

"To Hotel Anatolia. We're going to spend the night there. In the morning we'll pick up your men at the airport and leave for Polihrono."

"Will you give me a few more details about what we're doing so I won't look totally clueless to my men?" I sensed he was irritated, but I didn't let it get to me.

"Sure. We're going to attack tomorrow night. I'll know more specifics after meeting with Octavian and the *guys*. He'll wait for us at Villa Alexandra. The hybrids can be taken down by guns–that'll be your job, but the prince, all the Amestec, and any immortal that might be there must be engaged with a sword–and that's my job. We need to know everybody's position and then hit hard."

"Wait, I thought we were going to kill Prince Albert while you take care of Lord Martuzon!"

"Prince Albert is a half-immortal–he'll be mine too."

"What? Where did you get that idea?"

"From digging into the prince's family tree," I said, raising my voice a bit. "It's been confirmed that the prince's mother is Lord Martuzon's half-immortal daughter. She probably killed an Immortal to gain true immortality. Since she's a female, she might have some twisted powers she inherited from Milos, who inherited them from me. She's the one who made the hybrids, she's an Immortal, and she's Albert's mother. That's a fact, Julian."

"This is unbelievable," said Grant, becoming agitated as he was trying to read the street names on the GPS. "I'm sorry, Safira. I need a moment to digest all this–that a prince is half-immortal, that I'm here with some strange dead soldiers, an Immortal who flies a plane like he invented it, and his sister who makes a brilliant attack plan like it's nothing."

"I didn't need to make a plan before–I fight alone…"

"I don't doubt you, Safira, and your amazing abilities; don't forget that I'm putting the lives of my men in your hands. I'm trusting that you'll do your best to protect them. I'm just conflicted…but it doesn't matter."

"What would you have me do?" I felt my anger rising, but I did not let it all out. "I'm sorry, Julian, but I can't be your stay at home girlfriend. If you've started to regret coming with me, now's the time to go back to Atlanta. I didn't ask you to come."

As I said this, I heard Octavian's voice in my ear. "We all landed safely. I've got the satellite in position and we're heading to Villa Alexandra. I'll record the information and in the morning I'll rent the helicopter. You two need to make love before this mission is doomed."

"You don't have to listen in anymore, Octavian. I'm turning the transmitter off. We're all safe now," I said, as my frustration found its way into my tone of voice.

* * *

We arrived at Anatolia Hotel close to midnight. We went directly to our rooms with our key cards without exchanging any other comments. Grant's attitude toward me was silence. My last words to him didn't help to create a better atmosphere between us.

We had adjoining rooms and I could hear him pacing back and forth, and that made me feel guilty. I wasn't tired, but I was anxious to shower and change from my dress into something more comfortable. The agitated sounds coming from Grant's room were cutting to my heart.

When I was undressed and ready to step into the shower, I stopped. The sight of my dress lying on the floor brought back the same painful memories of one hundred and twenty five years ago–that moment of my being naked in front of Andreas and kissing him was burning into my soul.

What would it take to suppress that memory?

I slipped my dress back on and went to Julian's door. I got no answer when I knocked, but I knew he was there. I tried knocking a few more times before I turned the door knob. It wasn't locked and as I slowly stepped into the dark room, I saw him sitting on the side of the bed, holding his face in the palms of his hands. He spread his fingers a little and looked at me, but he didn't actually see me.

"You shouldn't be here, Safira," he said as he rose to his feet. "You know what it does to me to be around you."

He wasn't wearing his shirt and his low cut trousers were displaying the well-developed muscles of his abdomen. The sight of his beautiful body made me take longer pauses between each breath.

"I came to make peace." I said, as I remained uncomfortably in the middle of the room. "I don't want you to regret coming with me."

We were still some distance from each other, but our souls and bodies were struggling to stay apart.

"I've never gone on a mission before where someone I love was involved," he began to explain. "I don't know how to act–I don't even know if I'm acting normal. I don't regret coming with you. I know you're trying to keep me away from you because of this war, but I love you, Safira."

I stood there in silence for a few more moments, pretending not to hear his last words. "You'd better turn on some more light in the room, or my eyes will soon be glowing," I said, a little perturbed that my natural gift was coming out when there was no need for it.

He smiled, but he didn't move to the table lamp. Perhaps he wanted to see me like that, enveloped in the shadows. I leaned over to turn on the lamp that was resting on the end table by his bed, but he came closer to me and turned it off again. We were facing each other as his arms wrapped around my waist and he pulled me closer to him.

No, he wasn't the man from my old dream–I was aware of that but it didn't matter–he was the man who loved me.

I reached up and tenderly stroked his face. Both of his hands detached themselves from my waist and began moving down my hips to caress on my legs. He maneuvered my dress over my head and it fell to the floor.

I stood there naked before him, unwilling for him to stop. My breasts were touching his chest, and they soon disappeared entirely into his hands. His lips were softly touching my lips–these memories were drawn from the past, but simultaneously we were creating new ones.

For those moments I was transformed into nothing more than a vulnerable but desired woman, and not an ancient, strange shadow of a forgotten past.

"Julian, what are you doing?" I asked as he became bolder and undressed.

"Love before the war," he answered, and his tongue was invading my mouth. "I want to hold you, to feel you. At this moment you're mine, my love."

He picked me up and held me closely in his arms before he laid me on the bed, and then he stretched his full length out beside me. I felt his erection and sexual tension aroused in my body too.

My body was screaming to be invaded, conquered, and ravished. This time I didn't hold back.

He touched me gently, as his eyes were looking into mine seeking sign of excitement in them. His soft fingers were brushing over my breasts and hips as they slowly approached my lower abdomen. I was a bit tense at first, until my muscles relaxed and I could feel fire burning inside me.

He became more provocative as his tongue followed the same route as his fingers. As his tongue circled my nipples they stiffened, and I could feel them invade his lips.

It was obvious to me that he knew how to awake a woman's sexual instincts.

Finally, I totally relaxed under the tender touch of his hands. He wasn't rushing–just enjoying every caress and every kiss that he gave me in my most intimate places. When his tongue touched my clitoris, it stirred electricity coursing through my veins. I couldn't contain myself any longer. My fingers spread the lips between my legs as they parted widely for him.

"Oh, my God, Safira," he whispered and I felt his hard pressure inside me.

I wanted to scream, but instead I giggled as sweet ecstasy took over my body. His hands held my hips tightly as he gradually increased the movement of his body. My eyes were glowing wildly at times, as we achieved moment after moment of pleasure. Our bodies were sweating vapors as each climax rolled over us.

* * *

In the morning when I awakened, his arms were still around me and his hands followed my motions as I shifted in the bed. It was seven and we needed to be at the airport in two hours.

While Julian still slept, I covered my body loosely with my dress and left his room quietly to return to my room.

My bed was untouched, but I lay on it and stared at the ceiling. My body still felt the moment when we became one–new memories for a new life. I totally gave myself to him and it was wrong–but it felt right.

I showered and dressed–this time in a blouse and jeans.

When I went back to Grant's room again, I didn't knock, but I opened the door and entered. He was about to shower and came towards me completely naked. I pretended not to look, but he took me in his arms. He kissed me so gently, our tongues dancing together as he pushed me against the wall. I could feel his hardness struggling to penetrate me again.

"Why did you leave?" he asked me "If I hadn't found your shoes here, I would have thought that last night was all in my imagination."

"I did forget my shoes, Julian," I said, as reality was setting back in. "Right now we've got to pick up your men. And please, make sure your men take these *strange* things seriously."

"I want you to know," Julian began, "that last night was the most amazing time of my life. There were a few moments when I could hardly believe that you and I were making love over and over…"

"Julian, please, this isn't the time to talk about this…" I said blushing, a little embarrassed that most of the time I was the instigator of all that we did.

"Why not? Last night was proof that even though I'm just a mortal, you wanted *me*.

32

IT WAS A STRANGE FEW minutes of silence, to say the least, after the three Navy SEALs climbed in the back of my Land Rover. I was driving and Grant was sitting beside me. I recognized two of them, Conrad and Pollack, from that night at the farm in Germany, but at first they didn't remember me.

I kept my eye on them in the rear view mirror and I could observe their immediate reaction about me–disbelief and dislike.

"Pollack, Conrad and Hamilton, let me introduce to you to Safira Tash. She's the *guy* in charge of this whole operation," said Grant, as seriously as he could–but he turned and winked slyly at me.

Their surprise because of my presence and identity kept them quiet for the rest of the trip. I was sure they remembered me now and perhaps they even had second thoughts about *volunteering* for this mission with me. As we drove out to the countryside, they all used their cell phones to take a few photos, trying to act indifferent and cool.

I love this part of Greece, called Khalkidhiki, with its curving roads that take you past the most beautiful hills and blue waters. I love the little towns with their pastel colored houses and flat roofs, the wild flowers growing everywhere on the side of the road, and the sunny clear sky. We passed a few ruins, some immense gardens, and a few farmers in trucks who were carting their fruits and vegetable to the larger cities in the area.

The scenery reminded me of my Transylvania, and those memories made me smile. But now my little native province wasn't the way I remembered it, and perhaps I would never return to it. It was just another fond memory to file away in the photo album of my mind.

* * *

Villa Alexandra was a three story structure, on Theopollos street that backed up to the sea. We didn't need all the space in the house, but we did need privacy to prepare for the mission. Octavian had finished installing and displaying his monitors and computers by the time the Hummer drove into the parking area.

None of us had very much luggage, nothing more than a back pack, but I needed to unload our equipment. Once everything was spread out on the floor, the SEALs were surprised.

"There's a lot of weapons and ammo here," said Hamilton, a heavily built African American, rightfully concerned about it.

"Yes, it is, and we'll need all of it," I answered. "We are here to *eliminate* Prince Albert and his soldiers. Nobody will be left alive–this is not your regular surgical strike. Go ahead, start opening the containers."

As the tops of all three containers were unsnapped and their contents were exposed, I continued. "You all know these guns and you know how to use them. The plan for this mission is simple: once you're inside the house and you've gone to specific locations, you just kill whoever comes towards you.

"Don't be distracted by the look of these people–they're all very young, they've got fair skin, and shoulder length light-colored hair. They're nothing like you would expect to see, but they *are* lethal. Some of them will be females. They aren't easily killed, so make sure you fire several rounds into each one. Whatever happens, don't try to take them down by physical force.

"Hamilton, you're a big guy and these people look like they're pushovers, but they're very strong and very capable. Shoot them all, down to the last one–don't leave any of them standing! We've got six of them that are on our side–four males and two females. All of ours will have short hair, so watch out for them.

"We're going to proceed in two groups: all of you with Grant as your leader, and my brother and I will be the other group. There are some forces inside that place that require only my skills."

Pollack couldn't resist a smile.

"I promised Grant I'd make it easy for you, so don't be angry about that. I know you've all done more dangerous missions in the past, but you'll see that what's expected of you here is like nothing you've ever encountered. And it's entirely secret."

I thought, "They won't remember too much about this operation—I'll make sure of it."

I stepped to the back of the living room and into a small kitchen to try to find a coffee maker and satisfy my craving.

"Commander," I heard Hamilton asking, "What's Safira talking about? Who're we fighting here? Who're these soldiers?"

Grant answered slowly and calmly.

"Let's just say that they're an experiment that went wrong. They shouldn't even exist."

"Well, Commander, I see that you found your mysterious Red Cross nurse. So, who the hell is Safira Tash?" asked Pollack, "She's more than an experimental super fighter. I've seen her at work before, in Germany, and she's beyond human. And did you see her brother?"

"Don't worry about her, Pollack. It's time for us to do our part," continued Grant. "We're doing this for the good of humanity. No innocent civilian deserves to die in an act of war. Safira and Octavian may be super fighters but we're soldiers, too. We'll be fast and we'll be strong."

"Sure thing," I heard them all as they agreed.

I made my way from the kitchen out into the courtyard. The six hybrids sitting on the ground rose to their feet at the same time. Whoever had transformed these young people didn't give them immortality, but their humanity was stripped away. All I could see was just their empty corpses that moved like zombies and obeyed commands.

Mircea was the hybrid who had most recently been transformed, and I looked into his eyes to see if they still shone or if they were already hollow. I remembered his cry for healing and mortality.

"Mircea, look at me! These are your orders–protect the mortals at any cost. Do you understand me?"

"Yes, Lady Safira," he responded, bowing again. He knew who I really was.

"You're in charge of your soldiers now. After we kill the enemy, be sure the bombs are in position. If you survive the fight, I'll reconsider your fate."

"There is no reason for us to exist–we are useless in this world," he murmured. "You can keep us alive but we have lost our souls already. But please, make *her* stop this madness. My brother is in danger."

His eyes stopped shining. These were my soldiers now, and their future had been sealed.

"I *will* stop her," I promised. "You just be sure to follow my orders."

Then I looked into the girls' eyes and I touched their foreheads. I saw that their spirit was gradually awakening. I knew how remarkable their skills were, after battling them in the Samson's house.

"Dana and Dora, you two will fight with me. Come, we need to get ready."

The girls followed me back into the living room, like two shadows. Their soulless devotion was almost impossible for me to comprehend.

"Now, what exactly do you want me to do?" asked my brother, with a bold look on his face.

"You fly the helicopter over the site and land on the roof, than remain there to be our lookout and give us intelligence. The guys will force their way in through the front gate. It's the only way in except from above, and that's where I need to be."

I turned to Grant and the SEALs and continued to elaborate on my plan without hesitation. They were expecting me to be in control and give orders.

"This compound is very isolated and it looks like a typical villa from the outside. The front gate opens onto a courtyard, and from there you make your way inside, to the first floor. Here's how this place is different from a villa—when you gain access to the first floor, infinite corridors built deep inside the mountain will branch off in all directions. These lead to the soldiers' dorms, and according to Mircea, they may have over a hundred hybrids there.

"You've got to move fast because these hybrids don't require sleep, and you'll lose the element of surprise. I'm counting on them coming out of the dorms ready for a fight, so they won't try to take cover. Use that to your advantage."

"So this is like a fortress for them, a military base?" asked Grant, coming closer to the computer screen where Octavian was displaying the floor plan and layout of Prince Albert's home.

"Exactly," I agreed. "They're more prepared to be attackers, rather than being in a defensive mode, but they still have an advantage with their numbers and weapons. Take these devices and put them in your ears–they're close-circuit phones, and we can be in direct contact at all times."

"What about them?" asked Hamilton, pointing with his head toward the hybrids. Mircea, Gelu, Marin and Mircu were standing beside the front door.

"They'll go in first on motorcycles and take out the guards. They don't require any communication with us–they have their orders. You'll be in the Hummer. Remember, shoot and find shelter. No heroism, no hostages, and no mercy. Any questions?"

"What if we're injured?" asked Conrad.

"Let me know immediately so I can come and treat you. If that happens, try to get away from the action and into the Rover–it's armored. If everybody does exactly what I've said, nobody will get hurt."

The SEALs were ready for action. My brother was right–the mortals were courageous in the face of the unknown, even if they couldn't force a change in their destiny.

I was ready to face Milos Martuzon.

* * *

As with everything else I knew that this moment would come, and I had prepared myself for it for more than a century. My spirit would keep me bold and wise, but I didn't expect any enjoyment out of this battle. My powers would overcome everything that would come my way and my instincts would protect me.

"All right, then, everybody choose your weapons and ammunition. We've got plenty of both. As of this moment we are on the countdown."

Grant gazed at me with a mixture of love and concern. I didn't understand his lack of trust in my abilities at all. He had seen me in action, he had seen me doing things beyond a mortal's power, and still, here I was being suffocated by his constant doubt and his self-torment about my safety.

"Safira, may I have a word with you?" requested Grant.

I consented to his request in spite of my better judgment. I knew where all this was going. The SEALs nudged each other as their eyes darted back and forth between Grant and me as Julian followed me to the second floor and into a small bedroom.

"Actually, I wanted to apologize to you," he said, looking straight into my eyes. "I was trying to see the woman I love, but instead I see a warrior who is so much more capable and daring that I could ever dream of being. The truth is that you could never love me–I'll never be worthy of you. I just wanted to let you know that I understand what you think about me and I accept it. If I die in this battle, don't feel bad about it–I love you enough for the both of us."

"Julian, what are you talking about? This is nonsense. You aren't going to die here."

"You let me be near you just because I might look like Andreas, but I'm not Andreas. Last night you made love with *me*."

Grant's tone of voice came across both proud and accusatory. His soul wanted to be satisfied with words of love and comfort, to be redeemed from the agony of doubt.

"I'm sorry", he murmured, "but I love you. What now?"

I looked outside the window. The hybrids were on the motorcycle and the SEALs were getting ready to board the Hummer after loading their weapons and ammunition. From the rooftop I heard the helicopter's engine as it idled in readiness for takeoff.

"It's time to go, now. I'll see you later, Julian. God's speed, Commander."

I turned away from him and left the room. We separated in the hallway, and I went up to the roof while he headed for the street. He didn't need to tell me how he felt–I saw it in his eyes and in his face. Watching him run down on the stairs, I realized that I had gone too far to quickly restore my mind. Whatever I might have sought by allowing him too deeply into my life, *love* was hurting me and affecting my judgment.

Love didn't have an on/off switch for either of us.

As I climbed into the co-pilot's seat I saw Grant turn the ignition key of the Hummer. The roar of the motorcycles was annoying, drowning out even our helicopter noise–that was good, because we could land at the fortress with less chance of being detected.

We lifted off from the roof and I looked below me to see the Land Rover drive down the road behind the hybrids. Dora and Dana were sitting behind me, making no sound and ready to follow my orders to kill those who might have been their own friends and relatives. Fortunately, they had no remorse about it.

In twenty minutes the war would start. How would I be remembered by my fellow Immortals after this battle?

33

"I CAN'T LAND ON THE roof," said Octavian, as the helicopter rose a few hundred feet. "There's another helicopter parked on the right side. You and the hybrids will have to rappel. I'll try to bring you in close enough, but you've got to be fast–this machine isn't state of the art. Hurry, I'll crash it and jump too."

I dropped the ropes and the hybrid females rappelled to the roof. They landed well without hurting themselves.

"Octavian, you'll have to stay in the air as long as you can. Keep your distance and be careful–they've probably set up booby traps. Shoot at whatever you see out there…"

"Safira, you can't fight alone inside! I must come with you!"

"I've got enough help inside. Up here you've got an advantage–you can see and take out those that we're not aware of, and I need your precision. Keep the guys alive!"

"I'll come in as soon as I can. I'll let you deal with Lord Martuzon but Prince Albert is mine."

"OK. God's speed!"

My brother dipped the nose of the helicopter toward the roof again, and I jumped without the rope. I sailed out and flew through the air, twisted in the air to orient myself, and landed on my feet.

Out on the road, the four hybrids abandoned their motorcycles several meters from the house and they walked slowly up the street, two by two. Once they were at the gate, they opened fire randomly, mainly to call attention to themselves. The six hybrid guards from the courtyard were armed with M6 rifles, and they ran to the gate. One of them checked the image on their monitor and he saw the men as they approached the gate. He signaled for the others to take their positions and they opened fire from above the gate. Mircea knew about this strategy and he waited for their heads to peer above the roof line.

One by one, after an intense round of fire, the guards were terminated and Mircea was the first to climb over the heavy metal gate.

As soon as the gate was opened, Grant maneuvered the Rover inside the courtyard. They had about a minute to enter the building and prepare for battle, and I was sure that the first rounds of fire from Mircea's men had awakened most of the enemy soldiers. It would be so convenient if all of the hybrids would come out at once to meet the SEALs' firepower, instead of them having to go inside and hunt the enemy down. Many of them did come out to meet the attack, and they were among the first who were taken out.

The SEALs took their position behind the many stone columns and trees. Only my hybrids weren't concerned about their safety. Each of them was attached to a SEAL, and Mircea was side by side with Grant. When the gunfire started, many of the hybrids toppled into the street, but there were a hundred more inside.

Dana and Dora waited until I positioned the swords on my belt, and then they started to open fire on the door that opened onto the roof. I was sure that by now someone had been sent to protect that entryway, but no one appeared. It was imperative that I get down to that floor immediately, before those who lived there found refuge somewhere else or tried to escape.

I had no choice but to throw a grenade. The blast did little to destroy the door but the hole it made in the wall exposed the soldiers behind it. They fired, and the girls returned their fire.

I had left my gun on the floor of my room at Villa Alexandra, but Dana and Dora were all the firepower I needed. It was totally dark outside–my eyes were like lightening. I easily stopped all the bullets that were trying to reach me with the blade of my sword.

There was an unlimited amount of power that sustained me when my eyes glowed, and that's why I favor fighting in the dark. At the sight of the light coming from my eyes, the hybrids stopped and realized that they were being attacked by three females. In that moment of confusion, Dora and Dana opened fire again, and the soldiers met their fate in a hail of bullets. We went inside, crawling over their bodies, with the girls leading the way.

This was the floor where Lord Martuzon, Prince Albert, his mother, and possibly more Amestec were supposed to be. I heard the commotion on the first floor, but up here, all was quiet. We entered a few empty bedrooms, but they bore the evidence of sudden abandonment.

"Octavian," I signaled to my brother, "there's no one on the third floor. What do you see?"

"Go to the second floor," he answered. "I see movement there, but be careful–more hybrids are moving up toward you."

"Where are the SEALs?" I asked him–I just couldn't force myself to ask about Grant directly.

"We just entered the dorm area," Grant responded to me. "They're smart–they're trying to guess the route we're going to take."

"They aren't smart–they just know how to fight," Octavian answered.

"Try to keep yourselves protected," I said, "and don't go too far down any corridor. Give them time to come out to where you are, and watch your back!"

"Yeah," Grant answered, with some sadness in his voice, "your hybrids are doing just that, but I lost mine–Mircea is dead."

* * *

I went out into the hallway and looked down on the large stairway. A handful of hybrids were heading for us stealthily, trying to mask the sound of their footsteps. I didn't have the time to reflect on Mircea's death, but it didn't affect me as much as it did Julian.

"Julian," I barked into my headset, "you need to back away and let them follow you out. Octavian can help you by shooting them from the air. Make them come out to you and stay with the plan."

There was no response from him.

"Grant!" I screamed at him again. His silence frightened my spirit.

"OK," came his hesitant answer, "but going backward isn't easy. We've got a good position here."

Suddenly I realized, not without hesitation, that I had to relinquish control and let him take charge. I had to accept the intolerable notion that I couldn't be in control of everything, especially not over his judgments and decisions.

"Understood. Good luck, Commander."

*   *   *

At that instant a bullet shattered a window pane in the hallway and pierced the forehead of a hybrid who had reached the first turn of the stairs—my brother had shot him from the helicopter. The fifty caliber gun didn't need any backup from us on the ground.

Dora and Dana took turns shooting and covering each other with consistent and perfect timing, and the enemy had no chance against them. My presence and my touch had made the girls much stronger, while Octavian reinforced them from above.

"The corridor's clear," said Octavian. "Go to the last door on the second floor. Be careful—there's a hidden room somewhere on that floor and they can use it to trap you."

I was there in two seconds. Before I opened the door, a task that at this point seemed quite easy for me' I made the decision to send the girls down to help the rest of my team.

"Grant, the girls are coming to help you."

"Do they know a different way in?" he asked me. 'This'll take forever! Safira, the enemy's hiding. Is that possible?"

I could sense that Grant was frustrated and impatient. He wanted to hurry and get the job done immediately, like he was accustomed to doing in the past. I asked Dora about another entrance and she shook her head.

"That's the only way in. Stay where you are. The girls will flush them out."

I turned to Dora and touched her forehead. She looked at me and I saw a faint glimmer of life in her eyes.

"You and Dana go to the deep end of the tunnel, place the bombs, and get out quickly. Understood?"

She nodded, and I watched her and her sister shooting their way down to the first floor and to the SEALs' position. I knew I was contradicting myself, but my conscience struggled under the weight of the decision I had to make regarding them.

"Cover the girls," I said to Grant. "They're going in to place the bombs. Don't detonate them until you hear from me or Octavian."

"Copy that! What's your status?"

"I've located the enemy. I'm about to engage him."

I took another step toward the door.

"Safira!"

Grant's voice had changed—he was using the same tone he had talked to me with in those passionate moments in the hotel room. I closed my eyes, very much aware that whatever he was about to tell me would be heard by everyone.

"Yes, Grant," I answered a bit uncomfortable.

"God's speed," he murmured, and my soul was filled with emotions.

"Be careful Safira," added my brother, "I can't see inside that room—there's some kind of filter there—but I can hear you."

* * *

I took a deep breath and kicked in the massive wooden door. As the door fell from its hinges onto the floor, I stood in the doorway for a few moments. The room was richly lit, almost to the extreme—and it was obvious that I was expected. I stopped to look around, surprised by the enormity of this room.

It appeared to be used as a living room, with some furniture placed randomly around the eight granite pillars that were set in two rows, holding up the ceiling. The room was beautifully decorated in dark gold, with large mirrors and expensive oriental carpets. In each corner was a large ceramic column decorated with *bas relief* carvings of Grecian deities, with a bust of a ruler or king beside each them.

This was definitely the room they used for large gatherings and entertainment. I had hoped to find them in their private quarters on the third floor so I'd have a better chance of eliminating them. That they took refuge here was nothing more than a strategic move. I took a few more steps inside, wishing I had my gun so I could shoot out that annoying light. But, if they were ready to fight me, guns wouldn't be their chosen weapon.

"Lady Safira! So, it is true. You found me again after all," I heard a voice behind me. My heart stopped beating for a second and all my muscles tightened.

The man had positioned himself between me and the door—a common strategy. I turned my head slowly, and my first sight of him was through the corner of my eye. He wasn't too tall, but he was well built. His skin seemed to be transparent and I gazed into the dark pools of his eyes.

When I had turned my body entirely to face him, his smile vanished. His clothes were made of fine soft cotton, tan pants and shirt, like a military uniform, shirt unbuttoned to show much of his chest. A scar across his entire forehead appeared to give him a look of extreme bitterness. One hand rested on the head of one the busts and the other hand rested on the hilt of a sword.

It wasn't Lord Martuzon as I had expected.

It was Prince Albert, just as I remembered him from our first unpleasant encounter at the gala. I was disappointed but I kept calm. Perhaps I would have to kill every one of his offspring he would send my way until I had my chance to eliminate him. So be it.

"I must say that even though I wish the circumstances were different, you are welcome to my palace."

His English was a bit too slow for my liking, with a heavy German accent. Of course, I had an accent, too, but his English was difficult to understand.

"Prince Albert von Solberg, I thought you were looking for me. Are you surprised to see me?"

The man smiled again, with a sinister expression. It seemed to me that our dialogue was buying him time. As we spent another moment staring at each other, I wondered if he was going to attack me or if he was waiting for someone else to do it for him.

"Hm! I am surprised by your courage to come here, knowing you might not leave this place, and you have brought with you such a pitiful army of mortal soldiers."

"You're *mortal*, too—Amestec, isn't it? That's why you want me."

"Right! Do you remember this?"

He pointed to the scar on his forehead. In that moment it was all too clear to me where we had met before our encounter at the gala.

I had shot him at the Wagner's farm in Germany—he was the one who got away. Because he was half-immortal, he didn't die, he had just absorbed some of the energy I had released when I touched the soldier's wounds. He was the one who attempted to erase any evidence of the hybrids' existence, detonating bombs in the barn. I was sure he knew I was the one who had shot him then, and how close I was to defeating him now.

I was also certain that he had the Fire Sword.

"It was fate that brought us together so many times. I felt your presence in Germany and I went after you, but you escaped me in Atlanta at the ball. But I didn't leave empty-handed. I have what you were looking for. Mother warned me about you. She was so right to lure you here, where you cannot escape anymore."

"Who *is* your mother, Albert?" I asked him, barely able to contain my fury.

"Hello, Safira!" a heard a female voice greet me, from the far corner of the room. A young woman with long blonde hair, dressed like a Grecian goddess, made her way in through a disguised door in the wall.

At that instant I couldn't hide the surprise in my voice, and my brother heard it, too.

"Who's the female Immortal?" he asked.

My recognition of her made me realize that it really is a small world, after all.

34

"HELLO, ANDA KOVACK!" I RESPONDED in my most tranquil tone of voice, while inside my body all my nerves were stretched as tight as the corsets of the past.

"Ah, Lady Safira, you remember me," Anda responded, and the sound of her high pitch voice was so irritating to me. "So, we meet again after, how long – one hundred and thirty years? I see you are still dressed like the slattern you were then. Fate plays such tricks on us, sometimes!"

I waited for her to come closer to me. Indeed, it was her–the same face, the same age and the same indolence I remembered. How was this possible? My emotions rose with the multitude of questions I had about her immortality.

Did she kill one of my brothers? I should have felt something if that had been the case, but my senses were clear.

"I see time has been quite good to you, Anda," I said, and I defiantly moved towards her. "You must have been fortunate to get some of your youth from Milos Martuzon, but I suppose he didn't give you everything. So where is he now?"

"His whereabouts are not important," she said with indifference. "The present is my only concern, and things are better for me now that you are here. I have big plans for you."

"The only plan that's on your mind is to capture or kill me. If you kill me, your children will die."

"My brothers and sisters are of no concern," Prince Albert snapped. "Mother wants you dead only for me, so I can have immortal life and inherit all of your gifts, including being a Healer. Then—we won't need you anymore."

"Does she?" I asked, raising my voice. "I thought she had other sons. What about the ones you have with Milos Martuzon, Anda? Don't you care about them? What will your husband say about this?"

Anda slowly crossed the room to an old cherry wood chest and pulled out a sword, turning to me with smoldering eyes. I recognized it immediately. It was Lord Martuzon's— the blade that had killed me long ago. At this point I wholly braced myself to encounter Lord Martuzon—his spirit lingered throughout this place, but I couldn't say exactly where it was.

"My husband said enough when he was alive," answered Anda, pointing his sword at me. "Every day he told me that he loved me, but he wept and called your name at night. My breaking point was reached and one night, after we made love, I gave him an extra portion of wine and he told me everything. He said you were born an Immortal

Healer with the gift to make immortals, and he killed you. He loved you, but he killed you.

"I was quite happy to hear this at first, but then he told me that you did not die. He found an empty grave and no trace of you. Perhaps your mother resurrected you, or you rose from the dead with your own powers–he did not know exactly, but he wanted you back. He wanted to find you and bring you back to his palace. He thought you might be at some secret mountain in Liechtenstein, along with more like you. He wanted you in *our* bed. You were going to be his wife and I was to be cast away.

"I hated him at that moment. I was seven months pregnant with my first son, and I could not bear the idea of him setting me aside–to have you come back and take over my life. After he fell asleep, I took his sword and cut his head off, like he did to you.

"At that moment something strange happened! I felt a cold breeze invading my body and I felt my heart stop beating for a few seconds. Even though it was the month of August, my body was freezing and the child inside me was moving, seemingly in desperation. But everything became normal a moment later, except that I had just murdered my husband and now I was a criminal.

"That night I left the Palace, Oradea and Transylvania. I stayed for a while with some relatives in Budapest until my son, Artamian, was born. From there I moved to different places and different men–I had to secure our survival. After thirty years, I realized how fortunate I was to not age at all. Seventy years later, I realized that Milos Martuzon was not a liar–immortality did exist and I had it.

"My life was not easy, but I did not forget what Milos had told me about you and your other immortal brothers that were in hiding. If you were the real Healer, then you could make all of my children Immortals. But how could I find you? I needed a connection and access to Liechtenstein.

"One day, the husband I had then cut his neck shaving and I held my hand on the cut to stop the bleeding; a day later his wound had healed, but he became less and less connected to reality and life. After a year I left him–he was like a shadow with no life remaining in him. But that intrigued me, and I continued to experiment on other lovers, shaving and cutting their necks until I created the perfect soldier. I engraved the first letter of my name on their neck.

Maurice, one of my sons, found the young king of Liechtenstein for me. I had a plan and I followed it. My new name was Anna Bathory, a Transylvanian royal in search of a good mach.

"I met King Leopold in Paris thirty years ago and I was promised that I would be Queen. I became pregnant, but the King returned to his country without me; he abandoned me and his son. I did not take that kind of offense lightly. Albert, my son, needs to restore his dignity and take back the inheritance that his father refused him. He is the King's first born–he must be the King.

"But I suppose I should not hate you anymore–you did not have much luck with men either, and now I am like you. So I want to make you a proposal. Stay here with me, let us be friends, and help me with my plans. Together we are so powerful and we can do anything! Come with me and help me win Liechtenstein. We are going to build a strong and rich country and be feared among immortals and mortals alike. What do you say?"

As I listened to her story I remained tightly wired until she admitted to killing Milos Martuzon. Now I understood why I sensed his spirit all this time–it was in her, along with his twisted powers.

It was strange that this news affected me somewhat. It was a contradictory feeling to have pity on my fiercest enemy. Milos died because he confessed his love for me and wished for my return to him. I couldn't have planned it better. His immortality was short lived because he stole it from me. Like his father before him, he received fair punishment for killing an Immortal, even if it was done by his own wife.

My answer to her as she tried to lure me into a deliberate acceptance of giving up my freedom was the same answer I had for Lord Martuzon.

"Anda, we both know that you and I will never be friends. I'm here because you shouldn't exist and because you built a forbidden army. You must be punished and your army must be taken out. I've got nothing against your children, but if they rise against me or if they kill other Immortals, I will terminate them all. That's a promise."

"You killed Marcu already," she said, becoming angry and hateful. "Now it is *you* who will have to die for me to avenge him. I am not afraid of you. *I* will take you down, but it will be Albert who will cut of your head. That is *my* promise."

I had expected this kind of reaction from her. I had no doubt now that her intentions were to seek revenge against Albert's father, make her son a king, and attack the Secret Mountain. She cared for nothing more–certainly she didn't care about her other sons.

I turned to Albert, who was holding his sword in its scabbard, waiting anxiously for his mother to attack me. I moved slowly closer to Albert and I saw the scar on his neck and hand, clear evidence that she had tried her twisted powers on him, too.

But, as Octavian had observed, I always tried to play games with weak minds.

"Tell me," I asked, smiling at him and catching a glimpse of interest in his eyes, "would you rather have me or your mother? You know that I'm unique and I have more powers than she does. Her pathetic attempt to give you immortality has failed. If I kill her that will certainly be the end of you, too. If you kill her, you'll have immortality and you'll have me as your mate and my powers. So what's it going to be?"

Prince Albert turned from me to his mother and seemed to be conflicted by the choices I had given him. His hesitation by not showing a vehement reaction against my proposal infuriated Anda. Again, another man in her life, her own son, was choosing me over her.

The sight of such betrayal was repulsive to her.

"I am your mother, you idiot," she screamed at him in panic. "You cannot do that! Move to the door! I could not give him immortality," she said to me, "but he is as strong as you are, perhaps even stronger. You are just a Healer, not a Warrior. I murdered a Warrior and I have become one."

"You are not even good at creating hybrids, Anda. How many of those creatures have you made?"

"More than you think, and they are everywhere, with all my sons. There is no escape for you!"

"Wrap it up, Safira," I heard my brother in my ear device, "Conrad was shot. I'm coming in."

"Anda, I'll gladly let you prove what you are to me."

I pulled my sword and waited. I let her attack me and I felt immediately that she was not strong at all, but she had some training in fighting. I let her fight and she expended a great amount of energy, while I barely responded. Each time the blades of out swords met, I wouldn't push her too hard. She could feel my strength and she groaned furiously.

Unfortunately, time wasn't at my disposal. Conrad had been hurt and I didn't have time to play war with this woman. But the light was so disturbing. They had deliberately made the room so bright to keep my powers limited.

I moved away from Anda and I exploded a few of the decorative lights in the sconces on the walls with my sword. Anda followed me, swinging and stabbing in my direction. Albert remained against a wall, still not getting involved.

I had to get to the lights on the ceiling. I leaped to the highest chest in the room, and from there I flew into the air towards the hanging chandelier and pulled it off the ceiling. As its weight and mass crashed down, the floor shook. Now, half of the light source was gone and I could see more clearly.

"Albert, help me!" yelled Anda, frustrated by her son who was still rooted in place. Before he could react and help her, I raised my blade over hers, pressed it down, and decapitated her with one swing. Before her body fell to the ground, her eyes showed real astonishment.

This was the end, the real end for a woman who rose against her fate for so long with no victory. I knew she was not far gone. I could see her spirit, invisible to the naked eye, waiting for my redemption, but she wouldn't receive it from my hands. I let her go.

Prince Albert glanced at me, seemingly undisturbed. He pulled out his strange sword from its case. It was longer than mine, and the blade was a deep rusty copper, so unusual and unsettling. I knew it right away–without a doubt that was my lost Fire Sword. He hit me hard. I bent under the pressure but I got up quickly.

He was very strong. Perhaps the combination of Amestec and hybrid increased his potency. I returned his parries and our swords met, hilt to hilt. A sudden wave of strong heat coming from his sword almost burned my face.

I was fighting the Fire Sword but the sword was not yet showing its full powers. We were locked in place and staring at each other. His face was calm, but I sensed a great deal of tension in his body. He was uncomfortable because he was fighting with me–a woman who he must decide whether to kill or to keep.

I smiled and attacked him again.

"Safira, Grant's down! Repeat! Grant's hit hard."

Hamilton was yelling in my ear. I could hear the strident sound of intense gunfire. A rush of heat struck my heart like thunder because Grant didn't have a protector–Mircea was dead. I hit the Amestec even harder but he could stand up to me on the same level. This was like a training exercise for me, only now I fought like a Warrior. My body knew what to do, but my mind listened to my heart, and I became weaker.

"Safira," said my brother, "I'm forbidden to touch the mortals, and Grant is badly hurt. You must get to him *now*."

"I'm not done," I answered my brother, but Albert thought I was talking to him. At that moment, the massive sound of shattering glass made both Albert and me turn immediately and focus on the interloper, as someone sailed through the window.

"Yes, you are," answered my brother.

He was in the room behind me.

35

OCTAVIAN WAS BEHIND ME WITH his sword raised over his head. His shirt was ripped, hanging below his belt. His eyes were fearless.

"You must go." The sound of his voice was demanding but expressionless, like an echo. "I'll cover you, the Prince is mine."

Prince Albert was between me and the door, a position he liked to hold. My brother's intrusion seemed to appall and enrage him the same time.

"You are not going anywhere, Lady Safira," he responded with a grim smile as he lifted his sword to attack me. "You are not leaving. We have business to finish."

"Go now, Safira" yelled my brother impatiently, as the prince's fury seemed to rise higher against me and the man who was giving me orders. As Albert swung his sword directly toward my neck, I got a foot hold on the pedestal where I had broken the statue. I rotated in the air over him, leaving Octavian to face Albert's threat and I started to run as quickly as I could.

The Amestec froze, confused by my disappearing act, but then he started to chase me. My brother followed behind him. The prince growled as he chased me, perhaps furious by the unexpected intrusion of an Immortal Warrior. Somewhere between the floors I lost sight of them both. Perhaps Octavian had caught him.

On the first floor, there was still some random shooting between the hybrids and my soldiers, but the SEALs were out in the courtyard.

I made my way out to join them, at the same time trying to locate a loaded gun. Shots were being fired my way, so I took cover behind a fountain and tried to focus–the night was dark, but the courtyard was very well illuminated. To my right was the wreckage of our helicopter, with tendrils of flame beginning to emerge from the cockpit.

Hamilton saw me and called on my ear device.

"Conrad is safe in the Land Rover. He was shot in the shoulder. Pollack is beside the second fountain with a leg wound, but he can't move."

"What about Grant?"

There was total silence from the man.

"Hamilton!"

"He's gone. He's dead."

For that split second I went deaf–whatever Hamilton told me next, I couldn't hear. Death among the mortals wasn't an option—no one was supposed to perish, especially him.

My muscles were convulsing, but I raised my body and started running towards Pollack, who was the closest to me. I checked his wound—the bullet had passed through his leg without hitting a bone, so he would soon be able to put a little weight on that leg.

I pressed my hands over the entry and the exit points to stop the bleeding. He had lost a lot of blood, but none of the arteries had been hit and it was nothing I couldn't repair. I ripped off a part of his T-shirt and bandaged the leg. Ligaments had been torn in his wrist and I twisted them back in place. It was a superficial wound, but it was painful and it hindered his use of a weapon.

"Does it still hurt?" I asked, as I helped him to get up.

Pollack looked at me with his mouth open in surprise.

"Just a little twinge, but nothing like it was hurting a second ago," he admitted. "How'd you do that?"

I ignored his question. "I'll help you walk. Let's go!"

Bullets were coming straight at me and the SEAL from two directions.

"Watch out!" Pollack warned me.

Hamilton tried to cover me, but from where he was standing they were out of his range.

"Pollack, stay behind me and shoot when you have a chance," I told the Lieutenant.

I stood still to protect Pollack and I reached forward with my right hand. I caught the first round of bullets coming at us in the palm of my hand and dropped them intact to the ground.

More bullets were fired at us and I saw them as if they were in slow motion. I switched hands and I caught the rest of them with my left hand. Pollack stood there with his mouth still agape, too astounded to lift his weapon.

I grabbed his rifle and opened fire on the hybrids. A moment later, all was quiet—I had killed them all.

The sound of metal clashing against metal echoed in the night—two swords in the heat of battle. My brother and Albert had reached the courtyard and I turned to see them. The Amestec sword shot flames into the darkness each time it encountered Octavian's sword.

So, it was true, that was the legendary Fire Sword that Prince Albert had stolen from me. And my brother was fighting against it.

If he didn't win, I could lose him forever.

I helped Pollack get in the Rover. I pulled the medical kit out of the trunk and I checked on Conrad. He was more than happy to see me. I hurriedly stitched his shoulder wound, but he wasn't in danger.

"Did you see that?" Pollack whispered to Hamilton, who watched me, still trembling but fascinated as I patched up the young SEAL. "She caught those bullets with her bare hands! I swear to you, that's what she did."

"Calm down, Pollack," said Hamilton, probably in denial about the whole incident. "Safira, I think they're all dead. It's been quiet for a few minutes, now. If there are more inside, the bombs will destroy them when we detonate them. The girls installed them, but they didn't make it out. None of them made it! *Those* guys fought well!"

"Let me see your arm," I said. He had a small wound caused by a bullet that had ricocheted. I touched the edge of it with my fingers and stopped the bleeding. The man looked at me like he was in a trance.

"Hamilton, where's Grant? Please take me to him!"

The SEAL hesitantly nodded at my request. As we went back inside to the first floor I passed by my brother on the staircase, still fighting the prince. The Amestec was retreating, and Octavian knew that the Amestec was trying to make his way up the roof where there was a helicopter waiting.

Grant lay motionless on the floor covered in blood; his skin tone had changed to a pale, lifeless color. I held my breath. My own body was shaking and racked with pain, and my heart struggled with the agony of his loss. My eyes closed, and it took me several moments to force them to open back to reality.

Yes, this was real!

"I'm sure he didn't have a pulse," said Hamilton with a weak voice.

I knelt beside him and laid his head on my lap. I couldn't deny it—I love him, and I let him die.

I pulled up his T-shirt. One bullet had entered his heart beside the right aorta and one bullet had perforated his disk at L5, but it exited by the ribs. I touched that wound with the palms of my hands and I didn't feel any major damage. I applied pressure on it using the T-shirt as a compress, and then I checked his heart. I could feel the bullet still inside, so I started to enlarge the bullet hole with my fingers.

Hamilton backed away, frightened.

"What are you doing, Safira? The Commander is dead and you can't treat him." But I didn't listen. I pushed my fingers further into his heart until I found the bullet. As I slowly pulled it out, I was gratified to feel that it was intact.

"What's going on?" asked Pollack impatiently on the radio, concerned about us. "It's time to go! It'll be sunrise in three hours!"

"She's pulling the bullet out of Grant's heart with her fingers," screamed Hamilton, turning his back to me. At that moment he most certainly thought that I had lost my mind.

"Stay where you are, Hamilton!" I ordered him. "Don't turn around."

I put pressure on Grant's heart wound again. My hand rested on his wound and I did my part–I healed him. His wounds weren't threatening anymore. I was a Healer–I had healed him, but he was still dead. I wanted to scream and explode with grief but I couldn't.

My eyes closed, but they didn't weep–they glowed. I needed to see *him* for the last time.

The love I felt was all for this mortal, who had loved me and died for me.

"I love you, Julian," I whispered in an attempt to say goodbye. I love him, and now he will never know.

NO! I could *not* let him die.

A sudden impulse I couldn't control made my fingers move. My hand touched his open heart. Suddenly, a stroke of electricity and gray dust like ashes emerged from my fingers, like it did when I healed Rares, and it filled the wound. In slow motion, the blood vessels and the tissue grew back together like there was never a wound there.

Grant's heart slowly started a faint beat–his chest barely moved up and down as he began to breathe shallowly.

He was coming back to life, but I felt myself growing weaker–like I was dying.

Dizziness that I had never felt before made my head spin, making me lose my vision. I struggled to keep the feeling in my legs and hands, but my body was growing numb. I felt no pain of any kind. The feeling of physical nonexistence forced me to collapse beside Grant.

"Hamilton," I yelled with my last bit of strength, "Grant's alive! Help him!"

The SEAL turned quickly, determined not to comprehend my little freak show, but he saw that Grant's color indicated life. He knelt down and checked Grant's pulse, totally stunned.

"How's that possible? I've been in enough combat to know 'dead' when I see it. He was shot in the heart!"

He looked surprised to see me lying on the ground.

"Are you OK? Safira, what's wrong? Are you hurt?"

"I'm just a little dizzy, but I'll be alright before long. You must help Grant."

My explanation didn't convince Hamilton, but he didn't dare contradict me.

"Hurry! Take him to the Rover and drive straight to the military base on Cape Nikolaos. Grant and the other wounded need immediate medical attention."

"What about you? I'm not leaving without you."

"I've got to help my brother. There's a chopper up there–that'll be our ride. Give me the detonators. Go now, Hamilton. That's an order!"

Hamilton handed me the two detonator boxes and lifted Grant to his shoulder. He turned to me and saluted me for the last time.

"Bless you, Safira."

* * *

I saw the Land Rover pass through the compound's outer gates as I continued to fight to breathe. In the next moment, everything in my vision turned red. I couldn't distinguish anything except some of the major shapes in the area, like columns and doors. Instinctively I crawled as rapidly as I could up the stairs. Half blind, I dragged myself from floor to floor over debris and dead bodies.

At this point I was so vulnerable that anyone could have killed me.

An inward power that was growing with every movement was behind my desperate attempt to fight this weakness and make it to the roof, to my brother. He could heal me if he was still alive. With the last of my strength I reached the roof. My brother was still there.

Octavian was still fighting Albert, taking his time and prolonging the duel, as a cat toys with a mouse, oblivious to Albert's ruthlessness. He appeared to be enjoying the flames that were rising from the Amestec's blade. His fighting differed from mine—he is strong and he stays more grounded, while I am more aerodynamic.

As I slowly I began to regain some of my senses, my back pressed against a wall. Whatever I had gone through frightened me like nothing ever had before. It was something similar to what Serban had described to me about the old order of wounded Immortal Warriors who weren't healed—empty shells with lingering spirits.

My brother saw I was in distress and he became more aggressive towards the Amestec as his movements became faster. A few times Albert seemed to have the advantage over him, but I suspected it was because of the powerful sword he was wielding and not because of his skills.

The Fire Blade touched Octavian more than once, cutting him with slashes on his arms, torso, and legs. But in my own agony, I closed my eyes to blind myself of his distress.

I couldn't let him die either.

Although I didn't think that it was possible, my mind pushed my own spirit out of my body and into Octavian's. For the next few moments I felt that I could see through Octavian's eyes, I was him and I was fighting in his body. Indeed, his powers seemed to grow stronger.

With my spirit combined with Octavian's, the prince didn't have a chance. Octavian struck Albert's knee cap hard with his foot–his patented move–and when the knee cap broke, the prince collapsed to the floor. Octavian straddled the prince's shoulders, grabbed a shock of Albert's long hair with one hand, swung Albert's sword in an upward arc, and decapitated him.

It was over. Octavian ran to me, picked me up in his arms and walked fast to the helicopter. I felt like I was dying again.

"What happened to you?" he asked, visibly concerned as he laid me into the co-pilot's seat. "You didn't answer my call and just now I felt your spirit in me. How was that possible?"

"I don't know. Something strange happened to me right after I healed Grant. I went deaf and blind, and I couldn't move."

"I thought Grant was dead." He went around the helicopter and got in the pilot's seat.

"He was dead," I confirmed. "Octavian, what have I done?"

Octavian held me tight against his chest and touched my forehead. It was an emotional moment for both of us. As fearless as Immortals are, we are also the most sentimental of all humanity. I checked his wounds: a cut that looked like a burn above his left elbow and a deep cut on his right shoulder.

The wounds didn't heal with my touch, so the legend was true–this sword had magic powers to destroy us.

"It's time to go, Safira," said my brother pretending to ignore my terrified look. "The SEALs are all safe. What about our hybrids?"

I shook my head. None had lived through this battle and none had wanted to. I could feel my strength returning, but not my powers. I could see, but I still felt so weak–incapable of fighting for my life. But everything had come to an end and we won, even though I had almost died.

This compound had to disappear and no evidence could remain of our kind's transgressions. No one must know that we exist. That would stir the mortals' curiosity about us and about what we were capable of doing.

Octavian fired up the helicopter's engine, the one that Albert had intended to use for his escape. My brother had probably deliberately crashed our 'copter when he came to my aid.

In two more hours it would be daylight. All of this mountain fortress must disappear.

"I didn't sense any other Amestec and I didn't get another satellite image of them."

"There aren't any others, at least not here," I said. "This battle was all about Anda Kovack's and Prince Albert's desire to seek revenge and to claim Liechtenstein. The rest of her children are somewhere in unknown locations, perhaps still searching for me or the rest of us. They have hybrids too."

"That's expected. Are you ready to go home?" my brother asked, suddenly in a jovial mood. "Safira, we've got the sword!"

"The lost Fire Sword," I said, and tears of joy streamed down my face. "Look at your wounds—they aren't healing. You fought against a sword that could potentially destroy your body forever, and you won! Albert stole it from me, but it's ours now!"

My brother carefully stored the prize in one of the containers.

"Let's go home," I said, trying to breathe normally.

As we began our ascent, I pressed the buttons on the detonators. The two bombs the hybrid girls had planted detonated Albert's cache of ammunition and explosives, and everything in the palace and dorms was totally destroyed. I watched the immense flames that were visible for ten miles in silence.

My soul was burning, too.

36

IT HAD BEEN MORE THAN a week since we returned home. I tried to get back into my old routine, but physically I was weak and mentally I was still far away.

"Don't you think this battle was easy?" I asked Octavian while I went to make more coffee. I left the kitchen a moment later, forgetting what I was doing.

"There'll be many more battles," answered my brother as he finished preparing my coffee. "This one was only the first of many. It won't be long before we'll have to fight again."

"But we haven't done this the right way," I said exasperated, "something is just not right. I fought my war with mortals. I was supposed to be a Warrior and not a Healer, and you had to finish the fight for me.

"I watched you. You fought well and won one of the swords. I truly believe that Gallbor has great plans for you in the future. I'm so proud of you!"

"Thanks, but I'm not concerned about Gallbor's plans—he's not important to me right now. *We* did exactly what we had to do."

"I failed in every way and brought judgment down on me."

Octavian became frustrated and I regretted bringing up this subject. He brought me a cup of coffee, and when he sat beside me, I couldn't resist touching his forehead, even if my touch didn't produced the intended effect. I could walk and talk but I was just a powerless shadow.

"You gave me life and you saved me so many times," I said to him, "even when you didn't know it. That moment when I lost my powers and I lay almost dead on the first floor, I knew I must get to you for healing—and you did it. I wouldn't be here without you."

Octavian turned to me and touched my forehead too, and I felt it.

"Safira, you don't even know how strong you are. You saved me too, by giving me your spirit. Now, that's the kind of power that only our Master has. I wish I could bring you some peace. I feel your sadness."

"Every day gets better," I reassured my brother, but he didn't believe me.

* * *

Doctor Samson's funeral was this past Saturday morning. That event, as sad as it was, couldn't sadden my heart more thoroughly than it already was. I looked at Ms. Ruth for a few minutes and I could feel her pain—the pain of losing someone you love and to never again have that love returned.

Never–not in this life.

What a beautiful thing it was for them to have spent a lifetime with each other. On my time line, fifty years isn't much, but these mortals grew old together, and it's beautiful.

What could I to do with my everlasting life if I couldn't keep those I love?

I had heard no news from Julian since the night Hamilton took him on his shoulder to the Rover and they disappeared into the dark. I remembered that he was dead– I couldn't forget that moment–seeing his pale waxen face and lifeless body.

Had I lost Grant? Was I still a Healer when I touched him? Did they arrive in time to the military base where he could receive medical attention? I couldn't deny that I saw him breathing, that even Hamilton thought he was alive. But what if it was only an illusion? It's not known whether my healing power could resurrect a mortal. I had always believed that only the Amestec, who had half of our genes, could receive my gift.

Many questions remained, and there was no one I could go to for answers.

My powers were still gone. I had no understanding of what had happened to me. I had the expectation that like before, my body would heal itself. This body was now so weak and vulnerable–this body that for so many years seemed indestructible. I was barely alive.

"Drink your coffee," said my brother, "and don't worry. I'm sure Grant's fine. We would have heard something, otherwise."

"Octavian, what if he was really dead? Could I have done the impossible? In the midst of all that commotion, maybe Hamilton and I were wrong—no mortal had ever received immortality from a Healer before."

"Perhaps nothing is impossible anymore."

My brother's eyes shifted from me to Prince Albert's sword that was lying on the coffee table. He got up and pulled it out of its scabbard. He looked at it for a few seconds, fascinated with it and forgetting about me. I was intrigued.

"What do you feel about Grant?" he asked me a moment later, swinging the sword in the air.

"My spirit is numb and powerless. I don't feel anything about him. I feel that Gallbor's just keeping me alive, but he's not forgiving me for something I can't understand. Oh, I see you like that sword…"

"Why did you want me to have it? The Fire Sword rightfully belongs to you."

"Not at all—you deserve it. The first of the two we must have is finally home. Don't forget that we still have to find Nagoshi and the Silver Sword. I just hope he turns out to be just a mere mortal."

"Albert was strong, but not strong enough for me, and I felt disappointed when I fought him. I was glad to hear that Lord Martuzon had been destroyed, but I wonder if the outcome would have been different if I had challenged another Immortal."

I didn't share my brother's opinion. I got up from the couch and went outside to the deck. Looking at the lake always calmed me. My brother didn't follow me, but Lord Arthur did. As I sat in a deck chair, he lay beside me, and I petted him and stroked his soft silky fur.

I should feel differently, but I couldn't. The fact that I had feared Lord Martuzon for so long, and I feared him capturing me and making me his mistress, still lingered in my soul. He should have died by my hand, not from a swift sword strike from a jealous wife.

I was disappointed, too. I wanted him to see me alive and to see my hand raised against him. I had no doubt that he wanted me back with him. He loved me, and the fact that he admitted this to his wife cost him his eternal life. So, in a sense, that made me a widow.

Everything started with our oldest sin, since we were sent to walk on this earth. Mortals shouldn't love us, and we shouldn't get involved with them any more than what was required. Rules had not been kept and I had broken them all. Did I regret it? What was there to regret?

Love and a night of passion?

Julian Grant.

*　*　*

As the afternoon sun began to sink behind the trees that bordered the lake, I thought I heard the doorbell ringing.

My wishful thinking made me laugh at myself. What were the odds that it could be…?

Julian Grant…

Something in the air smelled differently. It was a quiet, warm late Saturday afternoon. My senses had to be very wrong. The aroma I detected shouldn't be so strong and fresh–not anymore.

As Lord Arthur and I went back into the den I heard Octavian talking with someone in the foyer. Apparently we had a visitor, probably Nelda. Since we returned home, she and my brother had been almost inseparable.

The aroma was even stronger inside the house–freshly bloomed lilac flowers. I knew exactly where the all my guns were hidden, but for this kind of visitor, a different kind of weapon was required.

The sword wasn't on the table anymore; perhaps Octavian had put it away. I felt that every fiber of my body had been awakened back to life, as if my entire protection system had been invisibly activated. I had felt nothing like that since I had touched the heart of…

Julian Grant!

Octavian came into the den alone. I saw that his demeanor had changed after I gave his face just a cursory glance. He was as disturbed by the aroma as I was, and we both knew what it meant.

"Grant is here to see you," said my brother, and I saw that he was still holding the Fire Sword tightly.

"What?" I couldn't dare believe what he was saying.

"He's alive, Safira, and he's in the foyer. Do you want to see him or should I send him away?"

Octavian was protective of me, and I understood. He was no longer just my younger brother, but he was my protector and my equal.

Everything had changed. This battle had changed all our lives, lives that had once been so settled and secure.

"Octavian what's that scent in the air?"

"It's Grant. Be careful! Should I stick around?"

"No, I'll be OK. Octavian, do you think that Grant already knows about it?"

Octavian bowed and saluted me the old way. This time he smiled, not without malice.

"Be at peace, my Lady. He'll know as soon he goes for a haircut."

My brother called for Grant to come in, and then he left through the garage door, apparently going to visit with Nelda. Grant came toward me with measured steps across the room.

He seemed to be unchanged, but his hair had grown tremendously in just a week. His blue eyes were looking at me intensely and I felt a sensation of panic. It was as if he had never seen me before–it was well known that some severe injuries could trigger amnesia.

The Julian Grant who stood in front of me wasn't the same one I had joined to battle Albert von Solberg ten days ago. This one was a stranger to me. How dangerous was he?

"Please forgive me for intruding," he began, and his words cut deeply into my heart.

"You're always welcome here," I responded quickly, without thinking.

I felt the small distance between us suddenly grow larger. He took another step toward me, and his beautiful aroma was driving me crazy. I hugged myself tightly with my arms in an attempt to remain calm.

"What did you do to me, Lady Safira?" His voice was soft and caressing, and at that moment I knew I wasn't totally forgotten.

"For you I am just Safira..."

"You know very well what you are for me. Hamilton told me I was dead, and the doctors at the hospital confirmed it."

"No, you weren't totally dead..."

"Not totally dead? How can you not be 'totally dead'? There's no such thing!"

"Please forgive me for endangering your life," I apologized to him.

"There's nothing for me to forgive. I volunteered to fight with you, remember?"

"So, everyone is alright?" I asked, even though I knew the answer.

"Yes, they are." He gradually made his way closer to me.

"What about you?"

He brushed his fingers through his long hair, and my breath slowly escaped from my lungs while I waited for his answer.

"I had to come back *here*."

I wanted to know how he felt about me, if he had had a change of heart, if I had lost his love and lost him, too.

"I brought your Land Rover back from Greece," he continued, and the words that he intended to be funny crushed my spirit. I struggled to smile at his comment.

"You're right. Your car's in the garage–I forgot about it. Here're the keys."

I walked past him, picked up his keys from the bowl on the kitchen island, and handed them to him. Our fingers brushed together and I felt the mating vibration flowing from his body.

I stepped back fast, wanting to run from him, but he was faster. He caught my hand and pulled me toward him. I could feel how much stronger he was–so much stronger than me.

Julian Grant wasn't the forbidden fruit any longer.

THE END

FUTURE BOOKS

The Immortal Warriors are also featured in the following books:

- ➢ BREAKING ROGUE
- ➢ BREAKING FIRE
- ➢ BREAKING DUSK

More information about these books can be found at:

http://www.intownbooks.net

FROM THE AUTHOR

Camilia John grew up in a house full of story tellers, so it was natural for her to start making up her own. At the age of seventeen she earned the Gemini award for writing in her high school. Although she has had success in fashion design and business, she is a writer at heart. Her first paranormal series is *The Exiled Immortals,* and will be followed by *The Invisible Kingdom.*

www.ingramcontent.com/pod-product-compliance
Lightning Source LLC
Chambersburg PA
CBHW062024170626
46813CB00001B/282